SAPPHIRES *and* SMUGGLERS

OTHER BOOKS BY LYNN GARDNER

Emeralds and Espionage

Pearls and Peril

Diamonds and Danger

Turquoise and Terrorists

SAPPHIRES and SMUGGLERS

a novel

Lynn Gardner

Covenant Communications, Inc.

Published by Covenant Communications, Inc.
American Fork, Utah

Printed in the United States of America
First Printing: January 1999

06 05 04 03 02 01 00 99   10 9 8 7 6 5 4 3 2

ISBN 1-57734-434-0

Library of Congress Cataloging-in-Publication Data

Gardner, Lynn, 1938-
Sapphires and Smugglers: a novel / Lynn Gardner.
p. cm.
ISBN 1-57734-434-0
I. Title
PS3557.A7133S27 1999
813'.54--dc21   98-53644
CIP

FOREWORD

With each previous book, I've spent many hours on location, soaking up the atmosphere, prying into nooks and crannies to discover the fun, interesting, and exciting places that give that city or area its special ambience.

I was scheduled to spend twenty-one days in Thailand and Sri Lanka researching this book. I'd spent weeks shopping for just the right clothes to wear in that hot, humid climate during the monsoon season. Using travel books and brochures, I researched the locations I thought would be the most exciting for the book.

Then terrible fires raged throughout Indonesia and Malaysia, blanketing the entire southeast Asia area with thick smoke. Planes crashed, ships collided, hundreds of people died, and thousands were hospitalized. My trip was canceled. By the time the smoke had cleared, I'd lost my window of opportunity to travel there because of other commitments.

But my daughter, Shelley, and son, Greg, have frequent opportunities to travel to both Thailand and Sri Lanka in their jobs monitoring the international garment industry, so I told them where the action was to take place, and they took the pictures I needed. The sights, sounds, smells, animals, and many of the people in the book are straight off the streets of those exotic cities.

Ananda, the taxi driver in Colombo, Sri Lanka, who drove Shelley five hours into the mountains to check a manufacturing plant, asked why she needed some of the pictures she was taking. When she told him her mother was a writer and she was taking the pictures for me, he told her he wanted to be in the book. So he is.

The monitor lizard that appears later in the novel was encountered by Greg near the Dondra Head lighthouse as he stopped to take pictures for me at that location.

Both Shelley and Greg have been in Colombo during or immediately after attacks on the city by the Tamil Tigers. All the information on the rebel fighting is right out of their journals or the newspapers.

My thanks to Greg and Shelley for their extra efforts to make my details right, and for all the additional material I could never have gleaned from travel books.

CHAPTER ONE

My husband of only six months was missing. It was unbelievably ironic. Surrounded by good-looking men celebrating my acceptance into Interpol on what should have been one of the happiest days of my life, I'd never felt more bereft.

Bart wasn't just absent on this auspicious occasion. He was lost. Unaccounted for. Whereabouts unknown. And had been for weeks.

He'd promised to be here tonight for this celebration. The fact that he wasn't filled me with foreboding. If it was physically possible, Bart would be at my side. That could only mean—

Dad interrupted my thoughts, raising his glass in a toast to me. Suddenly the doorbell rang.

I raced through the white marble foyer of Mom and Dad's Santa Barbara mansion, praying Bart had made it after all, jubilant in my hope that he'd come. Throwing open the door, I stopped, speechless.

The face behind the armful of my favorite peach roses was not my husband. The face with the winsome smile came out of the past . . . my intimate past. Milton J. Hollingsworth III, debonair and sophisticated from his dark, neatly coiffed hair to his expensive Italian wingtip shoes, was my former fiancé.

I stood, mouth open, unable to utter a sound, unable even to move.

"Good evening, Allison. From your expression, I take it this is something of a surprise. You didn't receive my message. Am I arriving at an inopportune time?"

Mom rescued me at that moment, sweeping into the foyer like a tropical breeze, rustling the potted palms as she came, her teal chiffon evening dress billowing behind her.

"Why, Milton, how nice to see you. You're just in time to help us celebrate Allison's latest accomplishment and finally meet her father." She linked her arm in Milton's and drew him across the threshold, closing the door behind them.

"And that accomplishment would be . . . ?" Milton asked as he lay the roses in my arms and kissed my forehead, placed a finger under my chin to close my mouth, then took my elbows in his perfectly manicured hands and stood back to examine me.

At least I wasn't embarrassed by my appearance. For tonight's celebration I'd exchanged my comfortable threadbare jeans and soft, worn sweatshirt for a long, emerald-green velvet sheath that matched my eyes and made me look a trifle taller than my five-feet-four inches, but was slightly more clingy than I would have liked right now. I'd dressed for Bart, not Milton.

"Allison is carrying on the family tradition. Come into the library. Jack was about to offer a toast."

Mom propelled us through white oak French doors into the music room, past the glittering golden harp and dazzling white grand piano, past the nine-foot Christmas tree decorated with elegant gold bows and miniature musical instruments, on through the ballroom to the library.

"Milton Hollingsworth III, I believe." Dad stepped forward and thrust out his hand. "You won't remember that we ever met, but I think I was introduced to you once as a colleague of Margaret's. At the time, it was best that everyone believe I was dead."

Milton grasped the extended hand. "It's good to meet you at last, sir, although you know, your daughter never did believe you were actually dead."

"What brings you all the way out to the West Coast?" Dad asked.

"I'm here on business, but since I was so close, I couldn't pass up the opportunity to stop and pay my respects to the man who bested me. And see Allison, of course." He glanced around the room, then at me.

I finally found my voice. "Bart's not here, Milton."

Mom stepped into the breach, handing Milton a stemmed crystal goblet filled with sparkling amber liquid, then Dad took over.

"Milton, you probably don't know any of our guests. This is Oswald Barlow, a new member of our group."

Oz stepped forward and stood, almost possessively, by my side, proffering a hand to the impeccably attired newcomer, his cold eyes scrutinizing the taller man.

"Allison and I were engaged before Bart's return from his unexplained absence," Milton said. "Her announcement of our broken engagement came by way of the television broadcast of their explosive wedding." He turned to me and smiled warmly, slipping his arm around my waist—an intimacy I could have done without in the presence of Bart's peers.

Dad continued introductions. "David Chen, Lionel Brandt, Rip Schyler, Dominic Vicente, and, of course, you know Jim Allan, Bart's father."

Each man stepped forward and shook hands with Milton, each with a glance at me and the same solemn question in his eyes. But no one asked, and an undercurrent of tension greeted Else and Alma, Bart's mother, who entered the library at that moment carrying trays laden with hors d'oeuvres.

Milton regarded tall, blonde, and elegant Else with masculine appreciation even as he greeted Alma warmly. "Mrs. Allan, you're looking even lovelier than you did the last time I was here." He took the tray from her, set it on the desk, then took her hands in his and kissed her forehead. "I'd hoped to finally get to meet your son, but they tell me he's not here."

I intervened before Alma could say anything.

"Else Elbert, I'd like you to meet Milton Hollingsworth III, a dear friend." As they clasped hands, each appraising the other with an interesting intensity, I explained to Milton, "Else and these five gentlemen comprise the rest of the Anastasia family."

"Anastasia . . . the Greek version of the Phoenix rising from the ashes. Correct me if I'm wrong, but the parallel is too obvious to miss. Anastasia is the resurrection, or survival, of Jack Alexander in Vietnam after a very nearly successful attempt on his life," Milton said.

"Right," Dad nodded. "I had to spend the last twenty years in deep cover. Now that Margaret's safe, we can operate in the open. We were just proposing a toast to our newest member." Every eye in the room focused on Jack Alexander, creator and head of Interpol's elite anti-terrorist division.

With steel gray eyes, graying hair, and a medium height and build, my father could become, with minimum disguise, any man, anywhere, which added greatly to his ability to survive the innumerable attempts on his life in the last twenty-five years.

Dad put his arm around Mom's waist and pulled her to his side in an affectionate hug, looking into her eyes for a long moment before kissing her cheek. The gesture spoke volumes to me of their deep love, their understanding of the precious nature of life, and his assurance to her that I'd be able to handle this dangerous new lifestyle I'd chosen. He raised his goblet.

"To Melanie Allison Allan, may she be ever watchful—ever ready, ever valiant. And may her daring impetuousness be tempered only by her common sense and wisdom—and obedience to her adoring father," he added with a twinkle in his eye.

Every glass was raised, every voice chimed in the toast, "Hear, hear," as crystal clinked.

Then the unflappable Milton did the unthinkable thing at a toast. He choked and coughed.

Mom glided to his side, laughing. "I'm sorry, Milton. You were expecting champagne. We should have warned you. It's sparkling cider. Allison has embraced a new religion that precludes alcoholic beverages. And since none of us need to be addled by alcohol tonight, we opted for sparkly instead of bubbly."

"A new religion?" Milton arched his eyebrow.

"I'm a Mormon. Bart and I were just baptized members of The Church of Jesus Christ of Latter-day Saints. I'd be delighted to tell you all about it, but first you have to tell me what you're doing here. Did you get your ambassadorship?"

"Yes, but not where I'd hoped. The President asked, as a personal favor, if I'd go to Sri Lanka until that country is stabilized. Then he promised I could have my original assignment, ambassador to England. Back to the old family stomping grounds."

"And your family's castle?" I asked, with an innocent smile.

Milton studied me momentarily, decided I was needling him about his family's lordly background and immense wealth—as I'd done from the beginning of our relationship—and pointed his finger at my nose.

"I think I've intruded on something. I'll leave you to your celebration, and whatever you need clear heads for, and call before I return to New York. Maybe we can have lunch."

I put my hand on Milton's arm. "Has the President briefed you on Sri Lanka yet?"

Milton glanced at Dad, then back at me.

"Why?"

I couldn't meet his eyes for a minute, twisting the emerald engagement ring that nestled against my engraved wedding band. How did you tell someone who had promised to love and take care of you the rest of your life, that the one you chose instead of him was not around to do the job?

Milton tilted my chin up, searching my face with his intense dark eyes.

I took a deep breath and looked at Dad for approval before answering. "Because Bart mentioned Sri Lanka in his last communiqué."

"How long ago?"

"Two months."

"Join us, Milton," Dad said, waving at the refreshments spread behind us. "You may have come at an opportune time for all of us."

Hors d'oeuvres were distributed to serving plates before everyone settled into the velvet easy chairs scattered in a loose circle on the luxurious Oriental carpet.

Dad took his place in front of the group, swallowing a pink shrimp on a cracker. He washed it down with the last of his sparkling cider and cleared his throat.

"Bart's infiltrating a branch of Hamas that's been terrorizing Israel with suicide bombings. Sheik Ahmad Yassin, founder and spiritual leader of the militant Islamic movement, has to be stopped before peace can be had between Israel and Palestine. Since his release from prison, the attacks have intensified. We are hoping Bart can destroy the organization from within." He paused.

"But?" Milton prompted, glancing at me.

"But we haven't heard from Bart for eight weeks—and his last communiqué came from Thailand, not Palestine where he was supposed to be—and it mentioned a possible destination of Sri Lanka," I answered quietly.

Milton sat, elbows on the mauve velvet chair arms, steepled fingers thoughtfully tapping his chin. "I'm afraid I may know why," he said. "As you're well aware, the civil war in Sri Lanka has escalated in the last few months with an infusion of foreign arms and agents."

Dad nodded. "I understand the State Department has just been alerted that organized terrorists could be behind it. If Hamas is aiding the insurrection, it'll be a blood bath."

"Already tens of thousands have died and over a million people have been displaced by the fighting," Milton said. "I hate to think what those numbers will be with fanatics involved."

It was bad enough that my husband was living with a bunch of crazed terrorists bent on destroying everyone and everything that didn't subscribe to their way of thinking. I dreaded the possibility of Bart being in the middle of a bloody insurrection. Inquiries through Interpol channels had produced nothing. Contacts with known snitches had produced the same. It was as though the mysterious Far East had swallowed my husband.

I knew Dad was worried, but given Bart's talent for survival and Dad's own experience in infiltration, he'd hesitated to send in the cavalry. Not knowing where to send them was another problem.

Why hadn't Bart called? Why hadn't he let us know where he was? How he was? It was to have been our first Christmas together. The feeling of foreboding that shivered through me banished all hope of a merry Christmas.

CHAPTER TWO

"We may have to regroup at this point," Dad said, pacing back and forth between the twin white wrought-iron circular staircases that led to the reading loft. "We've received word that the closing of the sapphire mines in Thailand may not have been because the veins petered out, as was reported. Rumor says the owners were forced to sell to a faction that's smuggling the gems out of the country to fund terrorist activities, along with the ever-present drugs from the Golden Triangle. I was about to give Allison her first assignment, but maybe we'd better rethink this."

"You were sending me to Thailand?" I asked, trying to keep the excitement out of my voice.

"To Sri Lanka and Thailand to check out the sapphire mines. Find out what's really happening. See if there is any terrorist connection. And check out the possibility of sapphires and drugs being smuggled into Los Angeles. But now . . . ," Dad's voice trailed off as he paced, deep in thought.

"There's no reason I shouldn't go," I started softly, but before I could even finish my argument, Milton, Oz, and Mom spoke simultaneously. Mom prevailed.

"There's every reason why you shouldn't go. No one in their right mind would send a new agent into a war zone on her first assignment."

Oz's argument was similar. "Not enough experience to go under fire on purpose."

Of all people, staid, logical, reserved Milton saw the emotional angle. "You'd be searching for Bart, and that could get both of you killed. You'd be leading with your heart, not your head."

"So who can you send instead?" I asked. "You and Mom will be tied up in Israel. You've just committed Sky and Dominic to Interpol Headquarters at Lyon, France, for the next ninety days. Else's assigned as a member of the royal ski party to protect the two British princes, and David's headed for Hong Kong. Lionel's busy installing his defense perimeter security system at endangered embassies, and Oz is . . ."

"Available for southeast Asia," Oz interrupted. "Jack, if you want some on-the-job training for your newest agent, you could place her in my care. We could get the information you need, and at the same time, keep an eye out for Bart."

I held my breath. As much as I wanted this assignment, I wasn't sure I needed it with Oz at my elbow for the duration.

"Oz, don't you have something going on in the Czech Republic?" Mom asked.

Before he could answer, a tiny electronic bell chimed over the intercom. A message was being received in the underground control center.

I flew to the ballroom with Dad close behind, the quick clip of my high heels beating a sharp staccato on the white oak parquet floor that was inlaid with brass musical symbols.

At one end of the ballroom, four sets of French doors spilled open onto a white marble patio at the front of the house. On the opposite wall stood an immense gold-veined white marble fireplace, over which hung a portrait of my mother when she was known as Margo, star of stage and screen.

The fireplace was my destination. Grasping the huge emerald eyes on the five-foot-tall gold peacock screen that decorated the open fireplace, I pushed one eye up and the other down, then slipped behind the gold filigree. As I stepped into the fireplace, which was large enough that I barely had to duck my head, the door to a hidden elevator slid silently open along one wall.

Dad arrived as I entered, and held the door for Mom, who squeezed beside us, plucking the teal chiffon out of the door before it closed on the armful of fabric.

"It could just be a message from Interpol, Bunny," Dad said softly, his hand gripping my shoulder and pulling me next to him in a comforting hug.

"I know, but it could be Bart. I wouldn't want to miss him if it was."

I counted the seconds it took for the elevator to descend into the cave beneath the house, my heart beating triple time. A rush of sea air, cool, moist, and salty, and the sound of nearby lapping waves greeted us as the elevator door opened silently in the dark tunnel that led to the control center.

Dad touched a small indentation in the rock wall. A soft glow illuminated the darkness, just enough to see, but not enough to reveal the cave to a passing boat. The twists and turns in the far end of the tunnel that accessed the Pacific Ocean prevented that.

We stopped about fifty feet into the tunnel—at the halfway mark—where Dad again touched an indentation that looked like a deep chisel chip in the rock wall. A door slid open on Interpol's West Coast control center, filled with computers, radios, and the latest communication equipment available.

I hurried to the computer that recorded all incoming messages. A jumble of letters and numbers spread across the screen. Mom typed instructions and the computer deciphered the coded message.

Five words flashed on the screen: *Anna. Galle Face Tuesday. Apollo.*

It made no sense.

"What does it mean?" I asked Dad, who was peering over my shoulder.

"It means Bart wants to meet an agent in Colombo on Tuesday." Colombo was the capital of Sri Lanka.

My heart leaped.

"What agent? Who's Anna?" I asked, breathlessly.

"Code name for Anastasia. He's asking for anyone available from Anastasia."

"That could be me. I'm available and you were going to send me there anyway. Are you sure he didn't ask for me?"

"We assigned you the code name Melpomena, since that's the Greek muse you were named after. If he'd wanted you, he'd have asked for you, Bunny."

I ignored that. It was the last thing I wanted to hear.

"I know Bart's Apollo. You're Zeus. Mom is Hera. But what or who is Galle Face?"

"Galle Face is an area in Colombo on the west coast of Sri Lanka," Mom said. "We use an old hotel there as a drop or meeting place."

I turned back to the computer. "Is that all? I don't get to talk to him? I don't get to answer?"

"Apparently he's afraid of being caught sending messages, or that they'll be intercepted, or he would have elaborated." Dad was quiet for a minute, chin in hand, eyes narrowed in thought. "I'm not sure he'd like it if we sent you, Bunny. He'd never take you into a danger zone, especially into the middle of a civil war."

"Am I, or am I not, a certified agent?" I asked. But before I could press it and force an answer from Dad, Mom typed more instructions into the computer and stepped back to watch the screen.

A jumble of letters, words, and numbers scrolled across the face of the computer, line after line.

"He sent this from a telephone in the lobby of the Oriental Hotel in Bangkok," Mom said, pointing to an area code, telephone number, and address, time, and date. "This code means he had someone with him and couldn't transmit more. These numbers signify he's accomplished the first phase of his assignment."

"I knew he'd do it," Dad said, smacking a fist to the palm of his hand.

"This means he doesn't know when he'll make the next communication," Mom continued, pointing to the next set of numbers. "This tells us that it's difficult to communicate. This informs us more instruction will be forthcoming in the next day or two. And this one's for your benefit, Alli. This means that he's physically and psychologically well. Normally Bart wouldn't bother sending that information."

I gaped, open-mouthed. "How can you tell all that from that conglomeration of numbers and letters?"

"You may have finished your Interpol training, Bunny, but you haven't started Anastasia's specialized education yet." Dad covered his eyes with one hand, rubbing his temples as if to ward off a headache. "I'd hoped you'd have the next couple of weeks to absorb all of our own codes and procedures. I should have known better. Nothing in this business runs on a convenient timetable."

Mom was at the computer again, asking for printouts of a list of codes and tables. Then she stepped back. "Time to start your homework. It's a good thing you're a quick study. There's a lot here to memorize in a pretty short time."

She stacked the pages as they came off the printer and handed them to me. I scanned the printout. There were number codes for everything—beginning with 00—Anastasia's code for "agent down" and ending with ZZ—"mission accomplished."

I was euphoric. The only thing better than having Bart here tonight was knowing that he was alive and well. The possibility of seeing him soon sent me over the top.

"We'd better get back upstairs," Dad said. "We still have a lot of work to do tonight before the team leaves."

"I thought the party was too good be true," I said, linking my arm in Dad's as we headed for the door. "This was rather out of character for you to call everyone here just to celebrate my completed training."

"Never underestimate a proud father," Mom laughed as she turned out the lights in the control room.

We rejoined the group in the library as they finished the last of the hors d'oeuvres.

"We just had a message from Bart in Bangkok," Dad announced. "He's inside. He asked to have Anna meet him at the Galle Face in Colombo on Tuesday."

"He didn't ask for Allison?" Oz voiced the question everyone was probably thinking, since they were all looking at me.

"He knew the timetable for my graduation," I explained. "Dad just told me I still have a lot of stuff to learn that's strictly Anastasia. Bart would know I hadn't had time to do that yet and that Dad wouldn't be anxious to send me until I was completely knowledgeable on all our codes and procedures. But I have until Tuesday. That's six days from now. That even gives me time to decide what to pack."

Only Mom and Else appreciated the humor in that statement, since the guys didn't have the agony of deciding what was appropriate, comfortable, and packable, as well as all the other problems that plague women travelers.

"*If* I decide to let you go," Dad said, reminding me he hadn't really given me the assignment yet.

"You couldn't consider *not* sending me, even if there was someone else who could go—"

Oz interrupted. "I can go alone."

I glared him into silence.

Dad dropped his head and ran his hand over his eyes again.

I linked my arm through my father's and spoke softly. "You knew when you gave permission for me to train as an agent that sooner or later you'd have to send me into an unpleasant situation. That's all Anastasia deals with. This time you have an agent free to accompany me. Next time you might not."

Else languidly stretched her long, lovely legs before curling them beneath her in the cream-colored velvet chair. "We'll have the princes in the Bavarian Alps for Christmas. I could hop over the border and take care of Oz's Czech assignment."

She dipped her head and winked a blue eye at me from behind the lustrous cascade of long, blonde hair. A partner in crime. Else was related to most of the monarchies in Britain and Europe, and served as a professional bodyguard for her jet-setting cousins. The stunning Norwegian was brilliant, musically gifted, an expert in self-defense, and lightning-fast with a gun—all wrapped up in the most elegant packaging you ever saw.

"And I'll only be a short flight away in Hong Kong if I'm needed," David Chen said softly. Quiet, serious David watched and listened and spoke only when he had something important to say. Thirty-five, slightly built, with black short-cropped hair and piercing dark eyes that could warm you through or chill you to the bone. I flashed him a grateful smile.

Sky said nothing. That didn't bode well for me. Rip Schyler was the scholarly father figure in our group: sixty, a doctorate in criminology and another in abnormal behavior; tall, solidly built, gray-haired, with sagacious blue eyes hidden behind horn-rimmed glasses. I had to take his silence as disapproval. I wasn't sure how Dad took it, or if he noticed.

All eyes were on Dad, awaiting his decision. I held my breath. Was he still seeing me as his only child, or could he think of me as his newest agent? Either way, I thought with a sinking heart, my chances weren't good.

"Well?" I stepped back and looked up at my father, trying not to feel like a teenager asking for permission to take the car, or sound like one either. After all, I was a twenty-five-year-old married woman.

Dad leaned against the wrought-iron stairwell, arms crossed, a frown creasing his face. I was afraid father feelings were about to overpower the head of Anastasia.

Before he could marshal his defenses, I took the offensive.

"Thanks, Dad. You know I'll be in good hands with Oz and David as backup." I kissed his cheek and looped my arm through his, turning to the group. "Of course, since I am an accredited graduate of the James Bond Spy School . . ." Everyone laughed and Dominic shouted, "*Ole!*" as the lithe, cocky Spaniard pantomimed a bullfighter evading a bull.

This was an inside joke. I was about to explain it to Milton, when he stood, and with the slightest semblance of a bow, backed stiffly toward the door.

"It looks as though you will be very well taken care of in your adventures, Alli. If you get to Sri Lanka and find you need the services of the embassy, look me up. The embassy, its staff, and the Ambassador will be at your service." He turned on his heel and strode smartly out the door.

I glanced at Dad's bewildered expression. He got that way when I outmaneuvered him, and Milton's sudden announcement hadn't helped. I whirled and raced through the ballroom, catching Milton at the front door.

"Hold it, Hollingsworth," I said, grabbing his silk and linen jacket by its expensive coat tails. "What was that all about?" He turned on me and shook his finger in my face.

"You haven't changed a bit. You're still winding people around your fingers, using them to get whatever you want—regardless of the cost."

I was stunned. "What are you talking about?"

"When you set your mind to something, you don't wait and consider the consequences before you jump in with both feet. Have you stopped to think what you're doing? Your impetuousness and inexperience could jeopardize the lives of innocent people."

"Milton—"

He grabbed my shoulders and shook me. "Have you thought about Oz, about David, and the other agents who will be involved in protecting you so you can have this little adventure? Are you trying to prove to that Neanderthal you married that you're every bit as brave as he is?"

"Milton—"

"It's one thing to bat your beautiful green eyes, toss your black hair coyly, and melt men's hearts till they'll give you the world and worship at your feet. It's quite another to toy with lives. This time you may not like the price, Allison. This could cost the lives of your friends. And the life of that buccaneer you're so fond of. But it could cost *your* life. And that's too high a price to pay."

His dark eyes were unusually shiny as he stared at me for a moment, then kissed me hard and wheeled out the door, slamming it behind him. The crystal chandelier tinkled above me as his car peeled out of the driveway.

I turned at the rustling behind me. Mom had heard his tirade.

"What was that all about?" I asked, sinking to the white marble stairs, perplexed at Milton's uncharacteristic outburst.

"That," Mom said, her teal chiffon dress settling softly around us as she joined me on the stairs, "was a man who is still very much in love." Slipping her arm around my shoulders, she added, "He could reconcile himself to a life without you as long as you were happy, but he can't stand the thought of something drastic happening to you, or to one you love more than him."

"I can fix that," Dad said from the door. "Allison just won't go to Sri Lanka."

CHAPTER THREE

"Dad. You can't mean it."

He pointed his finger sternly. "You railroaded me. You put words in my mouth that weren't there, and you know it."

"I was just helping you make a hard decision."

He reached out to Mom and me and pulled us up from the stairs. "I think maybe we ought to bring this before the group and see how they feel about it."

I wasn't sure I liked that idea at all. The conversational buzz died as we entered the library, and Else met me at the door.

"You didn't tell me you had such good-looking, highly placed friends, Allison," Else said quietly, curiosity lighting her intense blue eyes. "Tell me about him."

"Later," I whispered, "when we don't have an audience. But his mother would approve of your pedigree, and you'd make a gorgeous couple."

I avoided Oz's curious stare.

"I'm going to put this to the group for your opinions," Dad began slowly. "As you know, my perspective may not be all that clear and unbiased on this issue. Lionel, let's start with you. You saw Allison in action in Santa Fe. You're aware of what's going on in Sri Lanka. If you were in Bart's shoes, asking for an agent to meet you, how would you feel if Allison turned up instead of Dominic or David or Else?"

Lionel, true to his funny, flirtatious, French nature, winked at me. "It would depend entirely on what I needed that agent for."

Dad cleared his throat, harrumphing gruffly. Mom tried to position herself out of his line of vision so he couldn't see her smile. I knew immediately my father was already regretting his decision to allow me to become part of Anastasia.

"Yes, sir," Lionel said, futilely brushing at his tousled golden hair and assuming a serious expression. "I was impressed by Allison's clear vision of the problem in Santa Fe. If I were Bart, I'd feel her only liability would be her personal value to me. You, sir, would be able to evaluate that aspect more precisely than I could." He glanced from Dad to Mom.

Bingo. One point for me. Dad had given Mom assignments as dangerous as his other agents.

"Dominic," Dad said. "Your opinion."

"Allison stuck to her guns when we assumed you and Bart had crashed in the helicopter. She thought beyond the obvious, even though she was intensely involved, personally and emotionally. I'd be happy to have her persistence on my side."

"Else?"

"Allison's not afraid to follow her hunches. Her impetuousness could be an advantage in a tight situation, or a liability. She might compromise Bart's effectiveness inside that organization if he felt a need to protect her, instead of relying on her abilities and allowing her to help him. If it were me asking for an agent backup, I'd take Allison in a heartbeat. I'm not sure Bart would at this point."

"Thanks, Else," Dad said. "Sky?"

"You want my personal or my professional opinion?" the older man asked.

"Do they differ?"

"Actually, yes. Professionally, given Allison's inexperience, coupled with her high personal stake in the agent she'd be assisting, I'd immediately give a thumbs-down." Sky paused. "However, having observed Allison in Santa Fe, I'd personally be unafraid to have her back me up. She's not afraid to plunge in and take her licks, which I must say, surprised me." He smiled wryly.

I gave Sky a self-conscious smile and nod of thanks for his kind words, then turned back to Dad as he asked Oz for his opinion.

Everyone in the room sat relaxed in comfortable chairs, except Dad, who stood in front of the group, and Oz, who stood behind the chairs with his hands in his pockets. He did a visible "relax, you're on stage" change of posture seconds before all eyes turned to him. That didn't bode well for me. I held my breath.

"As you know, Allison saved my life with her quick reactions and accurate shooting in her first real confrontational situation. She gets double points for that in my book. On the minus side," he emphasized with a glare at me, "her impulsive nature, her brash disregard for her own safety, and her reckless disobedience of orders are definitely factors to be considered."

His eyes never left mine as he recited his litany of my weaknesses. Oz was sabotaging me!

"On the other hand," I said, staring right back at Oz and trying to keep my voice calm and steady, "if you were to go with me and teach me all you know, then I'd have a much better chance of becoming as good an agent as you are. How could I fail with you there to keep me out of trouble?" I turned a disarming smile on him, hoping he didn't know me as well as he thought. "The bad guys won't stand a chance."

"Is it my turn?" Mom asked. Attention focused on Margaret Alexander, second in command in Anastasia's hierarchy. I knew she'd pre-empted David to defuse the current arcing between Oz and me.

"You're on," Dad said.

"I'm not sure any of you can appreciate how hard it is to put aside personal feelings and approach this from a strictly professional point of view. It's much easier to think of all of you as my children, than it is to think of Allison as one of my agents. But after working shoulder to shoulder through our trauma and trials searching for Bart and Jack when they were kidnapped in Santa Fe, I feel sure Allison will conduct herself as a professional." She paused. "I'm acutely aware of her shortcomings, but I think our newest agent has enough moxie to turn those into assets, instead of letting them be liabilities."

I mouthed a silent "thank you."

Dad turned to the remaining member of the group. "David?"

"Allison gets my vote of confidence," David said quietly. "But I'm in accord with those who wonder if Bart would feel the same."

Dad stood, hands shoved in pockets, shoulders hunched, and a scowl on his face.

"When do we leave?" I asked softly. "And what are our orders, sir?"

Before he could answer, the intercom chimed softly. Another incoming message!

I kicked off my high heels, hiked up my long, slender velvet skirt, and raced from the library to the far end of the ballroom, nearly knocking over the filigreed peacock screen as I twisted the emerald eye elevator buttons, and was on my way to the control room before anyone else reached the fireplace.

The big, bright screen on the computer was filled with information, but it wasn't from Bart. It was an uncoded update from Interpol on the situation in Sri Lanka. The civil war had escalated in the last twenty-four hours. Guerillas had poured into Colombo, setting off half a dozen bombs, killing ten government officials and eight innocent bystanders.

Dad was standing at my side by the time I'd finished scanning the bulletin. One glance at the expression on his face sent my heart, and my hopes, plummeting.

He put his arm around my shoulder. "Sorry, Bunny. This changes things. It's one thing to have the guerillas contained in the northeast section of the country they've taken over; it's quite another to have them making blatant attacks on the capital. Looks like Oz had better go alone."

"Dad!"

"Don't, Alli. Don't make it harder on me than it is. I know how much you want to see Bart. But I can't send you under fire when there's no need. Whatever Bart has for us, Oz can obtain it. By the time he gets back, you'll be ready for the next assignment."

I faced my father with my hands on my hips, looking him squarely in the eye. "How many times did you use Mom on an assignment that didn't really require her, just so the two of you could be together? Be honest."

He stared silently back at me.

"How many times was the danger factor something you ignored, because you missed her so much you figured it was worth it to be with her?" Before he could answer, I pressed further. "And how many of those times did you wish you'd never taken the risk? How many times were you sorry you'd brought her into the operation?"

No answer.

"I rest my case."

"Margaret had more experience . . . ," he began lamely.

"Not at first. You finally sent her for training—after she had joined you on a number of assignments. Isn't that right?"

"How do you know so much about what we did? Your mother has obviously leaked secret and confidential information. She may get a demotion for this breach of security." Dad leaned down and kissed my forehead, then wrapped his arms around me in a big bear hug. "I know you aced every section of your training, and that says you're ready for your first assignment. I just wish it was something besides this."

"Actually, this may turn out to be a piece of cake," I said, reaching up to stroke his cheek. "Thanks, Dad."

"You're too much like your mother. You can weasel anything you want out of this soft old heart."

"I'll keep it our secret. Your group upstairs sees you as a hard-nosed, hard-driving, by-the-book taskmaster. I promise I won't let on what you really are under that gruff exterior."

The computer activated the printer, signaling a continuation of the message. Mom joined us, with Oz at her side. Dad pulled the papers from the printer and handed them to Mom and Oz to absorb while we read the update just coming in.

"*Your* daughter, Mrs. Alexander, is far too much like her mother for her own good," Dad said sternly, without turning from the computer terminal.

Mom looked up from the bulletin and winked at me. "Actually, I suspect she also has far too much of her father's tenacity for her father's own good."

"I expect all this banter means Allison is going to Sri Lanka in spite of the new eruptions in the civil war," Oz said wearily.

"You did volunteer to train me on my first assignment," I reminded him. "Is that offer still good or are you reneging now that things are heating up over there?"

"I didn't reckon on taking you into a civil war. Between the terrorists and the guerillas—"

"I promise I'll protect your back," I interrupted with a smile. "What more could you ask?"

"That you follow instructions," Oz scowled, pointing a finger at me.

I pointed right back. "At the cave, when we took those three terrorists, didn't I follow your instructions to the letter?"

"Yes."

"And the time that's got your dander up is when a man twice your size was ready to shoot your brains out, and I intervened, instead of sitting in the car like you'd ordered and letting him kill you. Sorry, Charlie. That kind of asinine order deserves to be disobeyed." My tone was louder and certainly angrier than I'd intended.

Dad turned to us in astonishment. "You two sound like teenage siblings. What's got into you?"

Mom linked her arm through Dad's and smiled. "You've hit the relationship. You missed the age by a few years, but it's an honest mistake, given the tone of the conversation."

Dad looked from Oz to me. "Well, since we didn't provide a brother for you, and you married the one you adopted for yourself when you were young, I guess I couldn't have chosen a better one for you now. Welcome to the family, Oz. Hope you can stand the heat."

"Thank you, sir. As long as I don't have to continually remember that she's your daughter, and I can treat her as I would my own sister—" Oz stopped, stared bleakly at me, excused himself, and left the control room.

I squeezed Mom's hand. "Thanks," I whispered, and we turned our attention back to the computer. I didn't want anyone else to know, even Dad, what the undercurrent was really about.

"Guess that's it," Dad said, retrieving the remainder of the bulletin. "Let's get back upstairs and brief the group. Wait. There's one more bit coming in. I'll bring it. You two go on ahead."

He took longer than a few minutes, and when he finally appeared, his expression was troubled. I looked at him closely, then glanced at Mom. She was talking to Alma and hadn't noticed his return.

As Dad stood before the group, he assumed the mantle of head of Anastasia once again. He seemed to be more comfortable with that than the role of father. Not surprising, since the former had been a much more active part of his life.

As I looked at him, little prickles of prescience tingled up the back of my neck. Something in Dad's demeanor had changed. Mom leaned forward in her chair, apparently trying to determine what was different about him.

Dad finished apprising everyone of the contents of the latest Interpol bulletin and was clarifying assignments. He paused when he came to mine.

"Allison, my original idea was to let you nose around the jewelry mart in Los Angeles and see if you could pick up any leads before you went to Bangkok. If they're smuggling sapphires and drugs through the Port of Los Angeles, we need to work with the Contraband Enforcement Team at Customs . . . arrange to have them increase the number of containers they check from every ship arriving from Sri Lanka and Thailand."

Dad was rambling, the papers in his hands shaking almost imperceptibly, both uncharacteristic of him. I sat up and looked at Mom. She uncurled her legs and came slowly up to the edge of her chair.

He passed a hand over his eyes and paused.

Chills swept over me. He'd been fine as we read the messages downstairs in the control center, but he'd pulled one more bulletin off the printer after we left.

I stood on legs that had suddenly grown weak, smoothed the emerald velvet gown, and walked the few short steps to take the paper from Dad's trembling hand.

A single code on the paper sent my world reeling.

CHAPTER FOUR

00—Agent down.

The words blurred on the page. I took a deep breath and willed my mind and body to overcome the hysterics I felt rush to the surface.

Shuffling frantically through the papers, I searched for Bart's first transmission. The location was the same. The time difference was under an hour.

"What's the Oriental Hotel? A dive in a bad part of Bangkok?" I asked, forcing a calm to my voice I didn't feel.

"No," Mom said, "one of the most famous hotels in the world. It's a posh place right on the river just down from the Royal Palace."

"What else does it say?" I thrust the paper at Mom to decipher.

"Nothing," Dad said quietly, slipping his arm around my shoulder. "The transmission was interrupted."

"How can you tell?" I looked at Mom for confirmation, not wanting to believe any of this.

"There's no sign-off. It's open-ended. Each agent signs his transmissions with a code so you know that's the end. This is Bart's sign-off on his first message." Mom pointed to the final numbers on the page.

"Who sent this?"

"There's no way of knowing," Dad said, "if an agent doesn't identify himself."

"Why . . . ?" I couldn't finish the question. I was afraid of the answer.

Else appeared with a snifter of brandy that she tried to press into my hands. "I think you might need this right now."

I shook my head. "No, thanks. That's the last thing I need right now."

Dad took it, drained it with one swallow, and handed the glass back to Else with a nod.

I reached for Mom's hand for moral support.

"Is it possible to rebuild the scenario? Figure out what he was doing from his first message, and project what might have happened? Was there anything else on the first transmission?" I was grasping desperately for straws.

"I'm afraid that's all there was." Mom's voice dropped to a soft, apologetic whisper. Her arms went around me and held me tight. But I didn't want sympathy. I wanted action. I wanted to do something—anything—to solve the problem rather than stand here and feel so totally helpless.

With a quick hug, I withdrew from Mom's embrace and turned to Dad.

"Where do we start?" I said, taking a deep breath. "Tickets on the first flight to Bangkok?"

Dad looked at me, his gray eyes cloudy and moist. "I don't suppose . . ."

"No," I interrupted. "There is nothing in this world that will keep me from going to Bangkok on the next flight I can catch." I reached up and kissed his cheek. "Not even you, Father dear. Now, will you help plot this enterprise before you take off for Jerusalem, or do Oz and I get to do our own thing?"

I turned to Oz. "You are still in, aren't you?"

"All the way, Alli," Oz said.

"Good. What do we do first? Contact allied agents in Bangkok who might know something?" I looked for help from the experienced members of the group.

The rest, who had remained quietly in the background, rallied around. Jackets were doffed, ties loosened, and chairs pulled into a tight circle. Dad's professionalism overtook his fatherly reluctance and he immediately began assigning tasks.

"We need to find out who sent the message and what happened. It had to be someone with a knowledge of Anastasia's codes."

Dominic took the first assignment. He left for the control center, with Else right behind him, to make reservations on the next flight to Thailand.

Lionel headed down to find out what activities might have been going on in Bangkok recently: terrorist operations, leftist groups, anti-monarchy rallies, anything that might turn up a lead.

As I watched them leave the room, I realized we were in the wrong place even for the planning end of this. "What are we doing up here, when everything we need is in the control center? Another message could come in and we'd lose precious minutes getting to it."

Mom and I took the small fireplace elevator with Oz close on our heels. Dad, Sky, David, and Jim took the larger elevator hidden behind the curved staircase in the spacious foyer. I never remembered to use that one. Alma stayed behind to clear the remnants of our celebration.

Some celebration this turned out to be.

There were no further messages from either Bart or Interpol. That computer remained ominously silent while the golden heads of Else and Lionel bent over their computers, keys clicking as they input data and waited for the export of information.

The raven-haired duo of Dominic and David Chen attacked their computers with different styles, but the same intensity. Everything Dom did resembled the way he'd approach a bull in a ring, with passion, grace, and finesse. David's approach was careful, quiet, and with a seeming detachment that belied his own passion.

Though Jim and Alma Allan weren't active agents, they were as essential to Anastasia as any of its other members. Jim and Alma were assigned the care and keeping of the multimillion dollar estate, and they manned the control center when everyone was out on assignment.

Else turned from her computer terminal and brought me back to the task at hand. "How fast can you pack? Singapore Air has a 1:35 a.m. flight into Singapore with a connection into Bangkok. It's the only one leaving LAX until morning."

I glanced at my watch. 8:15 p.m. I could leave right now without packing so much as a toothbrush. There was plenty of time.

"I can do that." I looked at Dad. "What do I need to be ready from this end?"

"You need a new ID since Hamas knows you're part of Anastasia, passports to go with your new ID, and incidentals to corroborate your new identity." He shuffled through a handful of passports as he spoke.

"Sky, we don't have anything we could use for Allison and Oz. Can you manufacture something," he checked his watch, "in the next two hours? They'll need to be at LAX by midnight at the latest, so they'll need to leave here by ten o'clock."

"I can deliver them in the helicopter," David said, looking up from his computer. "That will give them an extra hour on this end. Maybe we'll have some word from our contacts before they leave."

"I think the best cover would be husband and wife," Sky said, watching my face as he spoke. "If they go as writer and photographer on assignment from an internationally recognized magazine, that will get them into places they'd normally have a hard time explaining. Do you prefer *Travel and Leisure* or *National Geographic Traveler?* We have agreements to use their credentials."

"National Geographic. Can't we just go as an unmarried team? No offense, Oz, but I already have one husband I can't keep track of. I don't need another."

"No. A husband and wife are expected to look after each other and stay together more than just a casual team. It gives you a legitimate excuse to not leave the other when someone tries to separate you," Sky explained. "Remember the adage 'Divide and conquer'? That's one of the first things a subtle enemy will try to do. A less subtle one will just dispose of you without worrying about separating you. You'll need to stay together, especially since this is your first time out, Allison. But I don't have to tell you that." He gave me a gentle, chiding smile and turned to begin the paperwork.

Else took scissors to my hair, which had just begun to grow out from my last need for a disguise, and I once again had short-cropped, curly hair. No bleach this time.

Mom brought out the small cosmetic bag that was her disguise kit and provided me with brown lens to hide my emerald-colored eyes.

Using clippers, Oz gave himself a "buzz," eliminating the shock of sandy hair that never stayed put and was in constant disarray on his forehead.

Mom snapped Polaroid pictures of Oz and me and helped Sky put together passports from authentic U.S. government issue paper stock. By the time they finished, we were a well-traveled couple with two dozen foreign destinations behind us.

Dad passed out expense money in U.S. dollars, along with a small handful of baht, the Thai currency, and Sri Lankan rupees. He counted out five thousand dollars in one hundred dollar bills to me and ten thousand to Oz.

"That smacks of favoritism," I teased. "Oz has been a member of this family for only a few hours and he's getting twice what I get. Glad he wasn't around when I was growing up."

Dad shook his head and purposely ignored my needling.

While passports and IDs were being prepared, Dominic and Lionel were making little headway finding information on what was happening, or had been, in Bangkok.

Oz prepared a briefcase for me with my study materials on Anastasia codes, and I pulled together information on some high spots in Bangkok that would be worthy of a photo session. I chose one camera and left the rest of the camera choices to Oz, since he'd be the one most likely to use them.

Then the James Bond stuff appeared: a beautiful wood-grain pen that had a recording device in one end and contained a tiny capsule of gas in the other. Just one little puff, enough to bring someone down in close quarters.

A shiny gold compact turned out to be a communications system capable of sending and receiving scrambled messages that were bounced off a satellite to provide instant communication across the world. Its matching gold lipstick case hid a miniature camera.

What looked like a small monocular was actually a polemoscope, an optical device that allowed you to see what was going on to the side of you when you appear to be looking straight ahead. The last item was a special ceramic gun I could carry through airport security undetected, slipped inside the padded covers of a journal.

Else started toward the elevator with me to help me pack. Appreciating the effort, but preferring to be alone for a few minutes, I stopped at the door.

"Would you mind gathering what information we have on Sri Lanka? Since Bart had planned to be there on Tuesday with something for Anastasia, we may end up going there if we haven't found him by then." It wasn't a lie. I'd planned to do it as soon as I'd packed.

"Sure. Have you ever been to Bangkok?" Else asked as she headed back to the computer. Then without waiting for an answer, she tossed advice over her shoulder. "Remember this is the monsoon season, so take waterproof shoes if you have such animals, and don't pack any synthetics. Take only cotton or you'll melt. If you've got something with lots of deep pockets, that's best."

"Thanks. Any other timely tidbits?"

"Take a backpack, not a purse, and absolute minimum jewelry."

"Got it."

Instead of turning toward the elevator as I left the control center, I walked slowly toward the end of the cave that opened, after several twists and turns, to the ocean. It was here, only a few short months ago, I'd seen my father for the first time in twenty years, half dead from a bullet wound. He was lying on the tiny strip of sand twenty feet below me, waves lapping at his legs, and seaweed plastered on the bullet hole to keep him from bleeding to death.

Bart had carried him up the stone steps that led from the water, and Dad had managed to open the door to the control center before he passed out.

Where was Bart now? Was *he* lying in water with a bullet wound? I shuddered at the thought. Who had sent that message? And why hadn't they identified themselves? Was it someone Bart could trust? Were they taking care of him? Or . . . ?

Turning abruptly, I strode to the elevator and in less than a minute hurried out the front door of the mansion. I ran down the thousand feet of lush green lawn to the caretaker's cottage. Snuggled under huge Spanish oak trees, it was the perfect honeymoon bungalow. Unfortunately, we'd spent very little time here. There seemed to be a world full of bad guys bent on keeping us apart.

Upstairs in my bedroom, I hung the seductive velvet dress in the closet with a sigh. I'd bought it especially for tonight, for Bart's return. Would I ever get to wear it for him? No—*when* would I get to wear it for him? That was the proper form of the question.

I took off my emerald engagement ring and tucked it away in my jewel box, wearing only the platinum wedding band Bart had placed on my finger on our wedding day. We'd knelt at the stone altar in front of the waterfall and recited vows to love one another till death do us part. Later, we'd promised to make eternal vows in the temple, one year from our baptismal date. Please let us have now, and forever, I silently pleaded.

Dressing for comfort on the nineteen-hour flight ahead of me, I donned wrinkle-free chinos, a white tee shirt, and tennis shoes, then shrugged into a lightweight blazer. Then I packed light, tossing some clothes into a large sports bag that I could carry on the airplane: a pair of jeans, some cotton tees and blouses, a couple of cotton skirts, two split skirts, and one basic black dress that I could dress up if the need arose.

I tossed in a string of pearls and a pair of low-heeled pumps; they were dressy enough, but I could still run in them. A scarf, essential toiletries, my high-tech gadgets, and I was ready.

Almost. I turned off the light, knelt beside my bed, and poured out my soul to the loving Father in Heaven to whom Bart had introduced me. Without his help, I knew we'd never be successful in this undertaking.

Dear God, as many times as you've heard and answered my prayers before, it has never been more important than now. Please watch over and protect Bart until we can get there to help him. Don't let anything happen to him that he can't handle.

Even in my optimistic naiveté, I realized that if the enemy had gotten to Bart, there was every possibility he would simply disappear and never be seen or heard from again. It happened too often. If someone didn't want a body found, there were dozens of ways to dispose of it, especially in a city of over seven million people with countless rivers and waterways so close at hand.

I glanced around the room one last time. The twinkling Christmas lights, greenery, and red velvet bows I'd hung over the French doors and windows seemed woefully out of place. As I pulled the plug on the festive lights, plunging the room into darkness, it felt much more suited to my mood.

Black.

With less than a week till Christmas, it would take a miracle to find Bart by then, much less get back home in time to celebrate the holiday in our own snug little nest. Even the reminder that Christmas was all about miracles didn't lighten my heavy heart as I left our cottage and prepared for the nineteen-hour flight to Singapore.

CHAPTER FIVE

Armed with new identities as Amy and Ed Teale and the historical baggage that went with them, Oz and I bid good-bye to David Chen and disembarked from Anastasia's helicopter at Los Angeles International Airport, known universally as LAX. That was a real misnomer. Nothing about this chaotic, busy place could be considered lax in any way. Even at midnight, the traffic was unreal and the number of people embarking and disembarking from the continual flow of aircraft was incredible.

We checked in, confirmed our seating, then settled down in a quiet, secluded corner of the Tom Bradley International Terminal with the files of information we'd compiled in the last few hours.

"Well, *Amy*, you have about twenty hours to digest all that information. Margaret said you're a quick study, but you'd have to have a photographic memory to learn Anastasia's codes well enough to destroy those copies before we land in Singapore. And I'm supposed to spend some time reviewing basic Interpol stuff with you before we get there," Oz said as we started on the mass of paperwork.

"Give me eight uninterrupted hours with the codes. I'm a linguist, remember. I have a natural affinity for languages. They come easily to me, and codes are just another language. I'm not worried about the Interpol stuff. I've just come from weeks of cramming that into my head. It's all still pretty close to the surface."

Oz looked at me for a long minute, his expression of disbelief replaced with wonder. "You're really something, Alli," he said softly.

"Amy. The name is Amy," I reminded. "Alli is married to Bart. Alli loves Bart very much, and there is no room in her life for anyone else. She is a one-man woman. Totally monogamous. She does not have affairs. She does not flirt. She does not encourage amorous overtures. And neither does her alter ego. This is strictly a business proposition, *Ed*, and nothing will transpire between us that we would not be totally comfortable having Bart observe."

Oz looked crushed. "Alli, I'd never . . ."

I bit my tongue and reached for his hand. "I'm sorry, Oz. That was uncalled for. I know you're too honorable to take advantage of this situation. It's just that the tone in your voice . . ." I stopped, not knowing how to get out of this conversation.

"Sorry. I'll watch the tone from now on. But you amaze me. I struggled for days to learn those codes so that I had them cold. My mind just doesn't work the way yours does, sorting out clues and puzzles so quickly—storing and categorizing and coming up with the answer before anyone else has time to put it all together."

"You're a good agent, Oz. In fact, you have to be very good for Dad to even consider you for Anastasia, much less enlist you into his group. That puts you into the top two percent, I'd venture to say."

"Right behind you," he said ruefully.

"No. You're a much better agent than I'll ever be. I'm here because Jack and Margaret are my parents. There isn't another way in the world I could have been involved with Interpol, much less this elite group of brilliant people. My affiliation is due to that little thing called nepotism, and I know it from the bottom of my heart. I'm fortunate that Dad even considered letting me take the training. I'm sure it was for my own protection, since I'm now known to the terrorist organizations. My skills are very specialized and very few. One of them is languages. So if you'll go read a newspaper or take a nap, I'll set about learning this new one."

I buried my nose in the list of codes, oblivious to the people milling around us and the passage of time, moving only for the omnipresent janitorial staff to vacuum under our feet. Suddenly Oz bolted upright in the seat next to me and uttered an expletive under his breath.

"What is it?" I asked, looking in the direction Oz was staring.

"See the guy at the check-in desk? The one in the expensive leather coat? We just got a picture of him yesterday and a carmo bulletin."

"Carmo? Interpol code: send all relevant information you may possess about this person, his criminal record, true identity, and criminal activities. That carmo?" I asked.

Oz nodded tersely as he pulled a tiny notebook from his pocket.

"Who is he?"

"The head of a gang of jewel thieves from South America who have brazenly grabbed gems right out of the hands of salesmen and store owners. The gang consists of a couple of hundred former Colombian soldiers and police officers, based out of West L.A., working up and down the coast. Last year five hundred million dollars worth of jewels were stolen, and this guy is supposed to be the mastermind behind the thefts."

"What's their MO?" I asked, watching the big, well-dressed man giving orders to two underlings hovering nearby.

"Instead of two or three thieves tailing a salesman with a briefcase full of jewels, a dozen or more gang up on the poor guy, overpower him, grab the stuff, and beat him up. He's so confused by the number of assailants and the violence, he can't identify any of them." Oz flipped pages in the little notebook.

"He's checking onto our flight. What's his name?" I asked, putting aside the codes.

"Papio Moreno is his current alias. He's got a string of them, and we're not sure who he really is. They've blended into the huge Hispanic community in L.A. so they've been hard to catch. I'll call him in. I heard on the news there was a heist today. He could be taking the jewels out of the country."

"Who are you calling?" I asked as Oz punched in some numbers on his cell phone.

"Mike Woodings is the only L.A. detective specializing in this type of crime. Whoa—Moreno's moving. Tail him and see who he talks to, if there's any kind of exchange, and watch what he's carrying while I connect with the local fuzz and keep my eye on his companion."

One of Papio's men remained behind while Papio and the other left the waiting room area and walked quickly away.

Oz moved behind the pillar so Papio's man, who now stood looking over the passengers in the waiting area, couldn't see him, but

Oz could watch his reflection in the window. I swung my leather backpack over my shoulder, checking the accessability of my gun as I followed the big Colombian, his mustachioed sidekick, and their briefcases down the terminal. The sidekick with the big mustache headed for the coffee shop. Papio took both briefcases—and turned into the men's room.

I stopped abruptly. What should I do now? Leave and go for Oz, or barge in after my quarry? Frustrated, I paced back and forth outside.

A janitor ambled around the corner and parked his cleaning cart by the door. He stooped to scrape up some gum sticking to the floor, leaving the cart unattended.

I grabbed a dirty, threadbare jacket from the handle of the cart and put it on, zipping it up to my chin. Rummaging hastily on the lower shelves, I found a ratty old ball cap, which I pulled low over my face. I tossed my backpack on the cart, covered it with some towels, and shoved my gun in my pocket. Activating my radio locator button so Oz could find me, and taking a deep breath, I propelled the cart into the men's room before my better judgment stopped me.

Papio Moreno bent over the sink washing his hands, both briefcases open on the counter beside him. Another man, much smaller, with kinky-curly graying hair to his shoulders, examined the contents of the cases. Papio glanced in the mirror and the second man whirled to face me as the cart rattled in, interrupting their solitude.

"Get out!" the smaller man commanded, turning a hostile glare on me. I stared back. The man with all the kinky hair was totally bald in front.

"Must clean," I mumbled.

"Get out. You can clean later." He stepped menacingly toward me, his hand reaching inside his coat jacket.

Papio ducked his head and splashed water on his face, apparently confident his companion could handle the disturbance. Or did he not want to be recognized? Were they transferring stolen jewels? Was Papio selling them or preparing to take them out of the country?

Backing up to an empty stall where I could see the entrance as well as my targets, I pulled my gun.

"Interpol. Lie down on the floor with your hands behind you," I ordered, pointing the gun with a steady hand at the two surprised men. With my other hand, I retrieved my radio from my backpack. "Bring in the backup, Oz. Mr. Moreno's briefcase is full of sparklies that I'm betting don't belong to him. Watch for the sidekick with the mustache who went for coffee."

Papio Moreno wasn't a stupid man. He quickly recovered from the shock of being drawn upon, and just as quickly apparently decided I wasn't much of a threat, gun notwithstanding. In one smooth, swift motion, he slammed a briefcase shut and slung it toward me, discus-style.

In the split second before he released the case, I saw what he intended. Shoving the cleaning cart toward him with my foot, I jumped back into the stall just as the expensive leather briefcase crashed with incredible force against the door.

I lost my balance and fell against the commode behind me, flinging arms and legs frantically to save myself from a dunking. Scrambling to regain my footing, I rushed out of the stall in time to see the small balding, kinky-haired man rush for the door with both briefcases in his hands. Sprawled on the floor under the overturned cart and spilled cleaning supplies, Moreno vainly attempted to get to his feet on the slippery, soapy floor. He'd gone down hard and was hurt.

I raced after the escapee, yelling for Oz in the radio still clutched in my left hand. I needn't have worried. The little man with the briefcases collided with the mustachioed man and two full cups of coffee. Hot, brown liquid splashed everywhere. The two men went down in a jumble of arms and legs.

Oz arrived at that moment. "What's going on?"

"This gentleman was running away with two briefcases full of jewels."

"You were just supposed to observe," Oz said, removing the gun from the kinky-haired man's shoulder holster.

"I did. I observed a deal going down. I tried to ask them nicely to give me the jewels, but they threw them at me instead. What kind of help is coming?" I retrieved the briefcases and stepped back into the doorway so I could keep an eye on Moreno.

"Woodings is on his way. Where's Papio?" Oz asked.

"In here."

Using the gun he'd just confiscated, Oz directed the two men back into the men's room, away from the oglers who had congregated.

"What's his problem?" Oz asked, referring to Moreno as he signaled the men to lie on the floor with their hands behind them.

"He's cleaning up his act."

Oz stared at a very wet Papio Moreno, nursing an obviously hurt knee and ego, struggling to get to his feet with the help of the overturned cart. He stopped when he saw Oz and his gun, and began a litany of noisy complaints about the treatment of innocent travelers.

"Allison. Did you do that?"

"I asked them to get on the floor, and he threw a briefcase at me. I didn't want him escaping. We are here to catch the bad guys, right?"

Oz just looked at me.

"Was I not supposed to do that?" I whispered, so our prisoners couldn't hear.

"Who has jurisdictional authority here?" Oz asked quietly.

"LAPD. According to Article 2 and 3 of Interpol's constitution, our field of activity is limited to crime prevention and law enforcement in connection with ordinary criminal offenses. This was an ordinary criminal offense—jewel theft. So we are authorized to act in conjunction with local authorities, whom you were in the act of contacting."

Oz said nothing. He just looked at me.

"Did I do something wrong? Tell me. I don't want to jeopardize my career before it even starts. What's the matter?"

Oz shook his head. "No. You didn't do anything wrong. You did everything right. You just amaze me. You actually came into the men's room, interrupted a buy, incapacitated one man, and captured two others. All in under five minutes." He continued to shake his head.

"I just followed orders. Where are the police? That's our flight being called. We've gotta go."

"Go watch for the cops and bring them in. They should be here any minute. Woodings probably won't make it before we get on the plane. He was home in bed. Like most sensible people at midnight."

Papio Moreno's complaints were becoming too loud to talk over. In addition to his obscene language at being caught by *una niña pequeña,* he was making lawyer noises and demands for medical attention.

I tossed the jacket and hat I'd borrowed onto the cleaning cart, stuffed my gun in my backpack, and hurried from the restroom with the briefcases while the little funny-haired man screamed his irritation at being caught by a half-pint woman. I didn't hear Oz's retort.

Disembarking passengers parted on the walkway as airport security raced through the terminal. I directed them into the restroom and followed with the briefcases, keeping an ear out for the second boarding call on our Singapore flight.

While Oz briefed the two security men, we opened the cases to show the evidence. One was filled with little velvet bags. The other briefcase contained stacks of fifty- and one-hundred dollar bills with gems scattered loosely on top, apparently the ones Moreno had been showing.

I opened several of the pouches, letting the sparkling unset gemstones sift through my fingers. Some of the bags contained incredibly beautiful pieces of very expensive-looking jewelry, already set. These would be easier to identify than the unset stones. But since each valuable stone has its own characteristics, and all the larger, more costly stones have their identifying marks catalogued, even most of the unset stones could be returned to their owners.

The security men hustled their captives to the door and reached for the briefcases, obviously anxious to be away. They were no more anxious than I was to be done with this interruption.

"Here you go, gentlemen," I said, handing over the briefcases. "They've just issued the final call for our flight. We're outta here."

My statement came as a surprise to the security men, who apparently assumed we'd accompany them to the airport security office.

"We must have your statement," the shorter of the two insisted.

"You already have it," I said.

"But not in writing. You need to come with us, now, while the details are fresh in your minds."

Nothing was going to keep me from getting to Bangkok as soon as possible, not even security's insistence that we must accompany them to give our formal, written report to the police. They grew increasingly obnoxious about it, on the verge of becoming downright nasty. The fat one even made the mistake of taking me by the arm to escort me to his office.

I was about to pull rank, on the off chance that Interpol outranked airport security in this instance, when four uniformed LAPD officers arrived. The two airport security guards became overly eager to help, offering to take the men to the airport security office, along with the jewels, while the police took our reports.

The officers refused their offer, taking custody of jewels and men from airport security. One of the officers turned to me, expecting me to repeat my statement for him.

"I'm sorry, officer. I just gave that whole story to those two security men, and I have a plane to catch. You can get all the details from them."

Oz was giving his report to another officer as the intercom announced the final call for Air Singapore Flight 5. I waved good-bye and headed for my gate, hurrying through the jet bridge into the waiting aircraft with the last few stragglers coming on board.

If Papio Moreno managed to slip through the fingers of the intrepid LAPD because of my absence on the scene at this moment, so be it. Bart was my main concern. Moreno was now Detective Mike Woodings' problem. I'd delivered him. I hoped I had as good a result with Bart.

I pulled the files from my backpack, tucking it under the seat in front of me. Still no Oz. I scrounged a pillow and two blankets—airplanes were always too cold for me—and settled down for the nineteen-hour flight to Singapore.

Where was Oz?

The doors on the big jumbo jet were secured. The pilot gave his welcoming spiel as the folding connection between airplane and terminal was withdrawn.

No Oz.

Oh, well. With or without him, I was going to Bangkok to find my husband. I would have welcomed his help and expertise even if his constant proximity might have been a little uncomfortable.

As I buckled my seat belt, I thought of the Oz I'd first met in San Francisco—funny, mischievous, light-hearted, a friendly tease. Then Santa Fe had brought his declaration of love, and his fury at me when he thought I was putting myself in danger.

My mind went back over every contact I'd ever had with Oz. I'd never said or done anything, never given him the slightest encouragement, never once even thought of him other than as a friend and fellow worker. Oz was simply a very nice guy I had to work with.

Why did he have to tell me he was in love with me? He probably never would have revealed his feelings, but when it had seemed apparent to everyone that Bart had died in a helicopter crash during Anastasia's last assignment, he must have felt it was appropriate. It hadn't been. And it ruined a perfectly good friendship.

"Ladies and gentlemen, we've had a slight delay, but we'll take off as soon as we get a little situation sorted out with the local authorities," the captain intoned as a raven-haired flight attendant approached my seat.

"Amy Teale?" she asked quietly, bending toward me.

"Yes?"

"The Los Angeles Police Department requests that you delay your take-off until they can speak with you." Her voice was low with a soft accent.

"You're kidding."

"I'm afraid not." Her shining page-boy bob fell forward across beautiful high cheek bones as she shook her head. "The captain is holding here so you can get off."

"Well, you can thank the captain, but he doesn't need to hold any longer. I'm not getting off. I have something pressing in Bangkok."

"Would you come up and speak with the captain?" Her soft brown almond eyes were apologetic.

"Of course, but it won't change my mind."

I followed her forward to the cockpit. This delay was not on my agenda. There was only one item on that agenda, and that was to get to Bart as quickly as possible. A pox on Papio Moreno and the jewels. And the LAPD. And Oz.

Through the windows, I could see the long arm of the jet bridge stretching back toward the airplane. Reaching ominously to keep me from Bart.

CHAPTER SIX

The flight attendant handed me the phone. Oz was on the other end.

"Mike Woodings is on his way and would like to talk to you when he gets here. We could tie this up nice and neat for him and then take the next flight."

"Sorry, Charlie. I'm going to find Bart. There isn't anything I could tell Detective Woodings that I haven't already told security. They can repeat the details to the good detective. Or you can. But my husband is more important to me than a passel of thieves and all the jewels in the world. Will you please release this airplane for take-off?"

"Alli, there's another flight in a few hours. We can help put these guys away."

"Oz, if the police want my testimony, I will gladly send them a deposition, I will talk to them over the phone while we are winging our way to Thailand, I'll sign my name in blood and promise to come back and testify against the bad guys, but I won't get off this airplane. And I promise I'll devise some horrible things for you if you don't let the pilot taxi this bird immediately. Copy?"

Oz sighed. "Copy."

"Come and get on this plane—since they are holding it and they've reattached the tunnel—and we can talk to Woodings over the phone if it's so important. He certainly doesn't need to see us face to face and the police already have our statement."

Something just wasn't right here, but I couldn't put my finger on it. I couldn't see a single reason for delaying our departure just to talk to a detective who could get our story from the arresting officers. One word came into my mind. *"Leave."*

I turned my back so no one could hear and spoke quietly into the phone. "Oz, I'm getting a feeling about this that I don't quite understand, but I think you'd better get on board right this minute and let's get out of here."

Oz was quiet for a minute. "You've got a point. And maybe the cops had better get Papio Moreno and his friends out of here, too, and the jewels locked up. Papio may still have friends roaming loose in the airport, unless they deserted ship when they saw their boss get picked up. Give me the pilot."

I handed the phone to the flight attendant. "He wants to talk to the captain."

Instead of going back to my seat immediately, I hung around to see what would happen. The flight attendant had already opened the door to the airplane and was obviously waiting for me to get off. Fat chance. There wasn't a single thing in this world that would get me off this aircraft. And who would try besides Detective Woodings? Why would he think it so important to talk to us personally? It didn't make sense.

It had to be Woodings. No one else knew we'd caught Moreno and his cohorts. Or did they? Oz had used his cell phone to call LAPD. And talk to Woodings. Anybody with the right equipment could pick up any call made on a cell phone. They could also trace the number of that phone. And place a call to that phone. Mike Woodings had called Oz back and requested that we stay and talk—after their initial conversation.

Wouldn't Papio Moreno's organization use the latest electronic equipment to protect themselves, the proceeds from their heists, and their buyers?

I glanced in the cockpit. The captain, now off the phone, was giving instructions to the flight attendant. She quickly positioned herself next to the accordion tunnel and grabbed the door handle.

Heavy footsteps echoed in the connecting tunnel—running toward the airplane. I couldn't see who was coming because of the curve in the tunnel, but it was apparent the flight attendant was preparing to close the door immediately. Ready to keep someone out—or close it after someone boarded.

The captain clicked on the intercom, reported that the problem had been resolved and instructed the flight attendants to prepare for immediate takeoff.

It was Oz—looking over his shoulder—as he raced around the curve and bounded aboard. As the flight attendant slammed the door behind him, we hurried to our seats.

"What was that all about?" I asked, buckling my seat belt.

"How do you do it, Alli? Do you have a sixth sense?"

"What do you mean?"

"When you said you didn't have a good feeling about us sticking around, I scratched the itch I'd had when Mike Woodings called me back and said he needed to talk to us personally. I'd attributed the difference in his voice to the gruffness you have when you first wake up. But when you said that—and I thought for a minute—I realized the voice wasn't Woodings. He knew about two briefcases. I hadn't said what the jewels were in—just that we'd caught Moreno and a couple of his guys in the middle of a buy."

"So who was on the phone?"

"Who did you think it was?" Oz asked, leaning across the arm rest.

"The only thing that made sense was someone in the organization had to have intercepted your calls, someone protecting the buy electronically. When it didn't come off, they were prepared to do whatever was necessary to recover the jewels and money and get their guys off. Were those real cops or phonies?"

Oz smiled. "We're on the same wavelength. That was the conclusion I came to after I thought about it. The cops were real. Now that I look back, I'm sure the airport security were Moreno's men. They were in an awful hurry to get Moreno and the jewels off our hands, and us down to the security office, but they disappeared the minute the police showed up and refused their offer to hold onto the briefcases and the men. I think you're right about the organization protecting its own with a phony call from Woodings."

"What was behind you when you boarded the plane? You looked like you were running from the devil himself."

Oz adjusted his seat belt and made a show of settling in for the flight before turning to me. He gave me a slow, mischievous smile.

"I'll tell you, if you'll tell me about Milton Hollingsworth III."

"What's to tell?" I said, relaxing back into my seat. "He was a junior ambassador at the UN. We worked together for a couple of years."

"There has to be more than that," Oz insisted.

"He was a good friend—and the only man I felt really comfortable with." I picked up the codes and began to study.

"Come on. Let's hear the rest of the story."

"Go away. I need to learn these codes and my former love life is no concern of yours."

"Sure it is," Oz insisted. "When your life depends on the person who's guarding your back, it's important to know what makes that person tick. Fill in some of these gaps. Then I promise I'll leave you alone."

It was apparent I wasn't going to get any studying done till I'd satisfied Oz's curiosity. I stuffed the notes in the seat pocket in front of me and began. "When I was five, the military declared Dad dead, but I knew he wasn't. I felt deserted. Fifteen years later, Bart asked me to marry him and he disappeared for years. Now I'd been deserted by the only two men I'd ever loved. Needless to say, I wasn't long on trust for the male gender of the species."

I glanced at Oz, leaning across the arm rest, chin in hand.

"Go on," he urged.

"Milton was caring, attentive, and dependable. He said he loved me and that I'd learn to love him, and he was willing to settle for that. I accepted his ring, but I could never bring myself to set a wedding date. I guess I secretly hoped Bart would come back and want me to be waiting for him."

"And if he hadn't?"

"Hadn't what? Hadn't come back or hadn't wanted to find me waiting?" I asked, becoming increasingly uncomfortable with the tenacious questioning.

"Both."

"You're awfully nosy. I don't think this has anything to do with our working relationship," I protested.

"Humor me. I've always been curious about your relationship after the stories of your wedding. And a little envious."

"Oz . . ."

"No. No. Don't say anything." He held up both hands, fending off my impending eruption. "I just meant you have a relationship anyone would envy, and I hope when I find the right girl, we can have that kind of connection."

I sat back and closed my eyes. Maybe this wasn't such a good idea.

Maybe I'd do much better on my own, inexperience notwithstanding.

"You're not going to sleep before you tell me the rest of the story, are you?" Oz said, nudging me.

"If I tell you what you want to know, will you go to sleep and let me study?"

"Deal," he agreed.

"What do you want to know?"

"Would you have married Milton if Bart hadn't come back?"

"Probably not. His family is obscenely wealthy and his mother is the cream of East Coast society. She was always trying to make me over, to raise me up to her standard of perfection in everything. She had already planned a wedding you wouldn't believe. My wedding. And I didn't have a thing to say about it." I shook my head. "No. I couldn't have married him. I guess I just got tired of saying no to his proposals and figured sooner or later his mother would convince him that he was marrying too far beneath himself. The family actually has a title and a castle in England. I wouldn't fit in."

"Not even with a nickname like Princess?" Oz teased.

"That's Bart's pet name for me. When we were growing up, I looked on him as my knight in shining armor. He was always rescuing me from rattlesnakes in the hills around the estate and all the times I fell off horses and out of trees. There weren't many other kids around, so we hung out together." I laughed and corrected myself. "Actually, I hung around him, following him everywhere. He was four years older and I idolized him. He put up with me and was good-natured about his little shadow."

"Did you date?"

"No. He was in college while I was in high school. I dated guys my age. Bart was my big brother—my confidante." I paused, remembering late night sessions with Bart in the reading loft of the library on the estate, talking about every subject imaginable, thrilled that he was interested in my opinion, and hanging on his every word.

"And?"

"And what?"

"And what happened next?"

"By the time I graduated from high school and was getting ready to go to college, Bart had already finished his degree and was leaving for job interviews. He told me he'd been waiting for me to grow up so he could marry me, and he asked me to wait for him."

"And?" Oz persisted. "Don't stop now."

"I really need to be studying, Oz."

"You can. As soon as you finish. Did Bart give you a ring?"

"No." I squirmed in my seat.

"Did he actually propose—ask you to marry him in so many words?"

"No." Oz was asking tough, personal questions—questions I'd beat myself over the head with for five long years.

"But you felt that was a proposal?"

"I thought it was at the time. I hoped it was. Then as the months turned into years and I never heard from him—I never received even a postcard—I decided I'd misconstrued what he meant and read into his words what I wanted to hear."

"Did you date during those years?"

"Yes."

"And you never found anyone that swept you off your feet and made you forget him?"

"No."

Oz was quiet for a minute. I picked up the papers again, hoping the interrogation was over. It wasn't.

"Alli, will you answer something honestly for me?"

I looked at him. His expression was serious, his usual mischievous smile absent, for once.

"Depends on what you want to know," I said, dropping the papers in my lap again and trying not to show my irritation at the continued interruption.

"How many proposals did you turn down, waiting for Bart?"

"I don't think that's anything you need to know, Oz." I picked up Anastasia's codes, trying to put Bart temporarily from my mind and concentrate on what I'd need to know to find him.

"Sorry, Alli. It isn't any of my business. It's just that you're too beautiful to not have had men falling all over themselves to marry you, and I wondered how many you had to fend off, waiting for a man who'd been gone for five years, without a word, to come back."

"Oz!"

He ignored my chastising tone and pressed on.

"What happened when Bart got back? How did you feel when he showed up? How did he propose?"

Exasperated, I slapped the papers in my lap and turned to Oz.

"What you're really after is my motivation for waiting for Bart. Right? You want to know why I was so certain he'd come back to marry me that I waited all that time without a word from him."

The impish smile spread over his face again. "Tell me, and I'll leave you alone."

I twisted in my seat to face him, needing him to comprehend, completely, my one overpowering reason. "Love. One single word. I loved Bart. I'd never loved anyone else. I knew when he left that he felt the same way about me. The rest was trust—and hope. And that's what I'm running on right now. Love for my husband, and trust and hope that we'll find him. Satisfied?"

Oz nodded, then turned and settled back into his seat. "It's nice to know there's someone who knows exactly what they want, and won't settle for less."

I wasn't sure what he meant by that, but didn't waste time pondering it. I stood, stretched, settled back in comfortably, buckled my seat belt and buried myself in the codes once more. The study session lasted all of about five minutes.

"I know about your explosive wedding, but I don't know any of the events that led up to it. I promise this is the last time I'll interrupt you, but I can't sleep with all these questions running around in my head." Oz snatched the papers from my hands and held them out of reach. "Tell me what happened," he begged, flashing a boyish smile, "then I'll leave you alone."

I shook my head. "You're impossible. Promise this is the last?"

He nodded.

"I was alone on the estate when Antonio Scaddono's men took it over—and devastated to have Bart show up after a five-year absence as a member of a gang of cutthroats and kidnappers. He said he was working undercover with my father to catch Scaddono and needed my help. He wanted me to pretend that I loved him, to pretend to marry him. The wedding was to be the trap. Mom and I were to be the bait."

"Pretend that you loved him? Couldn't the big oaf see that you did?"

"He came on to me with such big brotherly concern that I thought that was our only relationship. I concluded he'd never be able to see me as anything other than his kid sister or his little tagalong."

"But you were willing to go along with the charade?"

"By then I learned that Mom was really Margo, the famous movie actress whose estate we had been living on. She had been hiding from Scaddono for twenty years. Scaddono had broken her cover and come to eliminate the only witness to his assassination of a politically important family in Vietnam years ago. I figured the least I could do was go ahead with the sham marriage to save Mom."

"Was that all it was? A sham . . . a trap?"

"I thought that's what it was. Dad thought it was the perfect solution to the problem. I told you about our connection. Even though he was 'officially' dead, all the time I was growing up, Dad always spoke to me through images and impressions. That's why I felt he was alive. With this ESP—or whatever it is—we communicated, and he always knew what was going on in my life. I just never saw him or knew anything about his life. Dad knew how I felt about Bart, so he figured this would kill two birds with one stone. He could catch Scaddono, and Bart and I would be happily married at the same time."

"And was Bart agreeable to this scheme? To the marriage as a marriage and not just a plan to catch a bad guy?"

"Wholeheartedly, it appears. At the time I felt he was doing it simply for the plan. He thought I was in love with Milton, and didn't care for him at all and was doing it entirely against my will."

"You communicate well, I see. When did you figure out it was for real?"

"Not until I said yes and he put the wedding ring on my finger. The look in his eyes conveyed what he'd been trying to tell me and I hadn't dared believe. Then he showed me the one he'd had made for me to give him. It had been engraved 'Property of the Princess.' That finally convinced me that he really did love me and truly wanted to spend the rest of his life making me happy."

"How did you feel?" Oz asked, studying my face intensely. "Did you believe him or did you still harbor a few doubts?"

"I believed him. With all my heart. It was the happiest moment of my life and I don't know if there will ever be another that can equal it."

Oz was quiet for a long moment.

"Tell me about your parents. I know all the legends that surround Anastasia, but I don't know about your parents' beginnings."

"Mom was actually Margo, the '60s star of stage and screen. She amassed a fortune, bought that fantastic property on the coast above Santa Barbara, and needed someone to design the home she had in mind. Just any architect wouldn't do. MIT graduate Jack Alexander, design engineer extraordinaire, was the man everyone said she needed, but he was in Vietnam with the Air Force Office of Special Investigations. She contacted him, and he came while he was on leave and designed the place. While they were working on the plans, they fell in love."

"I'm curious about the control center."

"Dad convinced Mom to build the underground control center for his clandestine forces, and he designed it right in with the original plans. Jim Allan is the electronics genius who installed all the secret passages and silent sliding panels. He keeps them working while Alma keeps the place polished to perfection."

As I closed my eyes and thought about Mom and Dad, scenes from their past flashed before me as vividly as if I had experienced them myself.

"Go on," Oz urged.

I described the images to Oz as they came. Margo witnessing a brutal slaying on tour with the USO in Vietnam; the assassin searching for her to keep her from identifying him; Margo resuming her pre-Hollywood identity of Margaret Karillides, marrying OSI investigator Jack Alexander, and living obscurely on base in Vietnam. Margo disappearing forever.

The next scene was always the most painful—the one I'd relived in nightmares all my life—Dad being blown to bits in an explosion. He'd escaped, but the military had used it as the perfect cover for him to infiltrate the group of terrorists he'd been trailing. He'd been so successful, they kept him undercover for years, destroying or dismantling one group after another. He became a legend for surviving innumerable attempts on his life.

Now my own husband was following in my father's footsteps—infiltrating a group of terrorists with the purpose of destroying it from within. I shivered. I didn't like the analogy.

"You can't be asleep. Talk to me. We have nineteen hours ahead of us. Tell me a bedtime story and I'll go to sleep so you can study."

"You already made—and broke—that promise."

"Hurry up and get to the end of the story," Oz grinned. "You keep stopping in the middle."

I sighed and continued. "I was five years old when the military announced the death of my father. Mom and I immediately moved to the estate to manage it for the absent Margo while Mom also pursued her career at the university as an expert in native culture and folklore. It was shortly after our arrival, in the reading loft in the library, that I received an impression my father was very much alive."

"Didn't you think that was strange?"

"Of course. But you can't know how comforting it was at the same time. And to a highly imaginative child, maybe not so strange. It wasn't until six months ago that I actually saw my dad for the first time in twenty years. All in one week I met my father face to face, discovered my mother was actually Margo—the film star who owned the estate—and married Bart, my best friend, my only love."

And he was down somewhere in a foreign country where he could easily disappear forever. I shut my eyes to hold back the tears that threatened to surface.

"I envy you and Bart," Oz said, his voice husky and quiet. "You're so much in love. But there's also the flip side of the coin. What will you do, Alli, if . . ."

I held up my hand as if to ward off the words, then picked up the neglected pages from my lap, and stared at them with tear-filled eyes.

CHAPTER SEVEN

I blanked Oz's question from my mind and tried to concentrate on the codes I needed to memorize, codes I'd need to know to transmit messages, to decipher messages, codes to understand what was going on and let others know. Codes to call for help—or to send good news.

Good news. Please let it be good news, I prayed, that I could transmit to Anastasia. News that I'd found Bart—alive and well.

I managed to get into a study mode, blocking every other thing out. Anastasia's codes were easier than Interpol's. The numbers made more sense. 00—agent down. 01—request back-up. 02—suspect apprehended. 03—suspect escaped. Etc.

Interpol's codes were letters, acronyms. *Odgep* was painting; *gakab*—photos; *edbal* meant "for your information"; *omoba* was theft; *ebvip* was short for "please keep us informed of any results of your investigation." There were five thousand five-letter combinations assigned to often-used words and phrases. On the surface, none of them made sense, unless you knew the acronyms in the language they were based on. All messages were relayed in the four official languages of Interpol: English, French, Spanish, and Arabic.

I'd been surprised when I began my training to find that Interpol was not an international "police" organization as I'd always thought, but an international gathering and clearinghouse for information. Interpol agents have no power to make arrests, and they do little work in the field. They spend tedious hours poring over hundreds and thousands of documents, photographs, and fingerprints, piecing together the puzzle that will help the police of the one hundred and seventy-seven member nations make arrests, solve crimes, and find missing persons.

The lone exception, of course, was Anastasia. Jack Alexander's tiny, elite group had been brought under the umbrella of Interpol after 1984 when the international organization declared terrorism a criminal activity and made combating it a major part of Interpol's mission.

Combating terrorism had been my father's life work. Mom had been involved with him for twenty-five years. Now my husband had taken up the cause. Me too, I guess. I'd always wanted to make a difference in the world, but thought it would come by helping to improve the lives of children in Third World countries through my work at the United Nations.

I glanced at my watch. We were five hours into our nineteen-hour flight, and I was tired of sitting. I climbed over Oz, who was sleeping, and headed up the aisle for some exercise. The cabin was dimly lit, most passengers sleeping in various stages of discomfort. A trip to the restroom, some stretching exercises at the flight attendants' station, and a couple of quiet laps around the cabin restored the circulation.

I studied the codes for another hour before sleep overtook me. I succumbed reluctantly, giving up consciousness only because I knew I'd need the ability to think clearly and the energy to act quickly that comes from a refreshing night's sleep.

My pillow shifting beneath my head and hands softly caressing my hair woke me.

"Sorry, Alli. I tried not to wake you, but I have a cramp in my leg."

I sat up. I'd been sleeping with my head in Oz's lap!

"How did that happen?" I asked, puzzled. I didn't remember moving the arm rest. I snapped it back down into place between us.

"You just looked so uncomfortable with your head against the window that I moved the seat divider and let you curl up on the seat with your head in my lap. You didn't object." Oz's gray eyes sparkled with amusement.

I didn't know whether to be indignant or grateful.

"Thanks, Oz, but you didn't have to do that. Everyone else was uncomfortable, too."

"I assure you, it was entirely my pleasure." His wide grin affirmed it.

There was no doubt. This was going to be a difficult trip.

After a quick excursion to the restroom to freshen up, I settled back in the seat next to Oz and studied my tickets.

"We don't land until 11:40 a.m. Singapore time, then we have a two-hour layover before our flight to Bangkok. We'll have lost most of the day by the time we finally get there. Why does everything have to take so long? Wasn't there a sooner flight out of Singapore?" I lamented, knowing all the while I was complaining that Else had expedited our trip as much as possible.

"It won't seem like two hours. Changi Airport's been voted the best airport in the world for nine years in a row. It's a fantastic place—with shower and sauna facilities, swimming pool, fitness center, putting green, Karaoke lounge, and even aromatherapy and foot reflexology treatment. If you have more than a four-hour layover, you can take a free tour of Singapore or rest at their Transit Hotel. You can wander through a science discovery center, an orchid garden and carp pond, meditate and pray in their chapel, watch TV, have your hair done, or hang out at the Internet Center and check your e-mail. And there are more shops and restaurants than you could possibly need."

"What I really need is to get to Bangkok immediately," I whispered, turning to the window.

Oz reached for my hand and squeezed it. "I know."

I patted his hand and withdrew mine from his. Had it been Sky or David or Lionel or any of the others, I probably wouldn't have bothered, but I was so conscious of Oz's feelings for me, I could hardly stand to have him touch me. I never wanted him to feel I was inviting his attention or reciprocating his affection in any way.

"Alli, are you really prepared for what we might find in Bangkok? Emotionally, I mean."

I looked at Oz. His face was full of concern and compassion.

"I know you can handle physically whatever comes," he continued, "but you love Bart so very much, I really worry about your emotional well-being. If—"

"If something has happened to Bart and I have to come back alone, my life will change drastically, I admit. But Bart has given me something precious—a chance at eternity."

Oz looked puzzled. "Meaning?"

"When Bart and I were baptized members of The Church of Jesus Christ of Latter-day Saints, it opened doors that every family should have. We can be sealed, joined under a covenant that time can't destroy and death can't break."

"You believe that?" He looked dubious.

"I believe it. Let me ask you this: do you believe God would bring two people together, command them to cleave only unto each other, bring children into the world to love and care for, and then dissolve that family unit upon death? Does that make sense? That you'd spend your whole life nurturing those relationships to have them end with death? To mean nothing in the next life?"

"I guess that depends on whether or not you believe in another life after this one," Oz said thoughtfully.

"Don't you?"

"Guess I've never spent a great deal of time thinking about it."

"Well, you've got time now. Give it a whirl, while I study some more."

I pulled another book from my backpack and opened it.

"That's not your course of study for this trip. What is it?" Oz asked, peering closely at the white leather book Bart had given me before he left for the Middle East, and I'd gone to learn how to play these ridiculous games my family played for a living.

"The Book of Mormon. I try to read a little every day."

"Is that the Mormon Bible?"

"No, Oz," I said patiently. "It's scripture—like the Bible. It testifies of Christ, just like the Bible does. Here, you read it for a few minutes and I'll study some more."

"No, thanks. Go ahead. I'll leave you alone and take a little nap."

At least now I knew what it took to shut him up.

Nineteen hours was a very long time sitting in one place. Too long. Movies, breakfast and lunch, hours sleeping, and hours of studying and memorizing the codes still left too much time until we landed in Singapore. Even the information I'd been absorbing on gemstones, fascinating as it was, could only hold my interest for so long. I was tired of studying, tired of inactivity.

And tired of being so very careful not to even brush against Oz. The stress of trying to avoid any contact at all was wearing on me. When our elbows touched on the arm rest, Oz would flash that impish smile that drove me crazy. Was the contact accidental or on purpose? I wasn't about to open that kettle of fish.

Three hours out of Singapore I went into the bathroom, meticulously tore the pages of codes into tiny bits of paper and flushed them down the toilet.

Finally the magic hour arrived and we were released from the bondage of the plane. As soon as we'd cleared Customs, I told Oz I'd meet him at our gate at flight time and fled to the peace of the orchid garden. The pond filled with gold and orange carp surrounded by greenery and exotic orchids soothed my troubled soul.

I couldn't sit. I'd had enough sitting for a lifetime so I walked, wandering around the ponds, one on each end of the Departure Hall, and where else I didn't know, until I found myself at the little prayer room. I went in and had a heart-to-heart talk with God.

"Father, I haven't the vaguest idea what I'm doing here. I don't know the first thing about the world of terrorists and wars and death and dying. Well, I guess I have just learned a couple of things, but I truly don't know what I am doing here. I know I'll never find Bart without thy help. And if it wouldn't be too much trouble, could it please be as soon as possible?"

I stopped abruptly.

"I'm sorry, Father. I don't mean to sound like I'm setting a timetable, because I realize that all things occur according to thy timetable, but if it doesn't really matter, can it please be sooner rather than later? Please?"

I sat, hoping to receive some affirmation that my prayer had been heard and would be answered. That was usually the hardest part. Just taking it on faith that the answer would be the way you wanted, instead of the way God thought it would be best for you.

I glanced at my watch, then bolted for the door. Our flight to Bangkok left in ten minutes! I should have checked in twenty minutes ago. If I hadn't already been in the Departure Hall, I'd have missed the flight for sure.

Oz paced the entrance to our gate, checking his watch as I raced down the terminal.

"Where have you been?" he scolded. "They're nearly finished boarding. I thought you were going to miss this flight."

"A herd of wild elephants couldn't have stopped me," I said, hurrying past as he turned to keep up with me. I didn't add that my own carelessness almost did.

"Where on earth were you?" Oz demanded as we settled into our seats near the back of the airplane. "I searched both terminals and both Arrival and Departure Halls. You'd just vanished."

"I was in the chapel," I said simply, not wanting to hear the chastisement I felt sure was forthcoming, and definitely not wanting to argue with him.

I got neither argument nor chastisement. When I finally glanced at him, he was just staring at me.

"This isn't good," he said after a long pause, "is it?"

"No."

We were both silent for an interminable length of time. I couldn't even guess what was on his mind, and I wasn't sure I wanted to know.

"I was so worried how you'd react if and when we found Bart, worried that you'd forget to act like a professional and leave someone dangerously vulnerable. But I'm the one who's acting unprofessionally. Emotions have no place in this business." Oz dropped his head and slowly shook it back and forth as he muttered almost inaudibly, "Why? Why?"

I didn't answer. I had no answers. Why do people fall in love with improbable people? The flight to Bangkok was filled with silent tension.

I studied the itinerary Else had mapped out for us. We were staying at the Oriental Hotel in Bangkok, where Bart had last been heard from. We were free to do whatever we deemed necessary for as long as it took in Bangkok. We also had open tickets to Sri Lanka if we found it necessary to keep the appointment set up for Tuesday at the Galle Face Hotel in Colombo. I prayed we could find him before that.

Traffic in Bangkok was unreal. I thought Los Angeles was bad. That was a picnic compared to this. Seventeen-minute waits at some stop lights, almost that at most others. Our driver informed us the best way to travel in Bangkok was by boat taxi or by foot. It was much less congested and much faster. I believed him. I could have traversed the distance from the airport to the hotel on foot faster than we made it by car.

The one-hundred-and-eighteen-year-old Oriental, queen of Thailand's luxury hotels, was set in a garden on the Chao Phraya River. No wonder so many famous people stayed in this exquisite setting. I pictured Joseph Conrad, Somerset Maugham, and Noel Coward taking notes on the fascinating patrons as they wandered through the beautiful lobby (no shorts, sleeveless shirts or thongs allowed—dress politely or you'll be refused entry). Graham Greene, John LeCarre, James Michener, Gore Vidal, and Barbara Cartland, as well as the others, had suites named for them in the original Author's Wing.

We were to be in the River Wing, built in 1976. We stepped to the desk and Oz began to register. Suddenly it dawned on me—we were registered as Mr. and Mrs. Ed Teale. We'd be staying in the same hotel room. This had been covered in my training. It was common practice for undercover agents. No one gave it a second thought.

But I hadn't thought of a situation where I'd be coupled with Oz. My partner was supposed to be Bart. My heart pounded in my ears. Panic rose in my throat. *You're supposed to be a professional, Allison. Act like it. Every agent faces this situation at one time or another. Deal with it like a veteran.*

"I saw the way you looked at that blonde as we walked in," I hissed, just loud enough for the desk clerk to hear. "If that's who you want to spend the night with, be my guest. I wouldn't stand in your way for the world."

Oz was speechless.

I turned to the clerk, busying himself with paperwork and trying to appear not to be listening.

"We need two rooms, please. Separate rooms. Not adjoining."

CHAPTER EIGHT

"Amy! What are you doing?"

"I wouldn't want to get in your way of having a really good time your first night in Bangkok," I said icily. "Or any of your nights in Bangkok, for that matter. So we'll solve that little problem with separate rooms."

I turned back to the clerk. "Can you accommodate us?"

"I'm checking, Madame," he said quietly. "Just one minute."

Oz grabbed my arm. I pulled away and held both hands palm up in front of me to ward him off.

"Don't," I said firmly but softly, trying to keep this strictly between Oz, myself, and the clerk. "You've made your bed. Now you can sleep in it."

"Do you want to be on the same floor, or do you prefer another, Mrs. Teale?"

"The same floor is fine. Just not the same room, thank you."

Oz was fuming. He'd probably never forgive me for this, but if I didn't, I was afraid I'd never forgive myself. He was so mad he couldn't speak.

We were led upstairs by a staff member who would wait on us hand and foot our entire stay. He was trained to remember our names, what we liked to eat for breakfast, and even what type of flowers we preferred in our room.

Oz stormed back to my room when he was gone.

"Would you like to tell me what that was all about?"

"Thank you for not making a scene when I did that. I appreciate it. And I know you're livid. I hadn't thought about us being in the same room. When it came right down to it, I just couldn't do it."

"Alli, I would never—"

"I know. I know. You are honorable and above reproach. But please hear me out. I don't want anyone, ever, to even insinuate that everything wasn't completely above board on this or any other trip. To do that, we simply avoid—how do they say it—'even the appearance of evil.' I know that nothing could ever happen between us, and you know that nothing would, but no one else—except Bart knows that. This way, we keep everyone straight."

"Are you, or are you not, supposed to be a professional? That was certainly not a professional thing to do. You called unnecessary attention to us, and we were supposed to stay together. Remember what Sky said?"

"I'm really sorry. I just panicked. I know we're supposed to be husband and wife and stay together. Bear with me, please, this time. I'll try to get things right from now on."

Oz's anger was defused by that, slightly. His feelings were hurt—mostly his male ego, I suspected.

"I admit it was a rotten thing to do to you in front of the desk clerk. I promise I'll try to make it up to you some way. But you understand, don't you, I couldn't stay in the same room, even if there were separate beds? I just couldn't."

Oz's shoulders sagged. He dropped his head to his chest and jammed his hands in his pockets.

"You win. I should have seen that coming. I should have been one step ahead, but it never entered my mind that you'd have second thoughts about staying with me. Sure says a lot about my character."

I shook my head firmly. "Don't, Oz. Don't try to make me feel guilty, or beat yourself about the head and shoulders for anything you've done. It's a fact of life. No matter who had come on this trip with me, I'd have done exactly the same thing. Even Sky, bless his fatherly image."

"Okay, partner," Oz said with a sigh. "What do we do now? Pretend you're lead agent and I'll check your methods."

"I want to find the telephone Bart used. I want to talk to anyone who might have been in the area and witnessed what happened."

"And how do you expect to do that? Walk right up to the concierge and ask who saw an agent taken down?"

"I'll think of something. What are you going to do?"

"Keep an eye on you."

"You don't think I can take care of myself?"

"When was the last time you were in Bangkok?"

"I've never been here before. This is my first time."

"Then sit down and let me fill you in a little on life in the big city. Especially this city."

Oz pointed to a little alcove with two easy chairs on each side of a lovely carved table. I sat, more on the edge of my chair than not, almost afraid to hear what Oz had to say. I wasn't sure he'd forgiven me, and I had no idea whether or not he'd try a little retribution.

"You know this is one of the jewel capitals of the world. It is also one of the slave capitals of the world."

"Slaves? In this day and age?"

"You are so terribly naive." He leaned back in his chair, covered his eyes with his hand, and exhaled deeply. Stretching his legs in front of him and draping his hands over the arms of the chair, he looked at me, shaking his head.

"Why did I ever agree to do this?" He took a deep breath. "Procurers go into the provinces throughout Thailand and buy men's daughters, their young daughters, or kidnap them, and force them to work in conditions of virtual slavery. Chaing Mai, in the north, is the official capital of Thai prostitution, but Bangkok is close behind. These girls have to work to buy themselves back, but they only have about ten to twelve good working years to save enough money before they're unemployable due to mental or physical disabilities acquired during their short working lives."

I was horrified.

Oz continued citing statistics, describing what was being done to change things, but I barely heard what he was saying. Naive was a kind word for what I was. I felt positively stupid to think I wasn't aware of something as big as this problem, as horrendous. When Bart had told me I'd lived a sheltered life, I had laughed. I'd been more than sheltered. I'd been blind.

"For that reason, I will not turn you loose on your own in Bangkok, especially at night, to poke around. I will be at your side, poking with you. I want to give you your head on this, so you can get a feel for the work, but I have to know every step you're going to take. Please don't try to ditch me. Please don't make me any more sorry that I came with you than I am right now. Will you promise me that?"

He sounded so very tired.

"Yes. I promise."

"I'll talk to the management about our 'photo layout' and the article we're supposedly doing. You can start poking around, but don't leave the hotel. And please let me know what you're about. Remember that we are a team and if we actually work that way, we'll be more apt to succeed than if we don't."

"Gotcha," I said. "Are we ready to start?"

"Ready."

I jumped to my feet and headed for the door.

"Got your camera?" Oz asked.

"Right here." I grabbed my backpack and produced the little camera I'd be using.

"And your gun?"

"Yes, sir. It's here, too."

"Let's do it."

We returned to the lobby on much more amiable terms than we'd left it thirty minutes before and parted company to begin the search for Bart.

I visited with the concierge, asking about the clientele, the activities, things I shouldn't miss, things we would make special note of in our pictures and article. Then I got down to what I really wanted to know: who usually inhabited the lobby about one o'clock in the afternoon on a Monday? That would be the focus of my story. Midday Monday in the life of one of the most famous (and expensive) hotels in the world. Weekends would probably be more exciting, but what about a Monday?

We were interrupted by an inquiry from a hotel guest, and while the concierge took care of the other guest's request, I stared around the elegant lobby, spotted the phones, and signaled the busy concierge I'd be back. Already I knew I wouldn't get what I wanted until the day man came on duty in the morning. Then I could probe for what I really needed.

I made a mental list of questions to ask: What usually happened? More people than usual in the lobby? Less? Anyone here every day at that time, day after day? Anything unusual or out of the ordinary happen? Of course, he wouldn't tell me if someone had been shot in their lobby, but I hoped he'd point out someone who could have seen whatever happened to Bart. What I really needed was some friendly, gossipy soul anxious to talk, anxious to tell a story.

The phone bank drew me toward it like a magnet—a perverse nightmare that beckoned and called and pulled as though phone cords had reached, snakelike, to entangle me in their tentacles and draw me to the very spot where Bart had been . . .

Had been what? What had happened here?

I examined each open booth, waited for the occupied ones to empty, and examined them. I wasn't sure what I was looking for. A mark left by a bullet, a piece of paper, a tiny splotch of blood missed by the immaculate staff. Nothing.

Of course, there'd be nothing. With a staff of 1,200 to attend to 398 rooms, there would not be so much as a speck of dust allowed to remain overnight, much less any sign of a violent disturbance.

Had it been violent? What kind of violence? Would Bart have still been at the phone? Had it taken place somewhere else, and had someone—who?—come back to these same phones to report it?

I sat down in an open booth and examined every possible angle visible from there. Moving restlessly about the lobby, I discovered the famous Author's Lounge with its bamboo trees, and the Monogram, a shop with antiques and home decorative items. The Pink Poodle featured haute couture, Tabtim Thai specialized in lovely neckpieces, Sartorial offered tailoring, and Cabochon Jewelers had exclusive jewelry, as did Royal Thai Gems just off the Bamboo Bar.

Who would have seen what had happened? Tourists patronizing the exclusive shops? Clerks? Shopkeepers? Passers-by? Hotel staff? But where did it happen? And *what* had happened? The magnitude of it all was simply overwhelming. We didn't have a single tangible clue. Just two heart-wrenching words: agent down.

The words pounded in my ears like a drumbeat. Where? How? Where was he now? Where? How? Where was he now?

Two hands came down on my shoulders. I nearly jumped out of my skin. I whirled around.

"Oh. You scared me to death!"

"Sorry," Oz apologized. "How are you coming?"

"I'm not. I don't have the foggiest idea where to start. At least, not tonight. There's a different concierge on duty in the daytime. And different staff. I don't know about the shops. I need to check their working hours. If we just knew what had happened and where, it would be so much simpler. At least we'd have a starting point. It may not even have happened in the hotel. Maybe it was out front and this was the closest phone."

"Want to discuss strategy over dinner? You haven't eaten that much since we left, and you need to feed those brain cells so they can get kicking."

As I started to object, Oz looped my arm over his. "We don't even have to leave the hotel. You can have your choice of several places right here—although if you leave it up to me, I'll take Lord Jim's. There's a superb view of the river, they serve the best mixed seafood grill around, and I just checked. We can get right in."

Grudgingly I admitted that I might be a little hungry, and I definitely needed the strategy session. In my training sessions, it seemed we'd had more to go on than the single fact that a message had been sent from a phone in the lobby of a great hotel. There was usually a body or a witness or . . . something.

I let Oz lead me to the restaurant. The tantalizing smells convinced me immediately it was the right thing to do. I was suddenly famished. We requested the secluded table in the corner, away from prying eyes and ears, with a lovely fountain splashing noisily next to us. Perfect background noise to prevent eavesdropping, if anyone was so inclined.

I ordered the seafood grill that Oz praised so highly and watched reflected lights shimmering on the river.

"Incredible view, isn't it?" Oz said.

"What? Oh, yes. Yes, it's beautiful. I wonder what he was doing here? Was he staying at the Oriental? Over three hundred dollars a night for a single is a bit steep on a lowly agent's salary. But then, since Anastasia has access to Mom's millions, he could have been here for two months and had one of the $3,000 suites for all I know."

"My guess is that this was a convenient place to make a phone call. The Oriental is one of the high profile places in Bangkok. Power lunches, meetings, conferences—all that. He could have slipped away from a meeting to send the message, been spotted by any number of people who would get paid big bucks to take out a member of Anastasia, and been hit."

"I've got to change my mindset," I said. "When I think of Bart infiltrating a terrorist group, I see him dirty and unshaven with a bunch of filthy terrorists hiding out in caves plotting to blow up the world."

"Try this scenario. Men in silk suits, custom-made in Hong Kong, or Bangkok, costing more than you spent per year in college, sitting around a carved teak table, planning terrorist activities from simple suicide missions in Lebanon that involve only one or two persons to activities the scope of the Twin Towers bombing in New York. Bart didn't come in as a newcomer. He infiltrated under the identity of an established but secretive loner with a reputation as one of the top professional assassins in the world."

I was wide-eyed. "I didn't know that."

"I'm telling you now. I'm supposed to give you information as I think you need it. You're back in training. How would Bart be able to assume this guy's identity and not be caught?"

I thought for a minute. "Bart would have the guy's ID—doctored, of course, and he'd have his background down pat. But if the guy was so secretive, why would he be meeting with the terrorists? It would blow all he'd tried to do by staying a loner."

"Good girl. Quick thinking. Say our guy wanted to make a change in his occupation—he's tired of living out of a suitcase, looking over his shoulder every minute. He wants a couple of big-paying jobs, then he's going to retire to a little vineyard in France and get out of the killing business. Hamas hires him to teach all his insidious little secrets to their men."

"Is that what Bart's doing?"

"He's supposed to be setting up classes, schools for terrorists, but we thought it would take place in the Middle East, not the Far East."

"Did he really take someone's identity," I asked curiously, "or did you invent the assassin and his reputation especially for Bart's cover?"

"The man and his background are real. Interpol lucked out and intercepted him before he made his last hit. He has the same general build and appearance as Bart, so it was the perfect in with the terrorists. In custody, he revealed the codes Bart needed to establish contact, and Bart assumed his identity."

"Then someone could just as well be after the assassin as Bart."

"That's true. Double jeopardy."

"Was he really going to teach all those terrible things and then turn those men loose on the world?" That would be too out of character for Bart—and Anastasia.

"No. We were supposed to get word of the times and locations of the schools; then, with a different scenario for each of them, pick up the 'students' and let the teacher get away. But we never got the calls. We don't know what happened, what changed, but something did."

Our dinner arrived, and as I picked at it, I thought of everyone who could be trying to harm my husband or the man whose identity he had assumed. The list was unbelievably long.

"Oh!" I nearly choked when the thought came to me.

"What's the matter?" Oz asked. "Swallow a bone?"

"We're in Bangkok! The Royal Palace! Sunny and Boomer! I haven't called them yet."

CHAPTER NINE

I couldn't believe I'd forgotten to call those two the minute we arrived in Bangkok. Actually, I could believe it. With Bart's dramatic disappearance, I could easily forget my own name.

Oz had heard about the kidnapping of the Thai king's grandchildren, but it was information relegated to a closed case and tucked in the far reaches of his mind. I refreshed his memory.

"It just happened to be the *last* time Bart infiltrated a group. He hired on as a sea hand on the *Emerald of the East* and sailed from Bangkok to Santa Barbara with the crew that Antonio Scaddono had sent to take over Margo's—Mom's—estate. Tony decided to make a little money on the side and grabbed a bunch of jewels from the summer palace and two children to hold for ransom."

"And they just happened to be a royal prince and princess?" Oz asked.

I nodded.

"I was able to spirit the two kids and the jewels away from the house and hide them in a tree until they could be rescued. Dad had known King Bhumibol Adjulyadej from a couple of previous incidents here, and he let him know his grandchildren were safe and under his supervision. Sunny and Boomer thought it was a great adventure and were even ring bearers at our wedding."

What a long time ago that seemed. Oz graciously didn't interrupt my memories during the rest of our meal.

After dinner, as we explored the hotel and gardens, it started to rain. This was the rainy season so I'd come expecting a good drenching. I got it. When it rains in Bangkok, it's as if the heavens open up and dump. And the water doesn't just come at you from above. Suddenly there are little rivers gushing up from everywhere and big, deep puddles covering everything.

I didn't remember ever being so wet. Oz left me dripping at my door and said good-night. I soaked my tired limbs in a hot tub filled with billowing bubbles and thought about our conversation. Something nagged at the back of my mind, something I knew I needed to remember to ask Oz before I began my morning. Something that flitted right on by and got away.

I was just dozing off when it came to me. I called Oz and woke him.

"Question," I said when he finally picked up the phone. "Can we ask blatant questions in this guise as photo-storytellers or do we have to play it cool and stay in character? I mean, can I just flat out ask about an incident that might have happened here yesterday, or do I have to pussyfoot around and go in the back door to find out if anybody saw anything?"

"Up to you," Oz mumbled. "After you've questioned someone for a few minutes, you'll probably develop a feel for what you can and what you can't ask that person."

"Thanks." Big help that was.

I slept fitfully. I'm sure I was awake more than I was asleep. I was so anxious to be out of bed and on to the important business of the day. I finally got up and read my scriptures until sunrise. Then, dressing in a cotton skirt and blouse so I wouldn't melt in the humidity, I hurried down to the lobby at the crack of dawn, waiting for the shift change.

Fortunately most of the employees had some knowledge of English or French. I talked to people in housekeeping, maids cleaning rooms, waiters preparing the dining rooms for breakfast, and even some of the shopkeepers as they unlocked their shops. No one knew anything. Or they weren't talking.

Deciding to find out what I could without addressing it directly, I interviewed the concierge about Mondays, all Mondays in general, and then last Monday in particular. When he'd satisfied all those questions, I tried a different tack.

"What do you do when there's a disturbance of some kind on the premises?"

The handsome Thai concierge, only a littler taller and probably a little older than me, smiled and his dark eyes lit up.

"Call house security first, of course. Disturbances are their business. Keeping our guests happy is mine."

"What constitutes a disturbance?" I asked.

"Would you like to talk to the head of security? Kim Kee probably has some interesting stories, although I'm sure the hotel would frown on any of them being published."

"Oh, I promise I wouldn't publish anything like that. I was just curious. Nothing negative would ever end up in the article."

Head of security turned out to be a large Japanese man who looked like he might be in training to be a Sumo wrestler. If he could get close enough to anyone to fall on them, they'd never rise again. I picked up the same thread of questioning I'd followed with the concierge—what typically happened on Monday, and had anything atypical happened this Monday?

He described some general types of disturbances—inebriated guests, a persistent vendor pursuing a guest, and the normal amount of shoplifters and pickpockets, although his security people were very sharp and usually escorted those types off the premises as soon as they were spotted, he assured me.

"Someone mentioned an incident this past Monday. Can we start there?"

"Umm," he said, watching me closely. "I believe something did happen down by the river."

I had noticed a loading area on the river earlier. I tried to appear nonchalant. "Yes?" I asked.

Kim Kee had been notified that some kind of altercation had been going on, but by the time he got to the loading area, all the parties had vanished.

"But you didn't see anything? Who might have been involved? What happened to them?"

"Nothing."

"Who turned in the report?" I was scrambling, scratching, trying to find even the tiniest clue.

"Don't remember."

"Do you keep a record of those things?" I persisted.

"Yes, we do." He smiled slightly.

"Could we check it?"

He shifted his bulk and looked at me. "Why do you want to know? Why are you so concerned with this? This is not the kind of thing the hotel would approve for your magazine."

"I promise I will not put any of this in the article." I looked at him, trying to decide what might convince him to help me. Money? Would he be insulted at being offered a bribe? The truth? Might sympathy work better?

"Come," he said finally. "We'll see what there is to be found."

Not much in his records, it turned out.

One of the gardeners had heard a shout and a scream. When he stood and looked over the bush he was trimming, he saw a man being helped to his feet by a very young woman. Probably one of the prostitutes that ply the area, the gardener thought, by the way she was dressed. She helped him into a water taxi and they left.

"What happened to the man?" I asked, trembling with the news.

My security friend pointed at the chair on the other side of his desk. "Sit, please."

I sat.

"Why do you want to know this?" he asked, placing his huge arms on the desk and leaning toward me.

"Because I'm a curious little writer who likes the stories behind the stories," I said, hoping he'd buy that. It was the truth. I always liked the back story more than the headline story.

"You asked about something that happened on Monday. You knew about the incident."

"My story is about a famous hotel on a Monday. Other writers do the glamorous weekends when the celebrities come. I thought I'd do something different."

He was quiet for a minute, thinking about my answer, while he watched me closely. "Is it important to you, to find out about the incident?"

I nodded, suddenly unable to speak. What an agent I made. Ready to dissolve into tears at the first news of Bart—if it was Bart.

"Tell me," he said, rocking back in his chair, tapping a pencil in the palm of one hand.

I swallowed hard, took a deep breath, and willed myself to act professionally, even if I didn't feel it at the moment. "A man made a phone call from here Monday afternoon about 1:00 and reported to his company that everything was fine. Thirty minutes later, another call was placed from the same phone. It said that he was . . . down. That was all. He didn't make the call."

"And you suspect foul play?"

"Yes. Could I talk to the gardener?"

My big friend tapped the pencil against his thumbnail and chewed on the inside of his cheek.

"What do you expect to find out from him?" he asked, cocking his head to one side as he studied me.

"A description of the man and the woman. If she's from around here, maybe he knows her."

"And then what?"

"Then I would try to find her to see what happened to the man."

"And if you found her, and she knew nothing?"

"If I found her, surely she would know what happened to the man—where he was—how he was."

Slowly the light dawned. This man knew the woman. This man was playing with me. Kim Kee knew about her and about Bart.

"Or do I even need to talk to the gardener? Maybe you have the information I'm looking for and we don't need to go any further than this room." I smiled a conspiratorial little smile and opened my backpack, letting my hand rest visibly on my wallet inside.

"Is his company willing to pay for information?" A slow smile spread across the ample cheeks as he watched my hand close around my wallet.

"Yes, they are."

"How much?"

"Depending on how precise the information is, it could be worth a great deal."

"What, in your estimation, would be a 'great deal'?" He leaned forward on the desk again, both palms supporting his triple chins.

"What is the asking price for the information?" I countered, not having the faintest idea what he would consider fair. I'd pay my entire inheritance, and then some, to get Bart back.

"What will you be paid for your article? A thousand dollars? Two? I think I could find the little woman. She is probably a very expensive prostitute and her time is costly. I think she would ask in the neighborhood of five thousand dollars for an interview." His eyes never left my face as he searched for some clue as to how that sat with me.

"It's a very small company. I think they'd be willing to pay three thousand dollars," I countered.

"Four."

"Thirty-five hundred," I smiled, aghast that I was bargaining for information on my husband.

"Let me see if I can arrange for her to be in the lobby later this morning. If she agrees to talk to you, and if she agrees on your price, where can I contact you?"

"Leave a message at the desk. I'm not leaving the hotel." I stood to leave on legs that quivered uncontrollably.

"Would you be pleased to leave a little earnest money so that I can convince her you are sincere?"

"Of course." I thumbed the money in my wallet without removing it from my backpack where he could see it, counted ten one hundred dollar bills, and laid them on the desk.

"You know, of course, that it is her decision to speak to you. She may want more money, or she may not want to see you at all."

"Please do what you can to convince her I need to talk to her. I'll look forward to hearing from you, right away," I said. Straightening my shoulders, I walked through the door and down the hall, aware of Kim Kee's eyes on me every step of the way.

Where was Oz? I couldn't wait to tell him what I'd found out. I stopped.

Just what have you found out? If your big friend is legitimate, and someone actually did get hurt by the river, that doesn't mean it was Bart. I took a deep breath. *Don't get your hopes up until you actually talk to the woman.*

Oz chatted amiably with the assistant manager near the reception desk. In a minute or two, I was able to draw him away.

We walked into the misty garden where we couldn't be heard, and I recounted my morning's results, trying to keep my enthusiasm and excitement in check.

"Good work." Oz nodded his head and smiled. "Good work."

"I didn't have any idea what kind of money . . . Oz, I was

bargaining! Bargaining for my husband. I can't believe I did that."

"You did what was expected of you in that situation. If you hadn't bargained with him, he might have upped the ante considerably, figuring he really had you over a barrel. This way it appeared that the information was important, but not vital. Now what's your plan?"

"Go sit in that lobby and wait for her to come. And hope it's soon. I'm not sure my nerves will handle this."

"You're doing fine. Do you want me to sit in while you talk to her or do you want to handle it yourself?"

I hadn't thought that far ahead. "I guess I'd sort of assumed that I'd talk to her. Is that all right?"

"I'll stay close in case you need me. I've got some phone work to do. And it would probably be a good idea if I was seen taking a few pictures. I'll keep an eye out for her while I'm working. Signal if you want my help."

I curled up in a quiet corner of the lobby to wait, going over and over in my mind how to approach this woman, how to get the information I needed. Would she even be willing to speak to me? And if she was, would she have anything helpful to tell me?

A phrase from my reading this morning flashed through my mind: "And I was led by the Spirit, not knowing beforehand the things which I should do." *Yes, lead me, please,* I prayed. *I certainly don't know what to do or how to broach what could be a very delicate subject with a most reluctant witness.*

Finally she came. I knew intuitively it was the woman I waited for as she approached the desk.

CHAPTER TEN

She was tiny, exquisite, like a little porcelain doll. Long, silky black hair hung all the way down her back, swaying as she walked. Her turquoise brocade dress, tailored to fit her curves perfectly, was split to her thigh, but her step was so demure, the leg was rarely visible.

The desk clerk pointed to me and as she turned, I gasped. She was only a child.

I rose to meet her, not sure how to greet this woman-child. She took the hand I offered, her eyes not meeting mine, but cast modestly downward.

"I'm Amy Teale," I said, wishing I could be honest with this young woman who held my very breath in her hands at the moment.

She shot a quick glance at me, then dropped her eyes again. "Mai Li," she said softly.

"Can we go in the garden to talk?" I asked, not wanting this to be any more public than it had to be.

Nodding, she led the way and we walked silently to a bench under a flowering flame tree.

"You were here Monday when something happened to a man by the river?" I asked, taking her hands in mine.

She nodded.

"Tell me what the man looked like. Did you take him somewhere? Is he . . . okay?" My throat closed up on that last word.

Finally Mai Li looked at me. "Who are you?" she whispered.

"If the man is who I think he is, I'm his wife. How did you get the number and the code?"

"What number and what code?" she said, straightening her shoulders and looking me directly in the eye. The timidity had been a pose. The real Mai Li wasn't a frightened little mouse.

I repeated the phone number, and the dread code—00.

She nodded, satisfied. "What is your husband's pet name for you?"

"Princess. Was it my husband? Tall, blond, with azure blue eyes?"

"Describe some very telling identifying mark."

The scars Bart received in the prison in Tibet were the most telling ID I could give her, but I wouldn't expect this exquisite creature to have seen them. Still, something made me describe them.

"He has scars crisscrossing his back, from his neck to his waist, from being whipped."

"Yes, it was your husband."

My heart leaped to my throat. Contradictory emotions raced through me. It was Bart. And this beautiful prostitute had seen his naked back.

"What happened? Where is he? Is he okay?"

Mai Li smiled. "You must never gamble. Your emotions speak on your face. Your husband was stabbed—but not seriously," she quickly reassured me. "I took him to my room and cleaned the wound and bandaged him. He stayed the night in my bed, but in the morning when I came home, he was gone. I don't know where."

I fought to banish the picture of Bart in this beautiful girl's bed, and of her tiny, delicate hands, washing, comforting, ministering to my husband. And what else? I shuddered at other thoughts that forced themselves into my mind. Unfair, illogical thoughts. Thoughts unfair to Bart's fidelity.

"When did you see him last?" I pressed.

"Yesterday morning."

"He didn't leave a message—or anything?"

"He left money."

My cheeks blazed crimson. I bit my lip. Bart would not . . .

Mai Li shook her head. "He was my friend. He gave me money to buy my freedom. That is how I happened to be with him when he was hurt. He was giving me money. He said he would be leaving and that he would give me as much as I needed so I could be free now because he didn't think he would be coming back for a while."

"Did he say where he was going?"

Mai Li shook her head and her hair fell forward, veiling her face.

"Will you tell me exactly what happened on Monday? Try to remember every detail. Something that didn't seem important might be the very clue I need to find him. Start from the first time you met Bart."

"I was to meet a client in the Author's Lounge. Your husband was there with another man, one with a very evil face. My client was late. Some drunks began harassing me and the tall, blond man with eyes the color of Ceylon sapphires took me from the lounge." She looked up at me with moist, dark, almond eyes. "He knew what I was, and yet he treated me like a lady. He wasn't embarrassed to be seen with me. He didn't take me to a dark corner or to his room. We sat in the lobby, we walked in the garden, and he asked about me." She placed her delicate hand over her heart. "Me."

"The inner you—your feelings?"

Mai Li nodded and paused, staring at her hands in her lap.

"He asked how you felt about what you do, and if there was a way you would not have to do it anymore."

Her dark eyes flashed with surprise. "How do you know this? Did he tell you about me?"

Sadness tugged at my heart. "I wish he'd had the opportunity. I haven't heard from him in over two months. But that's what Bart would do. He would worry about you in your particular situation."

She nodded, a kind of awe on her face. "He said that—that he would worry about me. He wanted to speak to my master, but I did not dare give him the name. He gave me money, twice what I would have been paid by my client, and sent me home. The next night I was meeting another client, and your husband saw us leaving the hotel. He called the man aside, whispered something to him, and my client rushed off with a horrified look on his face."

"And once again Bart gave you money and sent you home." I could imagine what Bart had told the poor man!

"Yes. This continued for several nights until my master heard what was happening. He confronted your husband. They did not know I heard their argument. Your husband offered to buy me. My master refused. Your husband offered . . . ," Mai Li hesitated, ". . . a great amount of money."

I smiled. My money—actually Mom's, which would become mine one day if my generous husband didn't give it all away and I didn't use the rest of it on bribes to find him. "And did your master agree to take it?"

"No. So your husband reserved and paid for my time for every minute that he was in the city." She glanced up with delight-filled eyes. "I've never had such a marvelous time. I've visited my parents in Chaing Mai. I flew on an airplane. I've slept alone all night and seen this beautiful capital by day. I have tasted what it would be like to be free." Mai Li put her hand to her mouth and looked at me.

My face must have mirrored the thoughts that flashed through my mind. Bart had bought and paid for time with this lovely woman-child. She was an expert at the art of pleasing men. Had she pleased him?

No, Bart wasn't the kind of man who would ever go to a woman like this, no matter how beautiful, no matter now available, no matter what the circumstance. I had to believe that with all my heart. I had to trust my husband. His integrity. His morality. His love for me.

"You must think that your husband—"

"No, Mai Li. I don't think my husband did anything other than show you great kindness. He isn't that kind of man. Now, finish your story."

"On the day that your husband was to leave the city, he came to speak to my master about buying my freedom. I waited in the garden to hear my master's answer. He refused. Your husband became angry and threatened to get my master fired. My master threatened to have your husband arrested before he could do that." Mai Li stopped.

"What happened?"

"Your husband left to find the hotel manager. He was knifed."

"By whom? Your master?"

"I did not see. I heard your husband cry out and I ran to the sound. He was lying on the ground, a dark red stain spreading over his jacket, his generous blood flowing on the stones."

I caught my breath as her graphic words stabbed at my own heart. "You said it wasn't serious."

"I thought he was dying when I found him . . . so much blood. I got his jacket off and we held it against his side while I helped him those few steps to the water taxi. He said it was not serious and instructed me to take him to my room and clean and bind him. I did. He was very brave, until I poured the antiseptic on his open wound. He passed out."

"Go on," I prompted. "When did you come back to the Oriental Hotel and call?"

"He sent me as soon as he regained consciousness."

"Did he tell you why he wanted the message sent?"

"He said it was in case the wound was more serious than he thought, that maybe someone ought to know."

"Mai Li, how bad was it?"

"It was a jagged cut, but not in a vital area. If the knife was clean, he will heal."

I dropped my head in my hands. *If the knife was clean.* What were the chances of that? "Then what?"

"He slept most of the night . . ."

"You stayed with him?"

"Yes. I sat on the bed beside him and prayed for him and read a book he gave me."

I tried to banish the vivid picture of Bart in her bed, of her curled up beside him. It had been two months since Bart had shared my bed. Stop it! I screamed at those images in my mind. Get thee from me! I concentrated on Mai Li's words as she continued, trying to rid myself of the jealousy that threatened to cloud my judgment.

"Toward morning he said he needed a painkiller. He gave me money and sent me to buy some. When I returned, he was gone."

"Did he leave on his own, or did someone find him and take him away?"

"There was no sign anyone had been there. His clothes were all gone. He had straightened the bed. On the pillow was the number of an airline and money to fly out of here to wherever I wished to go."

"But you're still here. Why haven't you gone?"

She looked away. "I wanted to stay until I was sure he didn't need me any more. I didn't want to be gone if he came back and needed my help. He had done so much for me. But I do not know why. Can you tell me about this man who risked his life for a lowly prostitute?"

"My husband believes that if you can do any good in the world, you should. If you can help someone, you need to. He was being a good Samaritan."

"Samaritan? I do not know this word."

"It's from the Christian Bible, a story of a man who went out of his way to help someone when no one else would."

"Yes. He is a good Samaritan."

"Will you leave Bangkok now?"

"Yes."

"Do you know where you'll go?"

Her eyes filled with tears, and she dropped her head slightly as she shook it. "I can't go back to Chaing Mai, to my family. I don't know where else to go."

"Would you like to go to America? Do you have any skills except . . . ?" I didn't exactly know how to finish that sentence.

She shook her head.

"Do you read and write English as well as you speak it? And do you have a passport?"

"Yes." Her face lit up.

"Then you could teach English to the Thai people in America. Get the next flight to Los Angeles. Here. As soon as you've made your reservations, call this number and give them your flight number, airline, and arrival time. I'll call right now and tell them you're coming. Bart's parents will pick you up at the airport. They will take you home and help you get settled in America and find you a job." I scribbled Jim and Alma's names and the number at the estate in Santa Barbara.

The light in her face dimmed considerably.

"Does that frighten you? To go so far away all alone?"

Mai Li nodded, unable to speak.

"Wait. How safe would you be if you were in the employ of the royal family?"

Her eyes widened.

Whoa. Slow down, Alli. Better talk with Sonny and Boomer before you make any promises.

"Mai Li, what will happen if your master finds you in the next few hours? Can you go somewhere that's safe? Somewhere I can get hold of you in a minute? How about my room upstairs?"

She looked a little uncertain. Because she didn't know whether she would be safe there? Or because she didn't know what I was planning for her?

"Do you want my help, Mai Li? Do you want me to get you out of your master's hands so you can be free to live your life as you wish?"

The frightened little girl who had always been told what to do battled with the woman who wanted to be free. I wasn't sure who would win.

"Yes," she said softly. "Yes, I would like to accept your help."

I dug deep into my tan leather backpack. "Here is the key to my room. Lock yourself in, don't answer the phone, and wait for me to come back. I will knock like this." I rapped on the bench to show her. "Don't open the door for anyone else. Now go, quickly."

Mai Li nodded, got up, and hurried toward the river. She turned as if to wave at me, at the same time looking around to determine if anyone was watching her. Then she doubled back into the hotel using a circuitous route. I sat for a minute, eyes closed, uttering a quiet prayer of thanks for this much news.

"Did she tell you what you needed to hear?"

I jumped at the voice so near my side. I hadn't heard anyone approach. Had he listened to our whole conversation? Did he know what we were plotting?

"She told me what she knew. It wasn't all I needed to hear, but it will have to do." I turned to look at Kim Kee. "Are you going to let her buy her freedom?"

Kim Kee's eyebrows shot up. He didn't answer for a minute. "She told you . . . ?"

"She didn't tell me anything about you. I assumed since you could put your hands on her in such a short time, that you knew her well. If she worked the Oriental Hotel, she would have to have your permission; otherwise, you, as head of security, would make sure she never stepped foot on the premises. Will you let her buy herself back?" I stood and faced him.

"Mai Li is very good. She makes a lot of money for me. I would suffer financially if I let her go."

"But you will, won't you? You will let that child go to try to live a normal life."

"How can she live a normal life, after what she has been?" he laughed scornfully.

"After what you made her!" I interrupted hotly. "What was her price? What did she originally owe you?"

He licked his lips, his tongue going back and forth on his bottom lip. He was doing a tally in his head.

"Never mind counting what you're going to lose. Here's the rest of your thirty-five hundred dollars, and another fifteen hundred to make a nice round five thousand dollars. Let her go. Please."

I was going to add, "You don't want to lose your fine job here," but I bit my tongue. I didn't need to provoke the man who might have stabbed my husband. I pressed the money into his outstretched hand.

He searched my face. What thoughts lurked behind those fathomless dark eyes? That I was a threat to him and his cushy job? Was he even now contemplating the same reward for me that he'd given Bart for interfering in his life?

CHAPTER ELEVEN

With a slight smile and incredible grace, Kim Kee wheeled his bulk around and stalked back to the hotel.

From another direction, Oz hurried across the garden to meet me.

"Did she know anything?"

I shook my head as we strolled back toward the hotel.

"Back to square one." I recapped Mai Li's story.

"No eye witnesses to the stabbing?"

"Probably not. Personally I think our fat friend in security did it to keep Mai Li on his payroll. We fenced a little, but he has no intention of letting her go."

"Whoa. You lost me on the last turn."

I looked into Oz's puzzled gray eyes.

"The head of security of the Oriental Hotel runs a prostitution ring. Mai Li is one of his girls. Bart was trying to help her buy her freedom. He threatened to go to hotel management if Kim Kee didn't let her go. I don't know how much money he'd already given her, but from her description, it was a substantial amount. Speaking of substantial amounts, I just gave Kim Kee all the money I had with me. Every penny. I'm broke."

Oz produced his wallet and stuffed some bills in my hand, never taking his eyes off me. He put his hands on my shoulders and stared into my eyes.

"So Bart wasn't taken down by someone who knew he was with Anastasia or thought he was the assassin." His voice was bitter. "It was all over a prostitute." He shook his head. "We lose Bart over a prostitute? And what plots are forming in that devious little mind of yours right now?"

I shrugged off Oz's grip and continued toward the hotel, picking a blossom from a flowering shrub as I swept past. Oz did a fast two-step to catch up.

"Don't tell me you're taking up the gauntlet?"

"Okay, I won't." I thrust my chin a little higher. "I need to call Boomer and Sunny before we leave for Sri Lanka and see if I can manage a quick visit before we take off."

"I'm glad you said 'we.' That means you are still considering me a member of this team. Have you already made our reservations for Colombo? Were you going to tell me before it was time to go or just assume I'd be at your side?"

I ignored the tone in Oz's voice.

"Of course I haven't made reservations. You're the lead agent on this case. It's up to you to say when we leave and where we go next. I just assumed you'd come to the same conclusion as I had—that Bart had a prearranged leaving time and sent Mai Li out so he wouldn't have to answer her questions when it was time to go or contend with her wanting to go with him. He was getting ready to leave, she said, and wouldn't be back for a while. Remember? The logical destination would be Sri Lanka, as that was where he wanted to meet someone on Tuesday. Today's Tuesday, is it not? So we need to leave as soon as possible to get to the Galle Face."

"What's on your mind? More than just getting to Sri Lanka and more than a quick visit to the royal children."

I sent a syrupy smile over my shoulder as I headed for the phone. "I'm going to call Boomer and Sunny. You can make our reservations, O Illustrious Leader, and if we don't have time for a visit, at least maybe I'll get to talk to them."

"Mrs. Teale," Oz said in a you-get-back-here-right-this-minute voice.

I spun around and hurried back, took his face in both my hands, looked Oz right in the eye, and kissed his cheek.

"Is that better, *Mr. Teale?* I'm sorry I forgot to kiss you good-bye. Do make our reservations."

I whirled away before he could stop me and hurried to the desk of the concierge.

"Is there some special way to contact King Bhumibol's grandchildren? They visited me in the United States and told me to call them if

I ever got to Bangkok. But I'm not sure how to go about it."

He didn't blink an eye. "I believe the family is in residence at the royal summer palace in Ayutthaya."

At my blank look, he offered, "About fifteen miles up river from here."

"Can you get a number for me, so I can call and tell them I'm in Bangkok? We may not be able to arrange a meeting, but I do need to let them know I'm here."

A good hotel concierge is worth his weight in gold, and like magicians, they make things appear, seemingly out of nowhere. It couldn't have been more than a few seconds before he had produced the number. The next part was not as easy.

Thai was not a language in which I was conversant. After many attempts to relay my request to speak to the young Bhumibol, I turned once again to the concierge and asked for his assistance. I wasn't sure whether the person to whom I was speaking couldn't understand what I wanted, or simply didn't think it was important enough to bother about.

Unfortunately, neither Boomer nor Sunny could be reached. Now what? I didn't want to go back to my room and have to rescind my offer of employment with the royal family. Why did I have to make such a rash statement? When would I learn to curtail my impulsive nature? If I had spoken with the children, I was sure they could have found somewhere for Mai Li. But again, would she be safe if she remained in Thailand? People could just disappear even if they were under the protection of the royal family.

I squared my shoulders and hurried up to my room to face Mai Li. What would I tell her?

I knocked, once, twice, three times, in the signal I'd devised.

"Yes?"

The confident reply surprised me. I'd expected a timid response. But if it were me behind that door, I'd have sounded just as she had. Smart girl.

"It's me. Let me in."

The door opened just a crack, the chain still attached. Then the chain was unhooked and the door opened just wide enough for me to slide through. She grabbed my arm and pulled me away from the door.

"I have been thinking," Mai Li whispered before I could say a word. "It isn't safe for me to be here another minute, for either of us.

I was leaving as you came. My master will suspect that you will try to help me and come looking for me. I wouldn't want to be responsible for anything . . . unpleasant happening to you."

"What would he do to me? He can't prove I've done anything more than speak to you."

"I must go. Now, before he has time to act. If I am to be free of him . . ."

"Did you decide where you're going?"

"No. Just away from here."

Suddenly a loud, authoritative knock rattled the door.

Mai Li jumped, her hand over her mouth, her eyes terrified. We both knew who it was before he said a word.

"Mrs. Teale? Are you there?"

"Get in the bathroom, quick. Turn on the shower, full force," I whispered.

Stripping my clothes off, I tossed them on the bed. The knocking sounded again, louder this time. I donned the heavy, plush terry cloth robe I'd discarded after my shower this morning as Kim Kee's voice bellowed on the other side of the door.

"Mrs. Teale, I'd like to talk to you. Please open the door."

"Just a minute."

I made sure Mai Li was out of sight, threw my bag on the bed, then opened the door just a crack, with the chain still attached.

"What can I do for you?"

"I have reason to believe you have something in your room that belongs to me. I'd like it back, please."

"What could I possibly have that belongs to you?"

"I want to search your room."

"Sorry. You caught me just getting in the shower. Could you come back later?"

"Mrs. Teale, if you don't open this door, I will break it down."

He could, too. All he'd have to do is flex his huge body against it, and it would collapse.

I opened the door.

"Thank you, Mrs. Teale. That was a wise decision." I smiled to myself as he slipped a key in his pocket. The key to my room, no doubt.

"I always cooperate with the authorities. Especially since I have absolutely nothing to hide." I wrapped the robe tighter around me. "Well, almost nothing."

He smiled at the little joke.

"What do you think I have that belongs to you?"

"I'll just take a look around and let you know when I find it." Kim Kee left a man at the open door and wandered about the room, looking behind the drapes, the chairs, and under the bed. Then he headed for the bathroom. I held my breath.

"Should I turn my shower off or will this only take a minute? I don't want to run out of hot water. We are getting ready to go, you know. My husband has the pictures, and I've been interviewing the employees. We have another hotel to cover tomorrow so we're leaving Bangkok in the next couple of hours. I need to get ready."

"Why do you and your husband have separate rooms?"

"Since it has nothing to do with security, I don't believe that's any of your business."

He opened the bathroom door and steam billowed into the room. He staggered back and wiped his face with his handkerchief. He let the contained steam dissipate for a second, then searched behind the door and any other possible place of concealment.

"Are you satisfied I have nothing of yours?"

He made his way slowly to the door, wiping his sweating face, still checking to see if there was some hiding place he could have missed, and grudgingly admitted that it appeared I didn't.

"Would you like to tell me what you thought I had that belonged to you?"

"Mai Li."

I laughed. "Sorry to disappoint you. That's all I need. Another pretty face for my husband to . . ." I stopped, as though I'd just leaked a secret. "Can I take my shower now?"

The huge man filled the door as he turned to me. "Yes. And you can leave Bangkok. Immediately."

I swung the door shut and locked it, then sank against it to let my quivering knees regain their strength.

Mai Li didn't come out of the bathroom, so I went in. She was nowhere in sight. I peeked in the steaming shower and found her huddled in a corner under a bath towel.

"He's gone," I whispered. "You can come out." I turned the shower off and Mai Li, white-faced and shaking, got to her feet, dressed only in a very wet, tiny, silk chemise. I handed her a dry towel and hurried to put my own clothes on.

As she came out of the bathroom, tugging her dress over her head, I motioned to her not to speak. On the little tablet by the phone, I scribbled a note. "He may have placed a bug in here. Don't talk. We'll have to write. Is there any way to get you down from here without being seen?"

Mai Li's almond-shaped eyes were almost round with fear. She shook her head.

I wrote again. "Do you think he really believes I know where you are?"

She nodded in the affirmative this time.

"Will he watch that close? How about the laundry basket, like the movies?"

That got a slight smile from her. And another negative response. What to do? What to do? Oz would be ready to leave soon, I was sure. I remembered there were almost hourly flights out of Bangkok.

I went to the phone and asked for Oz's room.

"Hi, sweetheart. Did you get our reservations? What time do we leave?"

There was silence on the other end of the line. "Sweety, are you there? I forgive you for ogling that beautiful blonde yesterday. I even forgive you if you did more than ogle her. As long as you were very careful doing it, you naughty boy. I'm almost ready to go, but I do want to pick up a little memento of our stay at the Oriental. I saw a lovely little thing in one of the shops downstairs and I just wanted to know if I have time to go down and get it."

There was life after all on the other end. Oz cleared his throat. "Thank you, *darling,* for your vote of confidence in me. Yes, we have reservations. We need to leave here in thirty minutes to make our flight. Can I help you with your shopping?"

"No thanks, sweety. I can manage it. You can stop by my room when you're packed and we'll go down together. Say twenty minutes?"

"Right."

I scribbled another note to Mai Li. "Do not even move. Lie very still on the bed till I get back."

She nodded. I quickly left the room, running down the stairs so I wouldn't have to wait for the elevator, and went straight to the Monogram, the little shop off the Author's Lounge that handled antiques and small home furnishings. There it was, still center front in the window. A beautifully carved teak chest, inlaid with mother of pearl and coral.

I called a sales person away from another customer who was undecided about which of two elaborately carved screens to take, pulled some money from my wallet and said I wanted to take that particular piece with me right now. While she took my American dollars and wrote out a sales receipt, I called the front desk and asked for a bellboy to come with a luggage trolley.

The young man appeared as she gave me my change and loaded my newest acquisition on his trolley. He followed me upstairs to my room with it to retrieve my luggage.

"Please, let this work," I prayed.

CHAPTER TWELVE

Oz was just leaving his room as we got off the elevator. We met him at the door to my room.

"Will you please wait right here for a minute while we finish gathering my things?" I asked the bellboy. "Then you can take them all down at the same time."

Oz relinquished his suitcase to the bellboy and followed me into my hotel room with the trolley. I shut the door, put my finger to my lips, and signaled "bug." Even if there wasn't one, and I wasn't sure either way, I didn't need to hear his reaction to what I was about to do.

"While I finish packing these few things, will you please do a quick check of the room to make sure I didn't leave anything behind?"

Oz stopped, rigid, in the middle of the room. His gray eyes darkened into two murky pools of disbelief that looked just on the verge of anger as he stared at Mai Li, huddled in the middle of the bed, then at me.

Throwing open the lid on the beautifully embellished trunk I'd just purchased, I started a nonstop monologue so Oz couldn't get a word in and there would be no suspenseful silence to reveal movement of more than two bodies in the room.

"Did I tell you, sweety, about Kim Kee, the head of security? You know I talked to him about finding the woman who helped that man disappear. He actually came up here thinking I had hidden her in my room. Can you imagine that? I almost slipped and revealed your weakness for a pretty face."

I tossed the plush cotton terry robe in the bottom of the trunk and grabbed the frightened Mai Li by the hand, motioning her to get inside the trunk. She hesitated only a minute. One look at Oz and she slipped silently into the safety of the trunk.

The medium-sized ebony trunk would have been a tight squeeze for even my petite stature, but Mai Li had such a tiny frame that she had no problem curling up comfortably on the bottom. I tossed her a pillow from the bed and quickly closed the trunk.

"Did you find anything in the bathroom or did I get it all? Oh, sweety, would you check the armoire? I don't remember whether I hung anything in there or not. I wish we had more time to spend in Bangkok. I really wanted to do some shopping in the floating markets. And I've always wanted to float lazily along the river and see the temples and the scenery and just watch the people."

Oz hadn't moved. He stood immobile in the middle of the floor, watching with a look of disbelief on his face that would have been comical in any other situation.

I continued the chatter. "Can we come back next year and do another story—this time on all the temples? In English, temple has such a high, spiritual connotation. There's something in the word itself that is soothing, peaceful. In Thai, it's simply *wat.* That's neither soothing nor peaceful, and it certainly doesn't carry any spiritual feeling. Isn't language interesting?"

One look at Oz and I knew I'd exceeded his patience on all counts. I slipped the little gold padlock through the lock and secured it. The key went into my pocket.

"Okay, sweety. I'm all packed and ready. Do you want to call the bellboy in so he can take our things downstairs? Did you already call a taxi? Of course, you did. You always think of everything. You do take such good care of me."

Toning down the acting, I said simply. "I'm ready now. Will you call the bellboy in so he can take our things downstairs?" I wasn't sure what Oz's boiling point was, but from his expression, he'd reached it. I canned the chatter.

In minutes we had checked out of the Oriental Hotel and were on our way to the airport. Oz hadn't yet said a single word, and from the way the muscles in his jaw were working, I didn't want to hear anything he might have to say in his current state of mind.

"It's interesting how a country that's ninety-five percent Buddhist and four percent Muslim can embrace Christmas decorations like they do." I continued to fill the silence with a babble of words, as much for the benefit of the taxi driver, who, for all I knew might be in the employ of the head of security at the Oriental, as to stifle my nagging conscience for what I'd just done to Oz.

"Did you know there are only about three hundred thousand Christians in Thailand—out of more than fifty-eight and a half million people?"

Oz was wearing down. I wasn't sure whether it was from my incessant chatter or because we were putting the Oriental Hotel behind us as quickly as was possible in the maddening traffic.

"Then again, since tourism is a major industry in Thailand, it would only be good business to decorate so foreign customers would be reminded to shop for more gifts," I reasoned aloud.

"What are you planning to do with the trunk?" Oz broke his silence with a question that sliced right through to the heart of the matter.

"Trunk? Oh, ship it home, of course. I don't think we want to drag it around with us, do we? What do you think? I wouldn't want it to get scratched and banged up—actually, I think I should have it wrapped for shipping. They usually have those little places in the airports that will take care of that. I hope we have time to find one . . ."

"You can't ship it home—like it is. And you can't wrap it—like it is—and ship it."

"Oh, I wasn't planning on sending the contents, if that's what you mean."

Oz breathed a sigh of relief and put his hands over his eyes.

"How does he do it?" He shook his head and looked at me. "How does he keep up with you? Where did he ever develop the patience to tolerate you? Are you always like this?"

For the first time all morning, I had nothing to say.

But only for a minute. Then I turned to Oz, put my hand gently over his, and whispered very softly, "He loves me. He truly loves me. It's not a simple attraction or infatuation. It's not a passing fancy. He loves me, warts and all. I don't know whether it's because of them, or in spite of them, but he loves me anyway. Just like I love him. You can't analyze love. Who knows why two people fall in love? Is it chemistry? Biology? Or is it the relationship of kindred spirits, bosom buddies, when nurtured, that ripens into the most beautiful, most wondrous phenomenon in the world?"

Oz had no comment. He just patted my hand and turned to look out the window.

I removed my hand. "Sorry. Guess I'm a little verbose today."

"A little!" He turned back and glared at me. "You are the master of understatement." He glanced at the driver, then dropped his voice to whisper level. The vehemence remained in his tone. "And if you call me sweety one more time or pull another stunt like this, I'll terminate this arrangement and send you packing so fast—"

I held up both hands. "Whoa. I get the drift. I'll mend my ways, I promise."

"You do have this all figured out? You have thought, in advance, how it will turn out?" He made a slight motion with his head in the direction of the trunk.

"Well, actually . . . ," I turned to look out the window at the bustle of brightly dressed people, the stream of cars, buses, and tuk-tuks, the little three-wheeled taxis that were cheaper, quicker, noisier, and more polluting than regular automobiles.

"Did you know the tuk-tuk is descended from the rickshaw? And that they tried to ban tuk-tuks from Bangkok because they're causing such air pollution?"

"I'm not interested in tuk-tuks or traffic. What's your plan? Not that I need to know or anything, since I'm apparently only along for the ride, but just so I won't inadvertently spoil any of your plans, could I be in on this?"

I looked at Oz. How could I tell him I hadn't planned further than simply getting Mai Li out of the hotel and the immediate grasp of her master? I had no idea what to do with her, or more correctly, what she wanted to do.

Nodding my head toward the taxi driver, I whispered, "When we get to the airport." We rode the rest of the way in silence as I tried my best to come up with a workable scenario for our trunk-bound passenger.

Mai Li took the problem squarely out of my hands. We deposited our luggage on a trolley, wheeled it to a rather secluded corner of the airport, and I unlocked the trunk while Oz stood guard, shielding the emerging girl from view of passers-by.

"Are you okay?" I asked, worried she may have suffered adverse effects from carbon monoxide in the slow-moving traffic.

"I'm fine." Mai Li looked at me, glanced around the terminal, and a slow smile spread across her face. I threw my arms around her and hugged her.

"We did it," I said, uttering a silent prayer of thanks for Mai Li's deliverance thus far.

"If you can stop congratulating yourselves for a minute, maybe you'd like to fill me in on the next step of this dangerous little adventure." Oz was not smiling.

Mai Li turned to Oz with more than a little trepidation in her expression. She pressed her hands together in front of her and dipped her head in a little bow.

"I thank you so much for your assistance in removing me from the grasp of my master." She turned to me. "I will take your advice and go to America immediately. If your husband's parents are nearly so kind as their son and his wife, I will not be afraid to place myself in their hands."

"Do you still have their number?"

"I memorized it when your husband gave it to me. It is with me always."

"Shall we go with you to get your ticket? Do you have your money with you?"

Mai Li produced a slim brocade wallet from her pocket. "I have my passport and my money. But you do not have to go farther with me. I need to learn to be independent."

"As soon as you know what your airline, flight number, and arrival time will be, call that number and tell them. Jim and Alma will meet you at Los Angeles airport. I'll call them right now and give them a heads up that you're coming."

Oz quietly interrupted. "We have to go. It's time for our flight." Then, as an afterthought, he added, "What are you going to do with your trunk?"

I stared at it blankly. There was no time to post it.

"I'll take it with me," Mai Li said. "I have no suitcase. If I travel with the trunk, there will not be so many questions. I took nothing when I flew to Chaing Mai and was the only one who did not have something to carry."

It was a perfect solution.

"Have them wrap it or box it so it won't get damaged when the handlers start tossing it around with the luggage."

"Yes." Mai Li's dark eyes misted.

"We need to go now," Oz prompted.

I hugged Mai Li once again and hurried after Oz. When I took one last look over my shoulder, she looked like such a lost, forlorn, little child, I almost turned around and went back.

"Mrs. Teale. You are a professional. Act like it," Oz said brusquely.

I opened my mouth to scorch Oz with an acrimonious reply, but bit my tongue instead. Granted, I probably *hadn't* been acting like a professional, but if that precluded being a humane, decent person who could take the time to help someone in need, maybe I didn't want to be a professional agent.

Our flight to Colombo was called again, and we were almost running now, Oz's longer legs outdistancing me in the dash to our gate. As we squeezed past two well-dressed gentlemen with their backs to us, I heard a familiar voice speaking quietly in Spanish. Glancing over my shoulder, I was astonished to see Papio Moreno leaning toward a younger man, deep in conversation.

It couldn't be. I stopped and turned back. It was. Papio Moreno in the flesh. The man we'd left in custody at LAX was in Bangkok. I hurried to catch up with Oz as he reached our check-in gate.

"Guess who had a get-out-of-jail-free card stashed up his sleeve, and lost no time in using it," I said as I stood next to Oz in line.

Oz's puzzled stare flashed from me to scan the faces behind and beyond us. "Who?" he asked.

"None other than Papio Moreno. We passed him in the crush of people at that last gate. How do you suppose he got sprung so fast? Or is it possible he was never taken into custody and booked?"

"You're sure it was Moreno?"

"Positive. Whoops. See for yourself. He's getting on this flight."

Papio Moreno queued up at the back of the line to board our flight to Sri Lanka.

"What if he sees us?" I asked, sidling behind a tall man in back of us.

"His problem, not ours. But speaking of problems, we need to talk about one of yours."

"Can it wait a minute? I need to give Jim and Alma a head's up about Mai Li."

I retrieved the gold compact, and while pretending to examine myself in the little mirror and powder my nose, I ran my fingernail in the engraving on the right side of the compact; that turned on the "send" aspect of the communications gadget. After a quick, whispered explanation to Jim Allan in Santa Barbara, I ran my fingernail along the left side to convert to "receive" mode.

"We'll take especially good care of her," Jim Allan said. "Glad to hear there's been some news of Bart. Good luck in Colombo. Let us know immediately what you find out. I don't need to tell you how worried Alma is."

We boarded the plane and settled into our seats near the back where we could talk more freely. I watched Moreno take a seat near the front.

"Okay. What's my problem?" From Oz's impenetrable stare, it was impossible to tell what was on his mind.

"I know that heart of yours is as big as California, and soft as cotton candy, but, *Mrs. Teale,* you simply can't go around adopting strays and taking them under your wing when we're in the middle of a mission. You lose concentration. You endanger them and yourself. And your partner, as well as the mission. This could have been San Francisco all over again, when you put yourself in jeopardy just to aid an old woman and her cats. Can you please refrain from becoming involved in other people's lives until we finish what we came for? Can you concentrate on the problem at hand and stop running off on tangents? Promise me that you'll stay focused on our goal . . ."

"Of course I'll stay focused on our goal," I interrupted through clenched teeth. I wanted to add, *you idiot!* "I've never lost sight of it for a second. You forget that I have a rather personal involvement in this goal. Would you rather I just left Mai Li where she was? No, don't answer that. Right now, I don't want to know how you feel about that or what you think I should have done. In fact, I don't want to talk to you at all till I calm down."

I dug into my backpack. "Here. Read a book on manners in Sri Lanka, or read my scriptures, or read a magazine, or take a nap. Or disappear. I don't care what you do. Just don't talk to me for a while, please, *Mr. Teale.*"

I was furious that Oz would take me to task for what little I'd done for Mai Li. Had I endangered the mission? Not that I could see. Was I overreacting? Maybe. But that didn't lessen the anger that boiled inside of me at being dressed down for a simple kind act. This was a mistake, this pairing for the mission. A serious mistake. It would never happen again. I'd make sure of that.

I opened the book in my lap, *Culture Shock: A Guide to Customs and Etiquette in Sri Lanka.* "Sri Lankans are some of the kindest and friendliest people in any country in the world," I read. That could very well change when Mr. Teale arrives on their paradisiacal little island.

"Sri Lankans are a conservative people. However, they are quick to anger." Oh, this should be a barrel of laughs. If Oz could drive me to the verge of murder, what would he do to someone who was "quick to anger"?

I tossed the book aside and watched out the window as we took off, leaving Bangkok behind. The muddy Chao Phraya River that emptied into the Gulf of Siam became a winding ribbon of shining satin twisting north through lush, green rice paddies and Thailand's bread basket central plain. The serene scene below did nothing to soothe the fury that still thumped with every beat of my heart at his words.

I picked up my scriptures and opened them at random. "See that ye do not judge wrongfully; for with that same judgment which ye judge ye shall also be judged." I slammed the book shut. That wasn't something I needed to hear right now.

But it was, and I knew it. I hated to admit it, really hated to admit Oz was right, but it wouldn't have done Bart any good at all if I had taken a knife as he had. There was no doubt in my mind that Kim Kee was the one who plunged that blade into my husband. And I *was* jeopardizing our mission getting involved with Mai Li. But how could I have done otherwise?

I closed my eyes and leaned my head against the window. What else could I have done? I pictured Kim Kee chaining Mai Li to her bed, starving her in reprisal for trying to escape. Or worse, Mai Li floating face down in the river.

Bart had tried to do the same thing for her that I'd done. What would Mom have done? And Dad? I couldn't picture either of them turning their back on Mai Li.

Opening my eyes, I glanced at the scriptures that had fallen open against my backpack—to the same page. Right next to the first scripture was another I had underlined one day. "Wherefore, every thing which inviteth and enticeth to do good, and to love God, and to serve him, is inspired of God."

Tingles ran up my arms. I didn't ever remember having such an immediate and forceful answer to a question. It *was* a good thing; I did it out of love; it was an act of service; and I certainly had had divine help or I never could have done it. End of story.

I handed Oz the Book of Mormon and pointed to the two scriptures. When he'd read them, I wrinkled my nose and tried to smile. Humble pie had a decidedly nasty taste and was extremely difficult to swallow.

"Sorry. I shouldn't have flown off the handle. You were right. But—so was I." I stuck out my hand. "Forgive me for that little explosion?"

As Oz started to shake my hand, someone stopped at our seats in the aisle. I looked up into the scowling face of Papio Moreno.

CHAPTER THIRTEEN

"Hola, Señor Moreno. This is a surprise. How did you manage to slip through the fingers of Detective Woodings? I thought he'd put you away for a nice long time."

"Nobody puts Moreno away," he growled in Spanish, leaning down so other passengers couldn't hear. "Butt out, *niña*. Stay away from me and my business. You won't like what will happen to that pretty face if I catch you nosing around. *Comprende?"*

"I understand completely, *señor*. But Sri Lanka is a very small country. You will pardon us if we inadvertently run across you as we conduct our own business, which, of course, has nothing to do with yours as we had no idea you were coming here."

With a black scowl at Oz and an oath I blanked out of my mind, Papio proceeded to the rear of the plane.

"The 'little girl' part I caught, and the 'understand' bit, but what was that last thing he said?" Oz asked.

"Nothing important, and I don't repeat that kind of language. Well. This is a new wrinkle. What now, O Great and Fearless Leader?" I said.

"Now we pass along this little bit of very interesting news to headquarters and see what they make of it. Maybe they have a few more pieces of the puzzle and can make sense out of all of this."

Oz pulled out the sterling silver cigarette lighter that was his version of the communications system and transmitted this most recent bit of news to Interpol headquarters in Lyon, France. The message was scrambled in transmission so anyone inadvertently tuning in, including the pilots in the cockpit, couldn't understand it.

In a few minutes, his cigarette lighter signaled an incoming message. Oz excused himself and went back to the restroom. He could send messages without attracting attention by simply putting the lighter near his lips as if he were idly playing with it. But he needed to be in a private place so someone nearby couldn't hear the lighter speaking back to him.

I tried to concentrate on the cultural guide to Sri Lanka while he was gone, not wanting to make any cultural faux pas. But I couldn't get into etiquette at this point. I kept thinking of the possibility that within just a few hours I might be with Bart again—I might see him, know for myself he was okay.

My thoughts got a little out of control at that point, so I turned to the printout of the civil war between the Tamil Tigers and the Sinhalese. In a nutshell, it boiled down to the minority Hindu Tamils being made to feel like second-class citizens to the Sinhalese Buddhist majority when Sinhala was decreed the official language of Sri Lanka. With this action, the minority Tamils were denied university seats, jobs, political power, and much more. When the Tamils demanded their own state in the northeast portion of Sri Lanka, it had been denied. Since then, there had been continual tension, increased violence, and outright war between the two native peoples.

When Oz returned, his one hundred forty-five pounds was wound tight with tension, and tiny beads of perspiration glittered on his forehead. He sat down, without comment, clenching and unclenching his fists, then laying one ankle across the other knee and grasping his shin with both hands. He just sat there, staring straight ahead, muscles working along his jaw, gripping his leg.

"Either you really banged your shin and it hurts like blazes, or you've just heard something that I need to hear and you don't want to tell me. I'm betting on the bad news. What did you find out?"

Oz smashed his fist into his shoe. "Fire and damnation! What am I doing here? This is going to be just one disaster after another."

I knew better than to speak. When he was ready, he could tell me. What had happened to the funny, light-hearted Oz I'd met in San Francisco? When had he changed into this tense bundle of agitated nerves that hardly had a nice thing to say to me anymore?

With a sinking heart, I realized when the change had come, and why, and I vowed yet again—although for different reasons than a few minutes ago—that Oz and I could never work together again. He was too concerned for my safety. Even that was simplistic. It was complicated by his feelings for me, and his guilt over his feelings for another man's wife, as well as his concern that he keep me safe for his good friend, Bart. No wonder this mission was driving him crazy.

"Papio Moreno is probably going to the Gem Congress in Sri Lanka organized by Victor Carranza, the so-called 'emerald czar' of Bogatá, Colombia. In the last six years, during strikes at gem mines, three thousand people have been killed. Victor has hired more security people than he has workers at the mines, and they have become a veritable little army. Victor is trying to polish the tarnished image of the gem trade with this International Gem Congress." Oz paused and finally looked at me.

"So I'm taking you not only into the middle of a civil war that's escalating almost hourly—the Tamil Tigers have just blown up the temple at Kandy that houses the sacred tooth of Buddha—but now we'll be in town with all the biggest buyers—and thieves—of jewels in the world." Closing his eyes, he leaned back in his chair.

I worked through the ramifications of this bit of news before I spoke, examining the problems we might encounter from every angle.

"This actually could be to our advantage, Oz. We're supposed to meet Bart—or retrieve something he'll have left at the Galle Face Hotel. We're also supposed to find out what's going on at the mines. Another time it might have been difficult to get in, but with the Gem Congress in progress, I'll bet they'll be open for the gemologists to tour. This could be a real blessing for us."

I placed my hand lightly on his arm and kept it there until he turned to look at me.

"I promise I'll do exactly as you say. I won't collect any more strays, as you call it, and I'll try to be the model agent."

Oz stared at me for a long moment before he put his hand over mine. His mouth turned up in a brief smile that didn't quite reach his troubled gray eyes.

"Thanks for the promise. I'll hold you to it, you know."

I looked quickly away, distressed by the raw emotion that burned in his eyes, the pain revealed in his face. I withdrew my hand and reached into my backpack for another book on Sri Lanka, using that as an excuse to avoid touching Oz.

"Have you formulated a plan, or will you just go with the flow when we reach Colombo?" I asked, keeping my eyes averted from his. Since I couldn't keep a physical distance between us, I had to keep an emotional one.

"First we'll check into the Galle Face and see what Bart has for us," Oz said. "That may determine our course of action. Else did get reservations for us, which was good, since it's apparent there's quite a crowd in town."

"Have you ever been here?"

"No. The FBI kept me rather close to home base."

"Listen to this description of the Galle Face." I read from the guide book: "'A much older hotel (1864) with more character than any of the big seven international hotels in Colombo. It was the superior establishment during the British colonial era and, though now showing its age, still has loads of colonial charm—from creaking barefoot waiters ambling along the terrace by the oceanside garden to some truly vast rooms whose bathrooms alone have as much space as the average room in a modern luxury hotel.' Definitely my kind of place. It says Bo Derek, Yuri Gagarin, Prince Phillip, and John D. Rockefeller are among the guests who've stayed there."

"They will have been in good company after your visit," Oz said.

I ignored the comment, not sure what he meant, and not anxious to find out.

"This is interesting. 'Marco Polo said it was undoubtedly the finest island of its size in all the world. Historians believe Galle may be the Tarshish of Biblical times—where King Solomon obtained gems, spices, and peacocks.' The town of Galle is just down the road from where we'll be staying. I had no idea there were eighteen and a half million people on that little tiny teardrop of an island. Here's another little gotcha: 'Sri Lanka is the world's largest tea exporter. It has the highest literacy rate of any developing nation. And—it has the world's first wildlife sanctuary, created in the third century B.C.'"

"I'm impressed," Oz said. "What does it say about the sapphire mines?"

I scanned the index and flipped pages, citing only the main points. "'Ratnapura is the gem center—every second person you meet on the street has the bargain of a lifetime for you wrapped up in his pocket.' There are a couple of long paragraphs on how they mine the stones—and a list of what's there. 'Rubies and sapphires are related stones and come in many colors. Red rubies, the most precious, aren't found in Sri Lanka, but pink ones are and can correctly be called pink sapphires.' How about that tidbit?"

"Okay. You've got my attention. What else?"

"'Sapphires come in yellow, orange, white, and most valuable, blue. Cat's-eye and alexandrite are found in some of the same veins as the other stones. Zircon can look exactly like a diamond except it's much softer, and can be yellow or orange on through brown and green.'"

"How about emeralds?"

"Not found in Sri Lanka. Lots of quartz—again different colors from purple amethyst to smoky quartz, to stones so dark they look black. 'Garnets are the poor person's ruby . . . Topaz is not found in Sri Lanka.' There you are. A quick course in gemology."

"Can I read it? I probably should know all the things you skipped over."

I handed the *Lonely Planet Travel Guide* to Oz, and buried myself in my other book to pick up a few words and phrases in the language—though it probably wasn't necessary since almost everyone was supposed to speak English. Still, it was generally useful, especially if the locals didn't know I could understand a little of their language.

As the plane began its descent, I could see a prominent green peak jutting above everything else on the island. A jumble of white, red-roofed buildings perched precariously at the very top. This had to be Adam's Peak, the most venerated place in what used to be called Ceylon and regarded by all Sri Lankans as a sacred place. Deeply indented in the rock at the top of the seven-thousand-three-hundred-fifty-foot peak was an imprint that looks like a footprint. Christians and Muslims say it's Adam's, placed there on his expulsion from paradise. Buddhist Sinhalese say it's Buddha's, made on his third visit to his island fiefdom, while the Hindus claim their god Siva left his mark there.

Even after the heat and high humidity in Bangkok, I couldn't believe the oppressive rush of hot, moist air that hit us when the doors to the airplane opened at the Bandaranaiki International Airport. The plane parked on the tarmac, and we walked across the sweltering concrete to a waiting bus that delivered wilting, sweating passengers to the terminal. Passengers disembarking from planes parked closer to the terminal simply walked across the blazing tarmac. There were no direct plane-to-terminal facilities in most third-world countries.

I wasn't prepared for the multitude of aromas that assaulted my senses—heavy, sweet fragrance of frangipani blossoms that couldn't mask the scent of overripe pineapple, exhaust and gasoline fumes, and even garbage off the airport perimeter.

Nor was I prepared for the high level of security. It took forever for our luggage to be off-loaded from the airplane. Then Customs had to check our bags with both an x-ray and physical search, ask what we were doing in the country, and how long we'd be staying.

Passengers were directed to the tourist desk, but instead of pointing out places of interest as was the norm, the agent drew a circle on a map around the top third of the island.

"This northern and eastern portion of the island is off-limits to all tourists. You may not travel to any part above this line. The Tamil Tigers have control of that area, and there is considerable fighting going on."

Making our way through English-speaking beggars and colorful snake charmers with hooded cobras swaying to the music of their flutes, we managed to locate the car that the Galle Face Hotel sent for us. The thirty-kilometer ride south to Colombo took an hour on the two-lane main road. We were stopped twice at Army checkpoints to look for bombs planted by Tamil Tigers. They held mirrors under the cars and searched inside the car, as well as our belongings again.

Just as I thought we were finally through with the interruptions, we rounded a corner and four soldiers with automatic weapons stepped into the road. The driver stopped the car. Three soldiers leveled their guns at us while a fourth opened the back door.

"Get out," the young Sri Lankan commanded in English. "With your hands held high. Stand away from the car, spread your legs apart, and lean forward with your hands on the car."

I glanced at Oz. He nodded to obey. I stood two feet away from the car, with my feet about that far apart, and leaned against the car.

"Further," the soldier ordered.

I moved my feet back another foot. He touched my leg with his gun. I bit my lip to keep from screaming. I moved my feet wider apart. That put me just enough off balance that I couldn't have moved fast to turn, to run, to react.

Two soldiers kept their guns trained on us and the driver while the other two did a thorough search of our belongings and the car. All the while, they kept up a steady stream of commentary, laughing as they pawed through my underclothes, holding up my lacy black bra on the barrel of a gun.

"Are these Sinhalese or Tamils?" I asked quietly.

Oz shrugged his shoulders. He didn't know.

I tried to catch the eye of the driver. His eyes were squeezed shut. His legs shook so bad the coins in his pockets jingled.

"If he's that scared, these can't be Sinhalese," I thought with a sinking heart.

CHAPTER FOURTEEN

Perspiration trickled down my face and down my back; I was sure it was puddling in my bra. The sun was unbearable, the car was hot to the touch, and I was scared spitless. I couldn't have come this far and be so close to meeting Bart, then have something happen less than an hour from our meeting place.

"Not now, Father," I prayed. "Please don't let these be Tamil Tigers. Please don't let anything prevent us from getting to meet Bart."

"What are you doing in Sri Lanka?" the leader of the soldiers demanded, examining our passports.

"We're here to photograph some of your historic buildings and your beautiful country, and write a story on the fiftieth anniversary of your independence," Oz said.

After several questions, the soldier finally seemed satisfied. "You may stand down," he said.

When I turned to face him, the stern, hard lines in his face softened just a bit. "Now I will tell you how to stay alive in Sri Lanka. Do not take pictures of any soldiers, checkpoints, or barricades. Do not venture beyond the lines drawn on your map. Stay alert to what is happening around you. Do not go near unattended trucks. And enjoy your stay," he added with an ironic half-smile.

We were allowed back into the car and waved on our way. The car behind us that had been held down the road by other soldiers crept slowly around the corner and took our place.

I leaned back in the seat, exhausted.

"Welcome to Sri Lanka," Oz said. "And your first real assignment."

"Thanks a lot," I replied, and turned to look out the window.

This is what you wanted. To be in the thick of things. To save the world from the bad guys. No, I corrected myself. This isn't the way I pictured it. I'd be beside Bart and we'd fight the evil in the world together. This certainly wasn't anywhere near the way I thought it would be.

We had cleared all the checkpoints and finally seemed to be making some headway toward the city. Then we came up behind an old man and an ox-cart. The side of the road was muddy. The cart was heavily laden and could not move off the pavement without sinking into the mud. We were forced to crawl along behind the ambling ox for several miles before we could pass. I remembered reading that animal carts have equal rights with cars. He probably wouldn't have moved over even if he could.

Traffic toward the airport was a steady stream of cars, buses, hand trolleys and ox-carts, bicycles and motor bikes. Behind us, a string of cars piled up, crawling along at the pace set by the ox in front of us.

To one used to California and New York traffic, this was a real study in self-control. Forcing myself to relax, to breathe deeply, to remember I was now in a different world where people did things more slowly, I finally was able to enjoy watching the human dramas that played out on the side of the road.

Sandal-footed Buddhist monks draped to their ankles in bright orange saris, with one shoulder bared, walked two and three abreast, most carrying large round fans. Elephants, with their handler, or *mahout*, either straddling their broad necks or directing from the ground, stacked poles or moved tree trunks.

Pineapple and exotic fruit, piled higher than my head, arranged along the roadside, had hand-lettered signs proclaiming ten baht, twenty baht, fifty baht, according to size. Old women carried brightly colored parasols to shield themselves from the hot island sun.

Finally, we reached Colombo. I was too wound up at this point to pay much attention to the city, the buildings, the people on the sidewalks. My whole being concentrated on the Galle Face Hotel and whether Bart would be there in person or would simply have left a message.

I prayed he would be there. I ached to feel his arms around me, to know that he was okay—to see for myself that the knife-wound hadn't been serious, as he had assured Mai Li.

"Where will we get the message? Will he just leave it at the desk? If he's been there already and we missed him, will he come back?" My pent-up questions tumbled out in a whisper. One never knew about taxi driver's loyalties.

"We'll check in, then ask if a message has been left for Anna. It might be instructions to meet him somewhere, or it could simply be a list of names and descriptions of the group he's infiltrated. Maybe even a list of the 'schools' they've set up and how we can dismantle them. It could be a lot of things, but, Mrs. Teale, it probably won't be Bart in person. Prepare yourself for that now so you won't be disappointed. He may be long gone from the island already," Oz answered quietly.

"Or maybe not, if the terrorist group is helping the Tamil Tigers."

"Let's hope that's not the case. Unfortunately, I'm afraid it is, but that will make it hard for Bart to get to us. The usual procedure is to get a kid off the street to deliver the message. He'd never have to come near the place in person."

"He won't know I'm here, will he?"

"No. He'll expect any of the rest of us, but not you. I have no idea how he'll take to the idea that I actually brought you here. I can't believe I did. I'll never do it again."

I ignored Oz's mumblings, and when we arrived, I leapt from the car and hurried across the red-brick entry to the huge triple doors that stood wide open. I could think of nothing except that Bart might be near—that he might even be watching as I left the car and dashed up the white marble stairs into the interior of the hotel.

We were stopped just inside the doors at a desk manned by a lovely Sri Lankan in a turquoise sari with gold bangle bracelets at her wrists. A sign on the desk said, "Please cooperate with security check. Thank you." Hotels were security conscious after the Intercontinental Hotel had been bombed twice.

Passing through that, I let Oz handle the registration. I was so nervous I couldn't stand still. I paced the two-story lobby, looking at every face, examining every corner, as well as the long airy wings that overlooked Galle Face Green, watching for the familiar tall, slender silhouette, the white-blond hair.

I backtracked down the front steps to check the marble seats on the veranda. No Bart. The white-haired Sri Lankan posted at the entry brought his hands together chest high and dipped his head in a shallow bow, his brown eyes crinkling in a friendly smile. I returned the salutation and the smile. A white bushy mustache covered the width of his face and curled up at the ends. His pristine white military-style jacket with red epaulets and gold buttons, and the long white draped skirt contrasted with skin so dark it looked like highly polished walnut.

I admired the exquisitely carved fifteen-foot-high teak front doors that I'd flown past without seeing when I first entered the hotel. I even scanned the etched marble list of famous people who had visited the distinguished Galle Face Hotel, "dedicated to yesterday's charm and tomorrow's comfort," during the years from 1864 to 1985. It was long and impressive.

Oz finally signaled he was ready.

"Was there a message?" I asked, trying to rein in my stampeding emotions.

"Not yet. I told them to let us know as soon as a message arrived for Anna. Come on. Let's go get settled in."

"Yes. Just in case Bart does come, I certainly don't need to look or smell like this. I'm ready for a quick shower and some clean clothes. Where are our rooms?"

A look flitted across Oz's face that stopped me in my tracks.

"What's the matter?"

"Unfortunately, it is room, Mrs. Teale. Not rooms."

"As in singular, not plural?"

"Exactly."

"Well, Mr. Teale, you can just march right back to that desk and tell them we need two rooms. Plural, not singular. Unless, of course, you'd rather I create another little scene like I did in Bangkok."

"Sorry, Mrs. Teale. There are only seventy-seven rooms in this establishment, and the other seventy-six are already filled. In fact, Else pulled some strings getting us the room she did. With the Gem Congress in town, rooms are at a premium."

"I won't—"

"Let's discuss this in our room, please, instead of creating a scene right here in front of all these people."

I couldn't believe it. This had to be some kind of nightmare. Soon I would wake and laugh at the absurdity of it all. I hadn't seen Bart for weeks. Now, when there was a slight possibility we could finally connect, I was sharing a room with another man!

The elevator was an experience—vintage 1860s that required an operator—or previous expertise with these antiquated beasts. I'd seen something similar in today's service lifts where you step inside, pull slats closed from the top and bottom, then work a handle instead of pressing buttons to attain the desired floor.

Using the huge old-fashioned skeleton key, Oz opened the dark-stained paneled door to an airy room that was large and spacious.

Just not large enough for both Oz and me.

"What do you think Bart will say when he finds us sharing a room?" I demanded as soon as Oz shut the door behind him.

"That we were lucky to have a room where we can wait for his message. You do realize that it's possible the message won't come today."

"Why not?"

"When you request a meeting or pickup of a drop, as Bart did, you're hoping that you'll be able to deliver as planned. That doesn't always happen. Especially when your schedule's controlled by another group, as Bart's probably is by the terrorists he's traveling with."

"And if the message doesn't come today?"

"Then we wait right here until it does. Even if it takes a week. If he has something so important to get us all the way over here—we'll wait until he can get it to us—no matter how long it takes."

"And where are you going to stay while we wait, if it takes that long?"

"Right here."

"Oh, no. No. Either you go, or I do. I told you in Bangkok, we avoid even the appearance of evil. That hasn't changed—especially if Bart comes. You think I want to share a room with the two of you?"

Oz clamped his teeth shut. He wheeled from me, stormed into the immense bathroom, and slammed the door.

I shut my eyes and sagged against the wall. This couldn't be happening. Please, tell me this isn't happening. In my worst nightmares, I could not imagine anything as bizarre. I'd been hoping and praying that my lost husband would reappear. If he did, I certainly didn't want him to find me sharing a room with Oz, even as innocent as I knew it would be—and as innocent as he would know it to be.

In the meantime, just in case Bart did make an appearance, I needed to improve mine. I unpacked my suitcase, hanging my things in the closet. I tossed a pastel plaid cotton skirt and a coordinating coral cotton tee on the bed nearest the bathroom and unpacked the books from my backpack.

When Oz emerged from the bathroom, I gathered up my clean clothes and toiletry bag and without a word, locked myself in the bathroom. The antique air-conditioning and plumbing would do. Actually, I was grateful for both, when I considered that all hotels in Sri Lanka, even in the capital city, aren't air-conditioned.

Thirty minutes later, much refreshed, and definitely in a better frame of mind, I found Oz stretched out on the other bed asleep. Leaving him that way, I quietly left the room and went downstairs to ask if the message for Anna had come yet. Nothing.

I wandered the verandas with their barrel-shaped captain's chairs and tiny round tables that were crowded with gemologists discussing acquisitions they hoped to make. No familiar face. I checked the lawn-level veranda with potted plants on a shelf near each tiny linen-covered table, and fresh flowers on each table. No Bart.

I strolled out into the late afternoon heat, seeking a little cool ocean breeze under the palm trees that shaded the black and white checkered patio. There was a breeze. It wasn't cool. This wasn't Santa Barbara, I had to remind myself. This was the tropics. Humid, dense, oppressive heat pressed down like a smothering blanket.

A bare-footed waiter appeared immediately at my side as I sat at one of the little patio tables just a few steps from the deep blue Indian Ocean. He looked as antique as the hotel itself. Deeply lined walnut-colored skin gleamed with perspiration. But his white collarless shirt was immaculate, and the brightly colored sari wrapped about his waist would have been the envy of anyone headed for Hawaii.

I ordered lime juice made with bottled water and watched the white waves roll onto the small strip of sandy beach.

My nerve endings were hot-wired. My entire system tingled. Sitting still was a major effort. I wanted to be up and moving, doing something positive, accomplishing something. Waiting was always hard, but this was impossible.

What if Bart didn't come after all? What if he couldn't actually get the message here? Or if it took days to arrive? How could I stand that?

I sipped idly at the drink, imagining Bart walking up the beach, or his hands on my shoulders as he slipped up behind me. I couldn't quiet the wild beating of my heart as I thought of seeing him again, of actually feeling his warm, solid body in my arms. And his arms around me, pulling me close, his breath warm on my neck. His lips on mine.

This is really what you need, Allison. Go ahead and get yourself all worked up to have him come—but be ready to fall hard when he doesn't appear in person.

What I really needed right now was a good run on the beach, but two minutes of that would have me ready for another shower and a new set of clothes. I'd have to settle for a walk right now. The run could come later.

I headed for what was called Galle Face Green, a long expanse of property between the old Galle Face Hotel and the contemporary Ceylon Intercontinental—the one bombed twice in the last year by the Tamils.

Half of the Green looked recently returfed, and the other half was a sandy wasteland awaiting new greening. The beach ran along one long boundary and the Galle Face Road along the other. Children played cricket with sticks and balls, people strolled along the beach, and the traffic noise from the road washed over all of it.

The Green was the cradle of all British sports in old Ceylon. Horse racing, polo, cricket, golf, rugby, football, hockey, and tennis all had their start on this stretch of open land.

An elephant lumbered down the Green, followed by a throng of laughing, chattering children. The *mahout*, or driver, motioned them away, but they ignored him and kept trying to touch the huge beast.

"Ride, lady? I take you for a ride on the elephant."

"Here? Now?"

"Yes, *noona*. You want to ride?"

"How much?"

"Only one hundred rupees, *noona*."

One American dollar equaled 54.15 rupees. That would be roughly two dollars. A plantation worker only made six rupees an hour, and a hotel receptionist 16 rupees, about thirty cents an hour.

"Too much. How about fifty rupees?"

"I take you for a long ride, *noona*. Worth one hundred rupees."

"Seventy-five rupees and you've got a customer."

The young, dark-skinned *mahout* thought about it seriously for a minute, then grinned a wide, white-toothed grin and signaled his elephant to kneel. He slid from the back of the animal, touched the trunk with his crook, and the elephant obeyed by offering his trunk as a stepping stool.

At the direction of the youthful *mahout*, I stepped onto the wrinkled gray trunk, at least two feet in diameter, and was lifted into the air like a circus performer, until I was high enough to scramble aboard the creature that was twice my own height.

It wasn't a comfortable ride, but exhilarating nevertheless. The elephant lumbered along the beach in a gait that produced a rocking, swaying ride. It's a good thing I didn't suffer from motion sickness.

Elephants are not smooth-skinned creatures. The short, prickly hairs scratched my bare legs. I'd just about decided my elephant adventure had been more than sufficient when the *mahout* signaled my mount to turn around. He was in the process of doing so when an explosion blasted the peaceful afternoon.

The thus-far docile beast beneath my legs shuddered a tremendous shudder from one end to the other, and whipped his head violently back and forth. I clutched at the ears that flapped furiously, slapping against my legs. Then before I knew what was happening, and before the *mahout* could react, my elephant went berserk.

He reached up with his trunk, wrapped it around my waist, and snatched me off his back. I was too astonished to scream, too frightened to move. He held me up in front of those intelligent dark eyes as if studying this thing he'd plucked off his back, as if trying to determine whether I'd been the cause of his fright.

I was aware of the young Sinhalese handler speaking to the elephant, aware of a change in the look in the depth of the beast's dark eyes. Then suddenly I was flying through the air, not gracefully like a bird, but flapping wildly, trying to right myself, trying not to land on my head, or the rocks that came rushing to meet me.

CHAPTER FIFTEEN

My head hurt. The pain was too severe to allow me to open my eyes. It hurt too bad to move or breathe. I lay, rigid, trying to remember why I should have such a headache. But my mind seemed too caught up in pain to respond to my query.

Someone held my hand, caressing it softly. I tried to open my eyes again, but the effort wasn't worth the pain. I quit trying.

Voices, far away, penetrated my consciousness. I tried to hear what they were saying but any kind of concentration left me breathless with pain. I lay still, aware the throbbing in my head matched the thumping of my heart. If I could get my heart to stop, maybe the headache would go away, too.

I drifted in and out of consciousness, in and out of pain, for what seemed a long, long time. The only constant was the hand that held mine, never letting go, and the stroking that continued, on my hand, my arm, or gently down the side of my face.

Finally the pain subsided enough to open my eyes. I looked straight ahead, not daring to move my head to one side or the other. I didn't recognize the room. Where was I?

I stole a glance out of the corner of my eye. A nice-looking stranger slumped in a chair beside me, his elbow on the bed and his forehead resting on the heel of one hand. The other held my hand. My fingers were quite stiff by now, and I flexed them, ever so carefully so as to not cause the pain to hit me again.

The head bobbed up and hopeful gray eyes stared into mine. A stranger's eyes.

"Alli. Oh, Alli. Thank heaven." The sandy-haired stranger picked up the phone and said, "She's awake. Will you call the doctor back?"

He hung up and turned back to me.

"How do you feel? That was quite a fall you took, I'm told. Right on your head. The doctor said you have a concussion, but your vitals were strong and you were breathing normally, so he left you here in our room instead of sending you to the hospital. He'll be right here to check you again, now that you're awake."

A little bell tingled in my head, sending a spasm of pain shooting through it again.

"You said 'our room.'" I spoke carefully, quietly, not wanting to chance a recurrence of the spasm.

"Yes."

I glanced around the room, lit only by a small table lamp. I'd never seen it before. Even in the dim light, I knew I'd never seen it before. I looked at the earnest face staring at me. A face I'd never seen before.

The door opened and another stranger appeared. This one was older, kindly looking, white-haired, with wire-rimmed glasses. He carried a black medical bag.

"I'm Dr. Armstrong, from down the street at the American Embassy. How's our patient feeling? Bit of a headache still?"

"Yes," I whispered, almost afraid to speak.

The doctor took my pulse, looked into my eyes with his little light, and asked about the pain in my head.

"Where am I?" I asked, after I'd made an unsuccessful stab at describing the indescribable pain I'd experienced, and the low throbbing ache I now felt behind my eyes.

"You're in your room at the Galle Face Hotel."

I glanced at the man still holding my hand. "Who are you?"

The gray eyes darted to the face of the doctor. The older American gentleman settled on the edge of my bed.

"What is your name?" Dr. Armstrong asked.

I opened my mouth to answer, but nothing came out. Nothing was there in that little compartment where I was stored. That little area of my brain that responded automatically to name, age, place of birth. I reached and groped but it was empty. I couldn't find my name. I couldn't find me.

I looked at the doctor, and then at the stranger who was clutching my hand tight now, squeezing it as if to press the knowledge that had vanished back into me.

"I . . . I don't know."

"Do you know your parents' names?" the doctor asked quietly.

I struggled to find faces, names, impressions, anything that would give me some clue. There was just a void, a nothingness that was frightening.

"You don't recognize this man?"

I looked again at the stranger. His eyes were pleading, his expression expectant.

"No. I'm sorry. I've never seen him before."

The man's only sound was a deep intake of breath. His gray eyes misted. He bit his lip, but still he didn't speak.

"Show her your passports, Mr. Teale."

Dr. Armstrong patted my hand as the sandy-haired stranger produced two American passports. He opened one. Amy Teale. He opened the other. Ed Teale. The picture was of the man at my side. The addresses were the same. I looked at the picture of Amy Teale. A brown-eyed woman with a cap of short black curls stared back me. Another stranger.

"Is that supposed to be me?" I asked, putting my hand to my hair. The hair style was similar.

The doctor asked Mr. Teale if there was a hand mirror in the bathroom. The man produced a backpack and drew out a small gold compact. He opened it and handed it to me. The face that stared back was the same as the stranger in the passport.

I closed my eyes, rejecting the pain that began to take over again, rejecting the idea that I could not remember my name or recognize my own face. Rejecting the terror that seized me.

"What happened? Why can't I remember? Why do I have this horrible pain in my head?"

Ed Teale answered first. "You were riding an elephant. An explosion startled him and he threw you. You landed on your head. Fortunately, you narrowly missed hitting some rocks, or the fall might have been . . ."

Dr. Armstrong took over when Ed Teale's voice faltered. "Apparently, the trauma to your head caused some temporary amnesia. Your memory will probably come back in bits and pieces in the next few days, or even the next few hours. After a good night's rest, and after the effects of the concussion subside, you'll probably snap back to your old self in no time. I'll come by again in the morning to see how you feel."

He patted my hand again, stuffed his stethoscope and blood pressure cuff back in his bag, and with a nod to Ed Teale to follow him, left the room.

I tried to sit up but decided it wasn't worth the effort. Moving my head very slowly, I searched the room for something, anything, that looked familiar. It was an attractive, spacious room. Two beds. Dark, glossy wood. High ceiling with an old Casablanca-style fan whirling quietly above. Cane and wicker furniture.

Ed Teale came back inside and sat down on the chair beside the bed. He reached for my hand. Reluctantly, I let him hold it.

"You don't remember anything?" he asked, his gray eyes searching mine.

"No. Nothing. It's like a curtain has been pulled over my memory, or it's been erased. There's just nothing there."

He sat quietly for a minute, his eyes on our interlocked fingers, running his index finger up and down over my hand.

"Are you really my husband? Are we really . . . married?"

His head snapped up as if I'd startled him.

"You don't believe the passports?" he asked quietly.

"I guess I'll have to believe anything you tell me. Why are we in a hotel? And where is it?"

"Colombo, Sri Lanka."

"Sri Lanka? What are we doing here?"

"We're photojournalists, on assignment to take pictures and do a couple of stories for *National Geographic Traveler.*"

"What was I doing on an elephant?"

"Riding it, the kid said. We'd just checked in, you showered and went downstairs while I took a nap. I'll never forgive myself for not being there with you. I should have been. I should never have let you out of my sight. I didn't think you'd go out alone. You'd promised . . ."

He paused, his hands trembling, his eyes filled with self-recrimination. He pulled my hand to his lips and kissed my fingertips.

"Promised what?"

"You promised to do exactly as I said. I just didn't think you'd go out alone."

"Why would I promise something like that? What kind of marriage do we have?"

The man looked at me with a strange expression. "There's a civil war going on in this country. You promised you'd follow my instructions so you wouldn't be hurt. There are soldiers everywhere. We were stopped on the way from the airport. The explosion that frightened the elephant was set off by the Tamil Tigers. They've infiltrated even the capital city."

"Then what in heaven's name are we doing here in the middle of a civil war? Do we do this kind of thing often?"

He handed me my passport. There were twenty or more foreign destinations stamped in the last few years.

"How long have we been married? Do we have any . . . are there any . . . children?" I was almost afraid to ask.

"No. We have no children." He smiled a secret little smile. "But we could work on that if you feel like it."

I turned my head away from his gaze. The innuendo wasn't funny nor did it seem proper right now. But surely, any married couple should be able to enjoy little private jokes.

"Is this our only job? Do we travel like this all the time, or do we have a home somewhere . . . ?" My head started throbbing again. All this was just too much. Then my stomach rumbled.

"You're starving. I'm sorry. I didn't think. It's been hours since we ate. I'll call room service and have them send something up. What would you like?"

Again my mind was blank. "Soup. A sandwich. Fruit. Anything. It doesn't matter." I closed my eyes and tried to find a picture from my past. What did I like to eat? What did my house look like? What kind of clothes did I wear? Was I a good photographer? Or was I a journalist?

When Ed Teale—I couldn't bring myself to say my husband—got off the phone, I asked him about my parents. "Are they still living?"

"Yes. Near Santa Barbara, California. They have a big house there overlooking the coast. Does that ring any bells?"

Still nothing. I picked up the passport again. Twenty-five years old. Where was the history that went with the woman in that picture?

Ed Teale walked to the window and stood silently looking out.

Suddenly I became aware of a physical need that I couldn't ignore. I knew I'd never make it on my own, but how do you ask a stranger to help you to the bathroom?

I turned slowly to the side and slid my legs toward the edge of the bed, then tried to pull myself up ever so gently. He was at my side immediately. I pointed to the bathroom. He slipped both arms under mine and eased me to my feet, so carefully, so tenderly, my head hardly knew it was moving. We stood by the bed for a minute, his arms around me, while I prepared myself for the next movement that I was sure would bring the pain pounding back again.

Ed buried his face in my hair and pulled me close to him. My hands went immediately to his chest to press him away. The look on his face as I stepped back out of his arms was a mixture of emotions—confusion, hurt, and—did I see a momentary flash of anger in his eyes?

I took a step toward the bathroom and my knees buckled. He caught me as I slid toward the floor, gently picked me up in his arms, and carried me into the bathroom. It was a huge room with an immense brass claw-footed bathtub and beautiful, old-fashioned fixtures.

"Thank you. I can handle it from here myself."

"You're sure? I can turn my head if it will make you feel any better, Mrs. Teale." He said it lightly, as if making fun of the fact that a wife was hesitant to undress in front of her husband.

"No, thanks. Shut the door behind you, please. If I pass out in some state of undress, leave me on the floor and throw a blanket over me."

He looked at me, shocked. "I will not."

"Go away, please."

He left me leaning against the sink. I stood there until a wave of dizziness passed, then unbuttoned my skort. It fell to the floor before I could catch it. I managed to ease myself onto the oak toilet seat, but wasn't sure I'd be able to get up again.

"Are you okay?" he asked through the door.

"Yes," I answered shakily, the pain resuming in all its fury. "Do I have any pajamas or a nightgown out there? If you can find some, will you please throw them in here to me?"

I tried to stand, to get to the door before he could open it, but my legs wouldn't cooperate and my head hurt too bad to move it.

The door opened a crack and something green and satin dangled in the room.

"Toss it to me, please."

"You don't sound very good."

"Toss it." I wasn't feeling very good. In fact, I felt like I was about to lose what I hadn't even put in my stomach yet. I caught the slinky green satin. Pajamas. So I was a pajama person. I'd been afraid when I saw them dangling inside the door, it might have been a flimsy little chemise. I stopped in the middle of pulling off my tee. Why should I care what I wore in front of my husband?

Because this stranger didn't feel like my husband. Because that's what he was to me—a stranger.

There was no mistaking his feeling for me. I could see it in his eyes, feel it as he held me. Who else but a loving, devoted husband would sit holding my hand for hours while I fought my way out of pain-riddled oblivion?

But I could find no feeling for this gentle man who so obviously had deep feelings for me. There was nothing.

I managed to get my pajamas on while sitting on the commode, but even though I finally got dressed, I couldn't get up.

"You're taking a long time in there. Are you okay?"

"I'm afraid you're going to have to come and help me. I can't stand up." In fact, I could hardly hold my head up. I was in a cold sweat, feeling a decided need to turn to the sink and throw up. But it was just far enough I couldn't make it from here.

The door opened immediately and Ed came in, deep concern etched in the lines on his forehead.

"Help me to the sink, please. I'm going to be sick." And I was. It was so embarrassing, throwing up in front of—why couldn't I think of him as anything but—that stranger?

He sat me down on the vanity stool, washed my face with a cool cloth, brought my toothbrush, and a glass, then moved me, stool and all to the sink, which he had already cleaned out. When I felt almost decent again, he tenderly picked me up and carried me back to bed. The covers were turned down this time, and he placed me on the smooth white sheets and adjusted two pillows behind my head.

Room service had delivered our dinner, but I didn't feel like eating. Even the thought of food made me wish I was still hanging over the sink.

"Have a spoonful of soup. Only one sip. If it doesn't feel like it's going to stay down, I've got a wastebasket right here handy. But try. One bite."

Just so he'd leave me alone, I consented to one sip. It stayed down. And it tasted good. He gave me another spoonful, and another, until the bowl was half empty. He broke off bite-sized pieces of some kind of bread, then sips of warm Coke to wash it down.

"Enough," I protested, wishing I could make the pain in my head go away as easily as the gnawing pain in my stomach. But he pressed one more thing on me—the pain pill the doctor had left so I could sleep. I accepted it gratefully.

"Now," he said, removing one of the pillows, "you can sleep. And when you wake tomorrow, you'll remember everything and . . ." He stopped, looked a little wistful, and leaned over to kiss me. I turned my head slightly and his lips touched my cheek.

"Thank you for taking care of me—Ed," I said, reaching for his hand.

"For richer, for poorer, in sickness and in health," he answered with a catch in his voice.

He turned the light off, leaving the curtains open to let moonlight illuminate the room. I closed my eyes and let myself drift on a black velvet sea. The boat rocked slightly, and I was aware of someone close to me in the rocking, swaying boat.

CHAPTER SIXTEEN

Sunlight streamed through the window, illuminating corners in the room I hadn't seen last night. My headache had subsided, but the memory of my past life was still a blank page—no pictures, no writing, no indication of who I was, what I was, or what my life was like.

Water ran in the bathroom. The stranger I was married to was apparently taking a shower. I sat up slowly, put my feet on the floor, and saw the tan leather backpack next to the bed. Leaning forward very carefully, afraid to start bad things happening in my head again, I retrieved the backpack and emptied it on the bed beside me.

Surely something would jog my memory, some clue to start the process of piecing together my missing self. Three books, two on Sri Lanka, and another, fell out. The third seemed to be a book of scripture. Gold lettering on the spine read: *The Holy Bible, The Book of Mormon, The Doctrine and Covenants, The Pearl of Great Price* at the top, and at the bottom, The Church of Jesus Christ of Latter-day Saints.

I shut my eyes and waited for my double vision to clear. The inscription on the inside was scribbled in a man's bold script. "To my beloved Princess: This book holds the key to happiness. It is a life script. May we follow the precepts as taught therein by the Master. All my love, forever, Bart."

Bart. Who was Bart? My husband's name was Ed. I wasn't solving mysteries. I was discovering more. But there was something about that book that gave me a small measure of comfort, the first I'd had since I opened my eyes last night not knowing who I was. Possibly my first clue to myself.

There was a gold compact, matching gold lipstick, a woodgrain pen, a fabric-padded journal—rather bulky for traveling, and a two-inch-long telescope. On closer examination, the wood-grained, gold-capped piece wasn't a telescope. When I looked through it, I could see things to the side of me, instead of in front. Odd.

Hoping to find the keys to unlock the sealed portion of my memory, I untied the slender satin ribbon on the journal with quivering fingers. The writing looked as though it had been done while traveling; the entries were brief sketches or impressions of people, places, monuments, cities, quotes, but nothing of a personal nature.

I thumbed through the book. There was something unusual about it—the size, the weight—didn't seem in proper proportion for some reason. The padded covers were far too thick. I was just trying to unstick the back pages that were clumped together when the bathroom door opened.

Ed Teale came out with a towel wrapped around his waist, and one in his hands, drying his hair.

"Good morning, sweetheart. I hope I didn't wake you. How do you feel?"

"Better, thank you." I averted my eyes, feeling like a voyeur, out of place in someone else's life.

He came close, smelling of soap and musky aftershave, and bent to kiss me. I offered my cheek instead of my mouth and saw a flash of disappointment in his eyes. He sat on the bed next to me and took my hand.

"I take it you don't remember me this morning, either," he said.

I shook my head and pulled my hand away, pretending to need it to show him the journal.

"I hoped to find something in here that would bring some memory back to me, but there's nothing about me. Did I write this?"

"Yes. You started keeping it to remind you of pictures we'd shot, additional information, and impressions to write about when we got ready to put the articles together."

"It's a strange kind of book for traveling—it's too cumbersome to slip into a pocket or even a small purse. Is that why I carry a backpack instead of a purse?"

He took the journal from me and tossed it on the bed behind us and leaned closer.

"Just one of your little idiosyncrasies. Want me to call for room service or do you feel up to going out for breakfast?"

"We can go out. Who's Bart?"

He froze, his expression blank, unreadable.

"Bart signed this book of scripture." I opened it and showed him the inscription.

Ed Teale stood, tightened the towel around his waist, and walked quickly to the closet to get his clothes.

"Bart's your brother," he said over his shoulder. "He just converted to the Mormon faith and gave that to you. He always called you his princess. You're very close."

"Tell me about him."

"How about over breakfast? I took a quick shower so I wouldn't use all the hot water. You never know how much you might have in these old hotels. Go ahead. It's your turn. Then we'll spend the rest of the day catching you up and trying to reconstruct those lost memories."

I looked through the clothes that were supposed to be mine and found a beige cotton tee and long, flared cotton skirt. It was like borrowing clothes. I didn't remember them. They weren't familiar.

"Not much selection here. Do we always travel this light?"

"Usually. We don't need to be burdened with unnecessary luggage on a trip like this."

I took the clothes into the bathroom and shut the door. I thought of locking it, but didn't, afraid of hurting my husband's feelings even more than I already had. Interesting. I could accept him as my husband now. Maybe that was how it worked. Just one little bit at a time.

When I came out of the bathroom, the doctor was talking to Ed in the sitting portion of our big room. They both stood.

"Good morning, Mrs. Teale. How's the head this morning? Still in pain?"

"Good morning. No pain, but I'm moving very carefully so I don't incite any."

"Sit right here. Let's get your vitals and see how my lovely patient is doing. Have you had any memory recall?" he asked as he fastened the blood pressure cuff around my arm.

"None."

"Well, these things sometimes take a few days." He declared me fit as a fiddle, but cautioned me to take it easy at first and not overexert. I might experience dizziness, inability to concentrate, insomnia, double vision, an unsteady gait, and even a change in disposition until the effects of the concussion wore off.

"In fact, my prescription is to simply laze around in our warm island sun, enjoy the beach and the surf and do nothing for the next twenty-four to forty-eight hours. Pretend you're on your second honeymoon, forget about your work, and just enjoy each other."

Dr. Armstrong left. He wasn't the house doctor as I'd thought last night. He was from the American Embassy just down Galle Road. Had he said that?

We opted to have our breakfast outside on the black and white checkered patio, under the palm trees, overlooking the ocean. Picturesque boats came and went, some small, homemade-looking catamarans, some larger two- or three-masted fishing boats, some brightly painted skiffs with fishing nets piled in one end.

Already the morning was hot and humid. Palms swayed and sang in the breeze off the ocean. Brightly colored birds flitted among the trees and darted in and out of the thatched-roofed picnic area just a small strip of grass away from the patio. While we waited for our breakfast, I tried to identify a few of them with the book in my backpack.

Ed was particularly enthusiastic in pointing out little iridescent sunbirds with sharp, down-curved bills that were bright spots in the sun. As we identified myna birds and swallows and the call of the house crow, it occurred to me we weren't getting to my questions.

"Tell me about Bart. Where is he? Is he older or younger than me?"

Ed turned his chair so he was face into the sun, closed his eyes, and leaned back. "He's four years older than you. You were raised together on the estate in southern California—basically alone. It's out of town and there weren't a lot of other kids around. You idolized him, followed him everywhere. He was a perfect big brother, answering all your questions, pulling you out of trouble, playing games with you. You think he's the greatest thing in the whole world."

"And is he?"

Ed sat up and looked at me. "What do you mean?"

"Is he really all that I . . . thought he was?"

My husband closed his eyes again and settled back in his sun-worshipping position. "Probably. He's about as nice a guy as you'll find anywhere. We're good friends. He'd do anything for you."

He sat up and looked at me, his gray eyes troubled. He looked away and rubbed the back of his neck.

"I'd better go check on our breakfast. Wouldn't want you to starve to death." He strode across the close-cropped grass, not bothering with the path that led from the hotel to the patio.

It was so strange not knowing anything about myself—being married to a man I didn't recognize, having no feeling for him—though it was apparent he was very much in love with me. And eerie seeing an unfamiliar face staring back in the mirror.

I searched my memory for the face of the brother who was supposed to be so special to me, for any recollection of those happy times Ed said we'd shared, but it was as though a chunk of my brain had been plucked from my head, leaving an empty portion, a void, where *I* should have been.

Ed returned with our ancient waiter in tow, carting enough breakfast to feed all the children playing ball on the green next to the hotel.

"What do I usually eat for breakfast?" I asked, overwhelmed at the wide array of exotic fruits, sweet breads, eggs, and juices on the tray.

"It depends entirely on your mood and your appetite," Ed answered with a broad smile. "Some mornings you down a glass of juice and run. Other days, you have the appetite of a logger, and consume everything in sight. I wasn't sure how you'd feel this morning, so I got a little bit of everything in case you were starving."

"How long are we supposed to be in Sri Lanka?" I asked, spearing something unidentifiable on the fruit plate.

"Until we get our pictures and story," Ed answered, heaping his plate with sweet bread and scrambled eggs.

"What are we looking for?"

"It's the fiftieth anniversary of the independence of Sri Lanka from British rule. We're going to tie that into the early Dutch colonization, then the English build-up of coffee and tea plantations, with photographs of the unique structures each culture left behind, as well as the early Lankan and Tamil temples. Sort of an architectural portrait of the country."

"Where do we start? And when? Is one of us the photographer and one the writer, or do we share the tasks?"

Ed looked up from his breakfast and smiled. "At least the fall on your head didn't change your habit of asking multiple questions." He leaned toward me and touched my hand lightly. "How do you feel? Any pain? Any memory recall?"

"Now who's asking multiple questions?" I smiled in return. "No real pain. Just a dull ache behind my eyes. And, no—no recall. Still nothing in the memory bank."

We ate in silence for a few minutes, a comfortable, companionable silence. I stole a glance at my husband as he stared out across the expanse of deep, blue water in front of us.

He was a pleasant-looking man with very short, sandy-colored hair, clear gray eyes, and an open, honest face. Slight of build, he was only a few inches taller and probably twenty-five pounds heavier than me.

"How did we meet? How long did we know each other before we got married? Where were we married?" The questions tumbled out before I could stop them. "It's so strange, being with you like this, but having no knowledge of our history. You're like an intimate stranger, someone I should know everything about, but instead I could have passed you on the street and never taken a second glance. It's so frustrating."

Ed put his hand gently on my shoulder. "Dr. Armstrong said your memory will probably come back bits and pieces at a time, possibly within the next few days." He withdrew his hand and turned back to stare at the ocean. "We'll just hope that it does."

The old dark-skinned waiter, immaculate in his white collarless jacket and colorful sarong tied at his waist, shuffled to our table again, offering coffee or tea. Ed held up his cup for coffee. When the waiter leaned toward my cup, Ed waved him off. "She doesn't drink coffee. No. No tea, either."

"Why don't I drink coffee or tea?"

"You're a Mormon. You also don't drink alcoholic beverages or smoke."

"What about you?"

"You and your brother joined the Church. I didn't."

"Why didn't you?"

Ed stared at his plate for a minute before he looked up at me. Just then a commotion on the green drew our attention. An elephant, ridden by a young native boy, lumbered onto the narrow strip of beach in front of us. The children had abandoned their ball game to chase the elephant, trying to touch it, to catch its spindly tail.

"*Noona!* You are well," the boy called. "I'm glad you live. Anouk is sorry he dump you on your head. I will give you free ride today to make up for it."

"That's the culprit who did this to me?" I asked, smiling at the enthusiastic but apologetic youth.

"Apparently. He was gone by the time they came to get me." He turned and called to the boy. "The lady doesn't wish to ride today."

"I take you free, *Noona,*" he insisted, urging his elephant right up to the patio.

"Not today. Maybe another time. My head is still recovering." I put both hands up to my head and held it as if I were trying to keep it from moving.

"I come back. Anouk will show you he is sorry."

We waved good-bye to the boy as he expertly guided the huge beast beneath him, and they ambled down the beach, taking the children and their noise with them.

"Did you say an explosion frightened the elephant? What kind of explosion?"

"A bomb. They think it was another one set off by the Tamil Tigers—on a truck parked in front of the American Embassy just down the street."

"Was anybody hurt?"

"As far as we can tell, you were the only casualty of that explosion. Fortunately, it was a lighter charge of explosives than the Tigers usually use, and traffic on the normally busy street was light."

"I'm glad no one was hurt."

We continued picking quietly at the plate of delicious fruit spread before us.

"Finished?" Ed asked as he pushed away from the table.

"I think so. I can't believe we put such a dent into that huge tray of food."

"I told you, you have a real appetite at times. I think it would be good for you to rest for a little while. Then maybe we can go for a short walk and work on getting your strength back up to par before we tackle our assignment."

"I'm not tired," I protested, but Ed was firm.

"The doctor said plenty of rest for a couple of days. That's exactly what you're going to do." He took my arm, draped it over his, and led me back into the cooler interior of the hotel. Inside I stopped for a moment to examine the huge wall-sized in-laid wood mural in the lobby, a melange of the cultural symbols of Sri Lankan history.

We strolled past the desk, pausing briefly; the clerk shook his head, and we headed back to our room.

"What was that all about?" I asked.

"I'm expecting a message. He was just letting me know it hadn't come in yet."

"Who from?"

"The boss."

"About what?"

"Probably some changes he's decided to make."

When we got to our room, Ed led me straight to the bed. Gently he sat me down, pressed me back against the pillows, and pulled my sandals off.

"You're treating me like a baby," I protested.

"No. I'm treating you like . . . the woman I love." The last words were spoken so softy I could barely make them out. "Now, can I get you anything?"

I relaxed against the pillows, thought for a minute, decided I wasn't sleepy, and asked for the book of scriptures from the backpack.

"You didn't finish telling me when my brother and I joined the Mormon church. You gave me the impression it was recently. And you never told me how long we've been married."

Ed handed me the book and headed for the bathroom. "Nature calls. Hold your questions and I'll field them all when I get back." He disappeared behind the closed door and stayed there for a very long time.

Turning the gilt-edged pages of the scriptures, I saw they were not well-worn, so either I didn't use them often or they were new. Occasional passages were marked in red pencil in all four sections of the book with cross references in the margins. I had studied in it. That little bit of knowledge about me was comforting.

Flipping through the pages, I read the marked passages, hoping to find some clue about myself, but it only created more questions. Why had I marked that verse? What made it special to me?

I closed my eyes, resting the scriptures in my lap. Something about this book gave me a connection to that part of me that was gone, the part I could no longer remember. I had no idea what it was, just that when I held the book in my hands, when I read those underlined passages, I didn't feel as lost, as adrift in an unfamiliar sea as I had since I had awakened with no memory.

When I opened my eyes, the bathroom door stood open and I was alone. My watch said two o'clock in the afternoon. I'd slept nearly four hours. The dull ache behind my eyes had subsided a little more. Now all I needed was my memory back and I'd be as good as new.

A run on the beach sounded really good right now. Well, maybe just a walk. My body was lethargic. It needed some exercise and I needed to start remembering all the things I'd forgotten. How could you possibly forget who you were? How could you not recognize your own face in the mirror or the husband you'd vowed to love till death do you part? I shivered at the phrase. Another mystery. Why that strange reaction to my marriage vows?

I sighed as I ran a brush through my short, dark, curly hair and stared at my reflection in the mirror. My passport said I was twenty-five years old. For twenty-five years I'd seen this face in the mirror, but there was nothing familiar about it at all. The brown eyes were as alien as the slightly turned-up nose with its light sprinkling of freckles.

After a long nap, my eyes shouldn't be tired, but they both felt like they had grains of sand in them. With my face close to the mirror, I pulled my eyelid away from my eye to find and remove the irritant.

The irritant was a contact lens! I popped one out of each eye into the water glass on the sink. My eyes weren't brown. They were green.

Emerald eyes, he had said. *You should always wear emeralds to match your marvelous emerald eyes.*

It was my first flash of memory. And the voice was not Ed's.

CHAPTER SEVENTEEN

Rummaging through my backpack, I found some contact lens cleaner tucked down deep in a pocket. Questions flooded my mind as I put the clean contacts back in my eyes. Why did my passport say I had brown eyes? Why hadn't my husband said anything? Didn't he know I wore contacts? Did he know what color my eyes really were? And why did I even wear them? They didn't seem to improve my vision at all.

My questions needed airing, if not to my husband, at least in the sunshine where I could examine them more closely. Ed wasn't in the lobby as I walked through, and I wasn't sure I wanted to talk to him just yet anyway. I needed time to think about these little discrepancies before I faced him again.

The thin strip of sand that passed for a beach in this area was empty to my left, so I turned that way instead of toward Galle Face Green, which still had groups of children playing cricket and families gathering for picnics or walks along the beach.

As I descended the sea wall stairs and passed the Indian High Commission, my mind was a tumble of questions, none of which my husband had seemed inclined to answer. Why?

It appeared most of the answers would not be forthcoming until my memory returned. I was agonizing over just how long that might be as I came to the end of my empty beach. A short road led from Galle Face Road to the beach, and beyond that the railroad edged along the beach as far as I could see.

Crossing the beach road, I turned onto Galle Face Road, wandering aimlessly as I pondered how to hurry the remembrance process.

"Allison. Wait."

I stopped and looked around. I was alone on the sidewalk.

"Allison," the voice called again. "Come in. Let's talk."

I looked up at the building in front of me. A distinguished-looking man stood at the gate to a high wall made from black volcanic rocks. With his dark-haired good looks, perfect tan, and confident stance, he could easily have been a GQ model. He motioned for me to come in. At least, I assumed it had to be me, since there was no one else within hearing distance except traffic in the street. I pointed at myself. He nodded.

This was the American Embassy, complete with Marine guards.

Dr. Armstrong appeared at his side and came quickly to take my arm.

"Mrs. Teale. How nice to see you up and about. How are you feeling?"

"Much better, Dr. Armstrong, and as soon as I remember who I am, I'll feel even better. You can't possibly know how disconcerting it is to look at the man sleeping in the same room and not recognize him as your husband."

As I spoke those words, the good-looking man joined us on the sidewalk, and a sudden frown marred his otherwise handsome features.

"Mr. Ambassador, this is the young woman I told you about who was thrown from the elephant. Mrs. Amy Teale, Milton J. Hollingsworth III, United States Ambassador to Sri Lanka."

I offered my hand and looked up into the surprised dark eyes of the ambassador.

"You must have mistaken me for someone else. As the doctor said, my name is Amy Teale. At least, that's what it says on my passport." I laughed. "Until I can remember something about me, I'll just have to believe what my passport and my husband tell me."

"Forgive my manners, Mrs. Teale. Instead of keeping you standing here in the heat and humidity after your ordeal, I should invite you in for tea. I'm more than a little interested in your story."

Holding my arm, with his other hand at the small of my back, in what seemed a surprisingly intimate gesture for a stranger, the ambassador led us into a sitting room. He signaled a waiting employee who seemed to know what was expected without verbal direction.

"Please sit here by me, and tell me what happened."

"I'm afraid I can't. I woke up in a strange hotel room, with a strange man holding my hand, and found I not only couldn't remember my own name, I didn't recognize my own face in the mirror."

"You don't remember anything at all?" he asked, leaning so close I could smell his expensive aftershave.

"Nothing. The good doctor says my memory will probably return in bits and pieces. I hope it hurries. You can't imagine how maddening it is to not know anything about yourself."

"Where is your husband?" he asked, his eyes filled with more than just a compassionate interest; the intensity seemed unusual from a stranger.

"Probably looking frantically for me about now. He's hovered over me continually since the accident. He made me lie down after breakfast for a little rest that turned into a four-hour nap. When I woke, he was gone. I decided I needed some fresh air and started out for a walk when you called to me. Who did you think I was?"

The ambassador's dark eyes never left my face. His gaze was so intense I felt my face flush.

"From a distance, you looked like someone I used to know. But her hair was long and her eyes were green. Her name was Melanie Allison Alexander, and she married a man named Bartholomew Allan."

He watched carefully how I took the information. I hoped my expression didn't give away the sudden turmoil I felt inside.

"That's interesting. My husband told me I have a brother named Bart." Before I could continue, tea was served on a huge silver tray from an exquisite silver tea service. "Oh, I'm sorry. My husband also told me that I don't drink tea or coffee. May I just have a glass of ice water with some lemon, please, if that wouldn't be too much bother?"

A single nod sent the neatly dressed young man out of the room. He returned almost immediately with a crystal goblet filled with ice water, and two slices of lemon on a matching crystal plate.

"What else has your husband told you?" the ambassador asked as he poured himself and the doctor a cup of tea.

"Not much, actually. Just that my brother and I are extremely close and we joined the Mormon church. My husband apparently didn't."

"I'd like to meet your husband. Will the two of you join me for dinner tonight? It will be very informal. I just arrived today. In fact,

I'm a day sooner than I was expected so I find myself with a free evening. I'd be pleased to have your company. About 8:00?"

"I'll have to give you a tentative answer until I check with Ed, but I don't know that we have anything planned for tonight. He was going to put off our work until he was sure I was strong enough to be on my feet for a while."

"He sounds like a very loving husband." There was an edge to the ambassador's voice that startled me. It wasn't sarcasm or irony, but something barely hidden beneath the surface that he hadn't completely veiled. Had he revealed it inadvertently, or on purpose?

I looked him straight in the eye. "He is. He sat by my side for hours holding my hand as I drifted in and out of consciousness—"

The ambassador interrupted before I could continue. "But he lets you wander loose in a foreign country with terrorists everywhere and no protection?"

I was the first to look away. Something about this attractive man bothered me. He was too persistent. Too inquisitive. And entirely too personal. He wanted too much, and there were too many answers that I didn't have. Was that my problem? I needed those answers, too.

I stood. "Thank you, Mr. Ambassador, for your concern and your invitation. I must be going. Ed will be looking for me."

"Let me see her to the door, Mr. Ambassador," Doctor Armstrong said, jumping to his feet. It was the first he'd spoken since we entered the embassy—I'd almost forgotten he was there.

"I'm glad you rested today," he said as he walked me down the sidewalk toward the Galle Face Hotel. Noise from traffic on Galle Road made talking almost impossible. "It would be good if you could put your feet up and rest again before dinner. Your body needs to be in a complete state of rest and relaxation so your mind can concentrate on calling back your memory. I know a young woman like you is used to being active, but if you can just focus on relaxing, I think things will come together for you much quicker. And I'm afraid you'll find that your body won't respond in its normal way to all that activity for a while."

"Thank you. Oh, there's my worried husband now." I waved as Ed hurried down the street. I offered my hand and the doctor took it in both of his.

"Remember, R&R will help more than anything else. Don't push it, don't try to rush it. It'll come."

As Ed raced toward us, Dr. Armstrong waved at him, then turned back toward the embassy.

"Where did you disappear to? I've been out of my mind with worry," Ed said, as he wrapped his arms around me, holding me tight against him as if to protect me from whatever I'd just exposed myself to.

"Having tea with the United States Ambassador to Sri Lanka," I laughed, extricating myself from the smothering embrace. As I explained what had happened, I pointed back to the gate of the embassy and found the ambassador watching us. I waved, pointed to Ed, and, linking my arm though his arm, started walking back to the hotel.

"And how did you find the ambassador?" Ed asked, his voice tight with tension.

"Charming, very good-looking, and intense. Yes. That's a good description. Intense. If his interest in my situation is any indication of his involvement with this country's problems, he'll be very successful—or drive himself crazy, one or the other. Oh, he invited us to dinner tonight. Said he'd love to meet you. Do we have other plans?"

Ed stopped, put his hands on my shoulders, and turned me to face him. "Would you like to go?"

I shrugged. "Why not? If you didn't have anything else planned, we might as well. You never know when you'll need to have the American Embassy on your side, and being personally acquainted with the ambassador can't hurt."

Ed searched my face, then turned, and taking my hand in his, began walking slowly. "You said he was good-looking. Did you find yourself attracted to him?"

I pulled him to a stop. "What kind of question is that?"

"If I'm still like a stranger to you, I'm just curious to see how you react to other men. You said he was charming and good-looking. As your husband, I'm a little paranoid to see who you might be attracted to."

"You can relax. He's not my type."

"What is your type?"

"Apparently you are. You're the one I married."

"If you can't remember anything from before last night, how can you be sure what your type is?"

"You must be my type. I don't think I would ever marry unless I was head over heels in love." I looked up at Ed. "How did I know that? Maybe I'm finally peeking through. Maybe it's beginning to come back."

I didn't like the turn this conversation was taking. It made me decidedly uncomfortable, but I had no idea why. Ed murmured something that sounded like "good," and we continued walking, finally reaching the green lawn that led to the hotel. I didn't try to instigate further conversation. It felt good to just walk. And Ed was a pleasant companion. Was that why I'd married him? He was a safe, pleasant person to be with? Whoa! Where did that come from? Safe? *Safe??*

"Did your message come yet?" I asked as we crossed the lobby, still troubled by the direction my thoughts were going.

"Not yet. They promised to call me as soon as it does."

"If you're thinking of putting me back to bed, forget it. I had a four-hour nap already, and we have a job to do. Isn't there something around here we can start on?"

Ed stopped. "The doctor said plenty of rest for a couple of days."

"Four hours is plenty. Can't we do something constructive?"

He looked at me for a minute, then shrugged his shoulders. "Okay. We'll get the cameras and go to work. But the minute you get the least bit tired, we'll quit."

We lucked out getting a taxi driver named Ananda who knew the city inside out. When we told him what we wanted to photograph, he immediately plunged into the thick of traffic and took us to the Colombo Fort and the Pettah. The former had been a fort during the Portuguese and Dutch periods, although today it was the commercial center of Sri Lanka. The Pettah was Colombo's bustling bazaar area.

In the next two hours we photographed the old lighthouse, which was now a landmark clock tower; the Queen's House, which was the home of the president; the Grande Mosque; the Jami-Ul-Alfar Mosque with its candy-striped red and white brickwork; St. Peter's Church; and the 1749 Dutch Wolvendaal Church. There were Hindu temples, known as *kovils* in Sri Lanka, with totally unpronounceable names, and Buddhist centers with beautiful frescoes and murals of the life of the Buddha.

Ananda was an excellent guide, with tidbits of information we'd never have discovered without spending hours in a library researching each of our photo subjects. He was a six-foot-tall cricket player who loved rock and roll and wanted to eventually move to France. He also had a delightful sense of humor, which was a great help in taking my mind off the headache that began to plague me again.

It was getting late, but Ananda insisted on one last stop at the most important Buddha center in the area, seven kilometers east of the Fort. The Buddha was reputed to have preached there two thousand years ago, and the dagoba was famous for its reclining Buddha image. Light and shadow play at that time of day gave us some extraordinary pictures.

I scribbled notes in my padded journal as Ananda wound through crowded streets trying to get us back to the Galle Face Hotel in time for our dinner appointment with the ambassador. That we made it was a testimony to Ananda's skill as a driver and his knowledge of the back streets and traffic patterns of Colombo.

"I will take you again tomorrow, if you wish," Ananda said as we pulled up to our hotel.

"Can you take me to the sapphire mines at Ratnapura?" Ed asked.

Ananda's smile disappeared. "We will talk," he promised before he drove away.

"Are you sure you feel up to this tonight?" Ed asked as I gathered my good black dress and pearls and headed for the bathroom to dress.

"I feel fine and will be even better after dinner. I'm starving." That was almost the whole truth. Fatigue seeped through my bones and my head ached again, but I was so intrigued by the ambassador that I couldn't stand the thought of canceling. Did he always take such a personal interest in his ambassadorial duties, or was there some reason he had a special interest in my case?

And was my motivation simply curiosity, or was there an attraction to the handsome ambassador that this married woman had better curtail immediately?

CHAPTER EIGHTEEN

Dinner turned out to be catered from the Galle Face Hotel and couldn't have been tastier. The conversation was scintillating, and I would have enjoyed myself immensely if my headache had subsided just a little. The ambassador and my husband engaged in some verbal sparring, but I couldn't put my finger on the cause of the undercurrents I felt as we got acquainted. They almost seemed to be talking in circles over my head.

"We were told at the airport to avoid the northern and eastern portions of the island. There won't be any problem with us going to Ratnapura to see the sapphire mines while we're here, will there?" I asked over dessert.

The ambassador glanced at Ed, then back at me. "Is this part of your photo-essay or just general sight-seeing?"

"Since the gem industry has such an impact on the economy of Sri Lanka, we thought that might warrant a trip there, coupled with the fact that it's supposed to be a spectacular scenic road, and one of the best views of Adam's Peak from the bottom," Ed said.

"All true," said the ambassador, steepling his hands thoughtfully. "But I'd be very careful outside of Colombo. The Tamils are on the move. This morning they blew up two ships off the Jaffna Peninsula and captured several others. They've been spotted off every coast this afternoon. Now they're moving into the southern portion of the island, which has been fairly secure thus far. If you insist on exploring, why don't you leave your wife in the capital? She could stay here in the embassy. Don't expose her to unnecessary danger."

"I didn't come to sit in a hotel room or the embassy while my husband has all the fun." I smiled, trying not to show my pique at his proprietary stance. "I understand you feel responsible for American citizens traveling abroad, and I appreciate your concern, but if Ed goes, I go."

Again the two men locked stares.

"Are your accommodations comfortable?" the ambassador asked, finally turning his attention back to me.

"Yes, thank you. We have a lovely room overlooking the ocean."

"You have plenty of room?" The question seemed to be directed to me, but his eyes were upon Ed.

"Yes," I answered. "The room is immense. Older, of course, but rather romantic."

At that, Ambassador Milton J. Hollingsworth III coughed suddenly, then he leaned forward, arms on the table, never taking his eyes off my husband. "Is this also a honeymoon trip as well as a business trip?"

Ed also leaned forward, resting his arms on the table, and in a level, controlled tone answered the ambassador. "No. This is strictly a business trip. We're on assignment. The pleasure we're having is in each other's company."

The ambassador stood. "I think Mrs. Teale would like to go now. She's been a good sport all evening, pretending to enjoy dinner, but I believe her headache is about to overpower her."

Startled, I looked up into dark eyes that seemed to see right through me. How did he know? He came around and pulled my chair from the table as I stood.

"Am I right, Mrs. Teale?"

My cheeks pinked as I tried to deny his allegation. I glanced at my husband. Ed stood up, obviously distressed that he hadn't noticed.

"You're right. My headache is about to overwhelm me. I'm sorry that it was so obvious. Forgive me for cutting our evening short."

The ambassador took my hand in his and leaned down to bring it to his lips. "Only to someone who was . . . ," he and Ed exchanged glances, ". . . attuned to you tonight. Please rest well, and I'd appreciate it if you'd keep me apprised of your itinerary. Would you mind checking in every night just so I won't worry that the terrorists have interrupted your work?"

"Are you always so interested in your fellow Americans?" I asked as we walked to the door.

"These are special circumstances, you must understand. I am very concerned about your welfare."

"Then we'll give you a good-night call so you can rest assured we're safe." I turned to him as we stepped through the doorway. "Thank you, Mr. Ambassador, for a lovely evening."

He shook Ed's hand, then took my hand and held it in both of his. "It was my pleasure, Mrs. Teale. I assure you, it was my great pleasure."

Eyes dark as midnight held mine until my husband took my arm and broke the spell. We turned, walked past the Marines standing guard, and down the sidewalk. It was strange. I hadn't felt like the ambassador was coming on to me, but only that he truly was concerned. But it was such a personal concern—almost an obsessive concern.

I glanced at Ed. He stared straight ahead. Even in the streetlight, I could see the muscle in his jaws working.

"He's a strange man," I said. "I'm sure he takes his work seriously, but there is a limit, you'd think, to how involved you'd get if you had several hundred people you felt that responsible for."

Ed didn't answer. He just looped my arm through his and kept up a brisk pace back to the hotel.

No message awaited us.

My husband still hadn't said anything as I gathered up my pajamas and headed for the bathroom. As I brushed my teeth, the ambassador's question about the honeymoon came back to me. Was that Ed's problem? The reason for his silence? Had he been feeling shunned since my accident?

At the thought, my legs buckled under me. I dropped onto the vanity stool. My husband had been very patient with me. He hadn't even kissed me, at least not on the lips, though I remembered that he had tried. Was I being unfair to impose that kind of restriction on someone who obviously loved me very much, even if I could muster no reciprocal feelings for him? Was I carrying it too far?

I finished brushing my teeth and getting ready for bed, involuntarily dragging out my routine. Facing Ed wasn't something I wanted to do now that I'd had time to think about this facet of our dilemma. But sooner or later, I had to emerge from the bathroom, so I took a deep breath and opened the door.

Ed was standing by the window, hands deep in his pockets, staring out into the night. I knew I should talk to him, but I couldn't make myself say the words. I wasn't even sure what words to say. I took the coward's way out. I crawled into bed and picked up the book of scriptures I'd left on the nightstand, the only familiarity I'd found since my accident.

Ed turned and looked at me, his face an expressionless mask. It gave no clue as to what he was thinking or feeling, nor any hints on how to begin to talk through this uncomfortable silence. I felt he expected me to say something, but what?

He stood still, watching me, his eyes never leaving mine. I held my breath. He moved slowly to the bed and stood looking down at me for a long moment before he sat down on the edge. He leaned toward me and raised one hand to touch my face.

"You don't have to be afraid of me. I won't touch you, I won't even kiss you, until you remember everything—and until you ask me to. Those are my two conditions. Your memory has to be fully restored. And you have to ask me to make love to you. You are as safe here as you'd be with your own brother."

I looked away, unable to stand the raw pain I saw in his eyes. His shoulders sagged and his head bowed to rest in his hands. I reached out to touch his arm. My fingers might have been a hot iron, he jumped so when he felt the pressure of them.

"I'm sorry, Ed. I know this isn't fair to you . . ."

He interrupted with a finger to my lips. "Shush. Don't say anything. Just remember that there is nothing I'd rather do than take you in my arms right this minute and show you how very much I love you. But because I do love you so dearly, I won't. You'll understand when your memory returns. So relax. Just concentrate on remembering who you are and let me help however I can."

"Thank you. No wonder I married you."

A look of pain flashed across his face as he lifted my hand to his lips and tenderly kissed my palm, then without a word, hurried to the bathroom and shut the door. The shower ran far longer than the hot water would have lasted, and before he emerged, I'd fallen asleep, dreaming of a tall, tanned man who rescued me from flame-throwing dragons.

I woke to the sound of gunshots and explosions in the distance. Ed was at the window, his bed not slept in.

"What is it?" I asked, joining him to see the lights out to sea.

"Probably the Tamil Tigers showing off their new acquisitions. There's a boat offshore firing some big guns, but they don't seem to be aimed at us. More than likely, the Sri Lankan Navy is engaging them. I'm not sure we should stick around much longer. I think whether our message has come or not, in the morning I'd better get you out of the country."

"Before we finish our assignment?"

"Your life is worth far more than any assignment, no matter who it came from. Get back to sleep, if you can, and we'll see if we can get reservations on a flight out of here tomorrow." He led me back to bed. "Will you be okay if I run down and check what's going on? The Foreign Correspondents Association is headquartered here in the hotel and some of them are always at the Sea Spray Bar. I'll go see if anyone has a handle on what's happening."

"Go ahead. For some reason, I can't seem to get enough sleep, so I'm sure I'll have no trouble falling off right away."

I didn't. And I dreamed again of the tall, tanned man. He was a knight in shining armor, rescuing a maiden surrounded by wriggling, writhing snakes, swinging his sword from side to side, slashing off the heads of the fearsome beasts just in time to save her. He swooped her off her feet and swung her on his horse. He was faceless. The maiden was me.

I woke in a cold sweat, sat up in bed, pulled my knees up, and wrapped my arms around them. I turned on the lamp to reassure myself there were no snakes in the room, and shuddered just remembering them. I hated snakes.

Ed's bed was empty, still made. The clock said four a.m. Where was my husband? I was about to get dressed and go find him when the door creaked open and Ed crept in. He stopped when he saw the light.

"Sorry. Did I wake you?"

"No. I had a horrible dream about snakes. But my knight in shining armor rescued me just in time." I started to laugh, but the look on Ed's face stopped me. "What's the matter?"

"Did you see your knight?"

"No. Why?"

"Bart has always been your knight in shining armor. Do you remember any more?"

"Nothing. What did you find out?"

"Our message came. We'll leave in the morning." Ed flopped on his bed and kicked his shoes off.

"What did it say?"

"We need pictures of some clothing manufacturing plants on the way to Ratnapura, as well as some of the mines, if we can get close enough. However, after talking to some of the journalists, I decided you're not going. The Tigers landed somewhere down the coast below Galle tonight and that's too close for comfort. You can stay here in the hotel and rest, if you prefer, but I'd rather you'd go next door to the embassy and let the ambassador entertain you while I'm gone. Then as soon as I get back, we'll leave Sri Lanka."

"Not on your life. You're not going to just park me somewhere and leave me while you go do all the work. I'm going with you."

"Amy. No." Ed sat up and swung his legs off the bed. "Are you sure you don't remember anything?"

"Why?"

"Because you are sounding exactly like your old self."

"Well, just because I can't remember who I am doesn't mean that I would act any different than I ever had, does it? I mean, just because a person forgets temporarily who they are, the basics haven't changed. Habits and characteristics shouldn't change, should they?" I sat on the edge of my bed and faced him. "Would they?"

"I don't know. I've never known anyone before who had amnesia. I don't know what to expect. I just know I won't take you into danger tomorrow."

"Where you go, I go. If you need pictures, I go with you. You're not leaving me behind. And if you try, I'll hire a car and follow you. I'm not a china doll, you know. End of discussion."

With that, I turned out the light and plopped back onto my pillows. After several minutes, I heard Ed stretch out on his bed. I lay awake a long time, knowing he hadn't gone to sleep yet either. I thought about leaving the Galle Face Hotel, leaving Sri Lanka, and couldn't picture a place to go to.

Was that why I felt this nagging reluctance to leave? Because it was the only known factor in my strange little world? I just knew I couldn't leave Sri Lanka yet. I didn't know why.

CHAPTER NINETEEN

Morning came too soon after all the interruptions of the night. I wasn't anxious to face it, until I heard Ed in the bathroom and knew if I wasn't ready when he was, I'd be left behind. I dressed quickly in a cool cotton blouse and light jeans while the shower was still running, deciding I probably wouldn't have time for one of my own when he emerged from the bathroom, preparing to leave without me.

That was exactly his plan.

"Sorry, Charlie. Whither thou goest, I will go." As I said the words, a brief flash of memory surfaced—a huge white stucco fireplace, Santa Fe style, and the warm secure feeling of being loved. Then it was gone. Closed down. Like clicking off the television set. Only an empty black screen remained.

I shut my eyes, willing the memory to return, any memory, but there was nothing. Ed stood watching me as I opened my eyes.

"Are you okay?"

"Yes. Just a quick glimpse of memory, one of the first I've had. But it was gone too soon."

"What did you remember?"

"Snuggling by a fireplace and being loved."

"That's all?"

"That's it. It was gone as quickly as it came. Do we have time for breakfast before we go?" I asked. "And did Ananda say he'd drive us or do we have to find another car?"

"I'm sure he'll take us—for the right price. As far as I'm concerned, he can name about any price and he'd be worth it. I felt like I could trust the fellow, and he's certainly a pleasure to be around."

"He's also a walking encyclopedia on Sri Lanka. But he didn't seem too keen on taking us to the mines."

"We're not going to the mines. You can pack your bag, because I'm taking you to the airport this morning. If there is any trouble, I don't want you anywhere near it."

"No. I'm not leaving you behind. Besides, I have the feeling that I shouldn't leave Sri Lanka just yet."

"Amy, I have an assignment to complete. I can't be here to care for you, and I can't leave you on your own. Either you go to the embassy and stay with the ambassador, or you fly out of here this morning."

"I can't tag along after the ambassador all day. He's a busy man. Why can't I come with you? If you're only going to be taking pictures, there's no reason that I can't come along and help."

"Reason number one: with the Tamil Tigers making inroads into this area, it's too dangerous. Reason number two: a severe concussion is nothing to sneeze at. You're supposed to be getting plenty of rest, which you can't do bouncing around in a car for hours on end. Reason number three: You need to see a specialist. There isn't one here. Reason number four: your parents—and Bart—would never forgive me if anything happened to you. I'm responsible for your well-being. Do I need to go on?" The impatience in his voice bordered on irritation.

"No need at all. None of your reasons are valid enough to send me away. I feel fine this morning and I'm not leaving Sri Lanka. End of discussion."

I grabbed my backpack, including some toiletries, none of which I'd had time to use, and headed for the door. "I can order breakfast while you make arrangements with Ananda. That will save a little time."

Ed's irritation became full-blown. "Go ahead. Order breakfast. I'll be right down."

When he came, it was with my bag packed full of my clothes.

"I've reserved a seat on the next flight to Singapore," Ed announced, settling into the chair opposite me and reaching for the plate of crocodile-shaped sweet buns. "You'll have a two-hour layover before your flight to LAX."

"Are you going to bodily carry me onto that flight? Because that's the only way you'll get me there, and unless they handcuff me to my seat, I'll get off that airplane before it takes off and come back here. Don't you understand? I can't leave Sri Lanka."

"Why?"

"I don't know why. I just know that I have to be here. It's the only thing I know for sure. I don't know myself, my history, anything about me. But I know I can't leave here yet. Besides, there's the issue of agency. As an adult, I do have some say in what I'm going to do."

Ed put his head in his hands and sat without speaking for several minutes. Then he leaned back in his chair and stared at me.

"You are the most obstinate person I have ever encountered in my life. And the most maddening."

"But you love me anyway," I teased, trying to temper my triumphant smile. "And you have to take me with you so you can keep an eye on me. Otherwise, you don't know what I might do."

Ed leaned forward, a wide smile that hinted of a small victory of his own spreading across his face. "Well, I finally got through to you. I'm glad you know I love you, even if you don't know anything else."

"Watch how you say that. 'Don't *remember* anything else' is the correct phraseology."

Breakfast and arrangements took only thirty minutes and we were off. For the exorbitant fee of nine thousand rupees, roughly one hundred seventy-five American dollars, a reluctant Ananda headed his air-conditioned Mercedes southeast out of Colombo on the left-hand side of the road, playing rock and roll tapes of American recording artists I'd never heard before.

Our first destination was a small town with a long name where a huge clothing manufacturing shop must have employed all the citizens from the surrounding area. Ed had to show papers that had arrived with our instructions before we were admitted to the secured area.

The fenced compound was abuzz with bad news. A truck filled with finished goods had been hijacked the night before, and the driver murdered. It was not considered the work of the Tamil Tigers, though most everything was blamed on them whether they were guilty or not. An organized gang of thieves worked the entire Southeast Asia area hijacking truckloads of clothes that could be worth as much as one million dollars per load.

Ed gave me instructions to wander and take pictures and talk to the employees while he was sequestered with the managers of the compound. For some reason, I had the feeling he wasn't gathering information on clothing production. That puzzled me. I had no basis for the feeling. Just a niggling little doubt somewhere in the back of my mind.

Ananda acted as interpreter. My few phrases of Sinhalese didn't serve me here.

The manufacturing shops were immense, long buildings with high steel rafters and ribbons of fluorescent lights high overhead. White-scarved, dark-haired women of all ages sat at row after row of sewing machines, assembling the name-brand products that would cost more in the United States for a single item than these people made in a month.

To call these sweat shops was a real misnomer. The work areas inside were tidy and clean. Outside, vegetables grew in neat, green, lush rows—the food that would be served in the immaculate dining room. Near a high stone wall, workers burned the remainder of bolts of fabric that was left from production. I wasn't sure if the high walls were there to keep out thieves or the wild animals that roamed the countryside, or to keep the workers inside.

As we left, Ananda informed me that it was some of all three, as well as to keep out those who desperately wanted to work there in order to feed their families. In third-world countries, these were often the best jobs in the entire area.

Everywhere the ground was not cultivated, the jungle growth crowded the edge of the road. In that jungle, leopards tracked the many species of deer indigenous to the island. The sloth bear, porcupine, jackal, and wild boar were inhabitants, as well as two species of crocodile. Ananda said there were eighty-three species of snakes, but only five were poisonous, and very common, he added as a warning. But king coconuts dropping from trees killed more people than snakes.

He spoke proudly of Sri Lanka's own sub-species of Asian elephant, but described the way they had been ruthlessly slaughtered—in twelve years Major T. W. Rogers had shot some twelve thousand elephants himself. Ananda laughed when he related that the major had been struck down by lightning. His grave had also been struck by lightning. Perhaps in this way, Ananda speculated, the elephants finally had their revenge.

When I asked Ed what he'd been talking about with the managers of the factory, he rambled on about production statistics and employee satisfaction solutions, but he avoided my eyes and changed the subject abruptly. I felt I wasn't being told the real story here. Why were we visiting factories? What did they have to do with the "architectural history" of Sri Lanka?

The feeling persisted as we visited two other similar manufacturing set-ups, and then drove on toward the gem mines at Ratnapura. Ed's questions to Ananda were pointed. What did he know about the people who ran the mines? Had the mines changed hands? Were they still as productive? Had mining methods changed?

Was this a journalist's curiosity for story background? Was this how we approached our photo-stories? Why couldn't I remember doing this before? Why had my entire existence become only a black void? All these questions only produced another headache.

Ananda continued our education of his beloved country. In 1960, Sirimavo Bandaranaike became the first elected woman prime minister in the world, serving twice in that capacity before being re-elected as current prime minister under her daughter, who was serving as Executive President of Sri Lanka.

I sketched a few brief notes in the unusual journal from my backpack. Writing in the car was mostly an exercise in futility. I probably wouldn't be able to decipher what I'd written later when I needed it, but if I could, the impressions would be valuable for the article. I studied the journal, wondering why on earth I had chosen such a bulky one to travel with—the inch and a half padded covers made the journal so big, it could only be carried in a roomy bag or backpack. Shrugging, I replaced it in the backpack. Just one more mystery.

Ananda maneuvered the car with great skill on the narrow road. There were actually only two main highways in Sri Lanka—both two-lane roads. When you left the main roads, all the other roads were so narrow that two trucks could not pass going fifty miles an hour. One had to pull off the road and stop while the other passed slowly and carefully.

Occasionally we had to pull over as a truck lumbered by, but in the five hours since we'd left Colombo, no one had tried to pass us.

Until we approached Ratnapura. Suddenly another car appeared behind us, honking impatiently for us to get out of the way.

I watched in amusement at Ananda's volatile reaction. His temper flared, and he uttered in Sinhalese what only could have been curses at the driver behind him, before pulling over to let the driver pass. As he did, a quick impression came to me. I was angry—very angry at someone sitting next to me—and I wondered how he'd fare with Sri Lankans' quick tempers. Then the impression was gone. Who was I angry with? And why?

As the car roared passed, I glanced at the man in the back seat who was leaning forward, looking at us. His expression showed first surprise, then hostility.

"Did you see that man?" I asked Ed. "He looked positively hateful. Why on earth would he be so irritated? We moved out of his way."

"Sorry. I wasn't watching." Ed turned to look out the window on his side, as if interested in the dense jungle that crowded the road.

But I'd seen the look that flitted across his face. He'd recognized the man in the car. Why did he lie to me? Little prickles of fear slid through me. Why would my husband lie to me?

I leaned my head back on the seat and closed my eyes, willing my memory to return—willing any memory to come and help me know who I was and why I felt like such a stranger in this body. But nothing came. Just the continued unease at the unknown.

"Ananda, I'm starving. When do we get to eat?" I asked as my stomach rumbled audibly.

"Very soon. We are coming into Ratnapura now. I will take you to the Rest House where they will feed you while you relax and enjoy the beautiful view. But I do not like the look of the sky. If it rains too much, we won't be able to get back to Colombo. The roads will flood and we won't be able to get through."

"I'd hoped to be able to finish up what we need to do today and make the early morning flight out of Colombo tomorrow," Ed said. "Let's hope it doesn't change our plans."

I had a clutching in the pit of my stomach when he said that. I couldn't leave Sri Lanka. I couldn't leave the Galle Face Hotel. I needed to do something important there. But I didn't know what. And I didn't know why.

Please, please, help me to remember, I found myself praying. I felt an intense sense of comfort at that prayer. But it triggered a myriad of questions. As they tumbled over in my mind, we pulled up to the Rest House in Ratnapura. And the heavens opened.

It was raining so hard I couldn't even see the building we were parked in front of—nor anything else. Ananda produced some umbrellas and got us inside, only slightly drenched.

"This is how we get ninety inches of rain per year," Ananda said with a hearty laugh as he shook the rain from the umbrellas. "All at once."

Ed conferred with Ananda while I explored the spacious veranda and found a gaily decorated Christmas tree. It drew me toward it, invoking a melancholy I couldn't understand as something unrecognizable tugged curiously at my heartstrings. Why this abject sadness at the sight of the tree? Or was it at the thought of Christmas? What were my Christmases like? Special? Barely observed or full of ritual and tradition?

I felt like a child, wishing on the star at the top of the tree, but my wish was not to find something underneath. It was to find me. I wanted to cry out in frustration! So many questions—and no answers.

When I finally pulled myself away from the tree, my husband had rented a room upstairs with an attached bath, which was a luxury, they told me, when you get away from the big cities.

"We're staying?" I asked, puzzled at the change in plans.

"Ananda says if the rain continues like this for even a couple of hours, we won't be able to get back to Colombo, and if we wait to see if the rain lets up before getting a room, there won't be any available. Besides, you look a little tired, and I thought you might like to take a nap while there's nothing to do but wait for the rain to stop."

"Thank you. You do take good care of me. But if I don't get something to eat right now, it will all be for naught. I'll perish from hunger before I could get upstairs to the bed."

"Then by all means, let's feed you." Ed put his arm around my waist, and with a gentle, caring smile, led me to the dining area.

How could he be so duplicitous? To appear so loving and caring one minute, and lie to me the next? Words pounded through my head till it began to ache again—deceitful, dishonest, deceptive, equivocate, prevaricate . . . lie. It didn't matter what you called it, it came down to the same thing. Why had he lied to me? And what other lies had he told me? What kind of marriage did we have if my husband lied to me?

I don't know what I had for lunch. I barely noticed what the room looked like where we ate. I mumbled something about another headache, which by this time was overpowering, and Ed took me upstairs. I managed to settle my head on the pillow without it splitting open, which was very much a concern until I had accomplished it. I felt my sandals slipped from my feet, a cover gently placed over me to ward off the chill of the hill country. When the door quietly closed and Ed left, I pulled off my still damp jeans and succumbed to the relief and oblivion sleep brought.

When I woke, the room was almost dark, filled with the gloom of a rainy afternoon. Rain still thundered on the roof and ran in rivulets down the windows.

Cautiously, I sat up. I was alone. Even my headache had abandoned me. *Thank you for small favors,* I murmured. Did I always carry on a dialogue with deity? In that case, I added a fervent prayer for remembrance of who I was and why I was really here, because by now, I had a recurring feeling that I knew nothing about photo-journalism, and my reason for being in Sri Lanka had nothing to do with that at all. But I still had no idea of the who, or what, or why of my real life.

Ed wasn't a meticulous packer. My clothes had been crammed, rather than folded into my bag when he'd packed them for me this morning, but one long skirt hadn't fared too badly. Paired with the blouse I'd been sleeping in, my outfit consisted of mix and match wrinkles.

I walked to the window and stood with my head pressed against the glass, unable to see out for the blinding rain, but not looking anyway. I was still looking inward, still trying to conjure up some image, any image that would give me a clue to me.

After several unfruitful minutes, and several more pleas for divine help, I wandered downstairs to find my husband and Ananda to see how they were spending the afternoon. As I descended the stairway, I heard Ed's voice, raised in anger. I stopped, just out of sight.

"When the deluge stops, you will leave," a man shouted. "You will get out of the country or your lives will be forfeit!" The accent was Spanish, not Sinhalese.

A door slammed. The only sound was the incessant beating of the rain against the roof. I didn't move, waiting for the next scene of the unbelievable drama—waiting, before I revealed myself, to see what would happen now.

A chair creaked and a quiet murmur of voices resumed in other parts of the Rest House. Apparently everyone had been listening to the interplay between my husband and the man with the Spanish accent. Who was he? The mysteries were becoming like the water outside, deeper and more plentiful. I didn't need more mysteries, when I was the biggest one myself.

I waited another minute, then continued downstairs and found Ed, sitting with a deck of cards spread in front of him on a small table in the corner, playing solitaire.

He looked up when I approached him, and stood with a welcoming smile, taking my hand to pull me down beside him on the rattan love seat.

"How are you feeling? Headache gone?"

"Yes, amazingly. What's going on? Have I missed anything exciting?"

"Not a thing. Boring afternoon. Ananda's gone to spend the night with some friends. Said if we need him to call."

"Those aren't the clothes you left in this morning," I noted with surprise. I hadn't seen any others in our room upstairs. We'd come with only my bag and backpack, because Ed had expected to put me on an airplane instead of bringing me along.

"No," Ed laughed sheepishly. "I had Ananda take me to the mines while you were sleeping. It was so boring here with nothing to do, I figured I might as well accomplish something and hoped the rain would let up a little. It didn't. I got drenched. His friend is about my size, so I borrowed some dry clothes."

"What did you hope to accomplish at the mines? Most of them are open pit—or open ditch-types, aren't they?" I stopped. "How did I know that? I must be remembering something I've read."

"You read it on the plane. It's in your book. If you want something to do, you could probably reacquaint yourself with all the things you learned about Sri Lanka before we came. Unless you'd like to take over my game here. I'm not having very good luck. It's beaten me all afternoon."

"Is that all you've done while I slept? Get drenched at the mines and play solitaire? No interesting company?" I waved toward the people in the dining room. "No interesting conversations? No fascinating items for the article? No intrigue?"

"Not a thing. When you get out of Colombo, most people don't speak English. Since I don't speak Sinhalese or Tamil, I can't converse with the locals. So it's been a totally boring day. But everything without you is boring. I'm glad you're awake and feeling better. This dreary day has brightened considerably since you walked into the room." He flashed a smile that should have brightened anyone's day—full of apparent sincerity and warmth. Except that I knew he was lying through his gleaming white teeth.

CHAPTER TWENTY

Dinner was not the relaxing, amiable event it should have been. I sought double meanings in everything Ed said. I no longer asked him about me, about us, about things we'd done. He hadn't been especially forthcoming with answers before, and I found myself unable to believe anything he told me now.

"You're quiet tonight. Headache return?"

"No," I shrugged. "Just not much to say, I guess. I keep trying to remember, but nothing comes. It's very discouraging, not knowing anything about yourself." I tried to smile and lighten the mood. "What would you like to do to while away the evening?"

"What I'd like to do, I've promised I wouldn't," Ed said with a rueful smile that spoke of accepted disappointment. "Looks like the most exciting game in town is a card game. What do you play?"

I stared at him. "Don't you know?"

He coughed into his napkin and countered with a sly grin, "We've never had the problem of time on our hands when we didn't have a very enjoyable activity to occupy us." He shook his head. "We've never played cards."

"I guess if I don't remember how to play something, you'll just have to teach me. Unless we need to spend some time working on the article. Would that be a good use of a free evening?"

"Not without a computer. I don't do longhand anymore. And you prefer the computer, too."

"Guess all that's left is cards. Might as well get started."

I decided it was no wonder we hadn't played cards. I had a hard time concentrating on even the most simple games long enough to give Ed a run for his money. My mind kept wandering—wondering, actually. Finally I gave up.

"Might as well go to bed. I'm not presenting any kind of challenge to you."

"If you only knew," Ed murmured.

"Hopefully the rain will stop during the night and the water recede enough for us to get back to the hotel in the morning." I stopped. "Ed, I don't want to leave Sri Lanka just yet. I don't know why, but I feel I need to be at the hotel—for something. Can we please stay a little longer? At least finish what we started here? Maybe by the end of the project, my memory will have returned."

He frowned. "I don't want you in danger. I'd rather leave without delay."

I didn't argue with him. We could broach the subject when the time came. However, I didn't intend to leave Sri Lanka.

"I'm going up to bed," I said. "Are you coming?"

"Not right now. Guess I'll tackle a few games of solitaire before I come up. Give you time for your nightly bathroom routine and to get into bed." He touched a hand to my hair and rumpled it slightly. "Don't wait up for me though. If I start winning, I may play a few more hands."

Something told me he wasn't coming to bed. He had other plans for this evening that didn't include me, and that didn't include playing solitaire either.

I wandered upstairs, wondering what Ed could be planning. What can you do in the pouring rain? Well, I might just have to find out. I brushed my teeth, washed my face, and tried to decide if I should wait up here in case he came to check on me, or go where I could watch him.

No. He probably wouldn't come to make sure I was asleep before he carried out his plans for the evening. I'd been falling asleep as soon as my head touched the pillow for two days now. He would count on that.

As I headed for the door, on impulse, I scooped up my backpack. I crept to the stairs, but couldn't see him from there, so I sidled down the stairs, trying to appear casual and inconspicuous to anyone who might see me.

I was right. Already he had his own clothes back on, still showing signs of his earlier dowsing. His borrowed clothes were folded in the corner of the love seat, waiting his return, no doubt. Or was he leaving the Rest House and not planning to come back for me?

He picked up a flashlight from beside the deck of cards and headed out into the storm. None of the patrons in the other room noticed him leaving. They didn't seem to pay any attention to me, either, as I grabbed the umbrella Ananda had left by the door and followed Ed into the torrent.

Rain in the tropics is like a Texas downpour. The sky seems to open and all the water in heaven flows out. And just as the heavens are limitless, so is the amount of water that can cascade down for hours, or even days, on end.

I knew I had to stay close enough to see that tiny beam of light through the downpour or I'd be lost forever. There were no other lights visible. Nothing to see where I walked. I could only follow in his footsteps and hope I didn't fall in a hole or off a cliff.

The umbrella wasn't much help, except possibly to keep my backpack from being soaked, too. Huge raindrops splashed back up to my knees, drenching my skirt at least that far. Rain blown sideways curled in around the umbrella and doused most of the rest of me. But I never took my eyes off that light in front, that one point of reference in the wild, wet, dark night.

We seemed to be going downhill. And we were moving fairly fast. Ed was no slouch in the walking department. Then again, he could see where he was going, shining the light on the road in front of him. I had to just hope there was nothing between him and me. I watched to see if he varied from his straight line, hoping to give myself time to dodge whatever he had sidestepped to avoid.

A dozen scenarios for the reason for this furtive trip slipped through my mind as we trudged on for what seemed hours, though it surely couldn't have been that long. Occasionally Ed stopped, shined his light around as if to get his bearings, then plunged ahead again. The further we got from the Rest House, the closer I tried to get to Ed. He couldn't hear my footsteps because of the rain, and I didn't want to chance losing him if he suddenly darted off the road and out of sight.

Dr. Armstrong was right. I didn't have either the stamina or the steady gait necessary for this kind of outing just yet. I hoped we weren't going much farther. But we did.

I'm sure we must have walked at least two miles when he stopped, shined the light around, and plunged into the darkness off the road. By this time I wasn't far behind him, but he had the advantage of the light. A half a dozen steps off the pavement, I stepped in a hole, and cried out as I tried to stay upright.

Ed whirled and shined the light right in my face. Something glinted in his other hand. It was a gun! My husband had a gun pointed at me.

"What are you doing here?" he demanded.

"Following you. Trying to find out why you lied to me. Trying to find out what secrets my husband keeps from me."

Suddenly a stream of light stabbed the darkness down the road. A car was coming. Ed leaped forward and grabbed me, dragging me behind him as he flashed his light frantically looking for a place to hide. The umbrella had to go, but trying to fold it while being yanked on the run through blinding rain, undergrowth, and knee-deep puddles was more than I could handle.

As the car turned onto the dirt road we'd just abandoned, Ed threw me to the ground behind a small palmetto with drooping leaves and dropped beside me. Headlights swept the area. The umbrella gave up the fight and folded obediently beneath me as I fell.

"I can't believe you did this," Ed hissed in my ear.

"I can't believe you have continually lied to me," I replied, brushing away the long grass that tickled my face. "What kind of marriage do we have, anyway?"

"Not now. What am I going to do with you? I can't take you into this."

"Well, you're not leaving me alone in the dark, in the rain, and especially not in this long grass. How many kinds of snakes did Ananda say there were?"

"Come on. We've got to keep up with that car."

Ed dragged me to my feet before I had a chance to get there by myself, and jerked me back to the road—if you could call it that. It actually felt more like a river. Water was at least ankle deep, and I had the feeling it was getting deeper all the time, and running, like we were.

I slipped both arms through the straps of my backpack, and did my best to stay upright as we stumbled after the slow-moving car. Several times one or the other of us stepped in a hole, maintaining our balance only because of the grip we had on each other.

Ramshackle buildings loomed in the headlights. The car slowed, pulled just beyond the buildings, and stopped.

"Find a place to hide, and stay there till I come for you," Ed whispered, pushing me toward the buildings.

"Not on your life, buster. I'm closer than your shadow. Just consider me an appendage from now on."

"Allison, do what you're told," he hissed.

"What did you call me?"

He cursed under his breath. "Never mind. Just stick close and don't make a sound."

Allison. He called me Allison. My mind raced as we skirted the buildings, getting as close to the car as we could. Was that a slip? Was Allison his lover? Unfortunately, I didn't have time to consider the ramifications of that.

The car door opened and the interior light revealed the angry man who had passed us on the road to Ratnapura. The man my husband had said he didn't see. As the man yelled at his driver to get the umbrella so he wouldn't get soaked, I heard a Spanish accent. This was the man at the Rest House—the man who had threatened us if we didn't leave immediately.

I had a sinking feeling—and it had nothing to do with the fact that I was now in water up to my knees. Why hadn't I simply gone to bed in that nice, dry room? I could be sleeping peacefully now, oblivious to the rain and to the very real possibility of encountering snakes or alligators or any number of things that belong on the other side of the fence at the zoo. Or worst of all—dangerous human animals.

As the men entered one of the little one-room shacks and lit a lantern, we maneuvered through the water to the window. The man sat at a small desk, looking in drawers, rifling through papers scattered on top, while his driver stood guard with a gun tucked into his belt.

Suddenly another car approached, its lights slicing through the liquid darkness. Ed didn't have to jerk me to the ground. I hit it before he did. Face first in a muddy puddle.

The man who emerged from his car and dashed into the hut was tall and slender, dark-haired as well as dark-skinned, and appeared to be in his forties. The man who waited, who stood to face the newcomer as he entered, was as tall, but broader through the shoulders and chest, and could only be described as a big man. His clothes were expensive and well-cut for his body. He might have been good-looking if his countenance had been pleasant, but he seemed to sport a perpetual scowl.

It deepened as he faced the dark, slender man.

"Where are the stones?" he demanded, loud enough for us to hear plainly even over the rain. "I thought you were going to leave them here for me."

"Even this rain won't keep out thieves, and as you have noticed, there's no lock on the door. Only a fool would leave anything of value in this place."

"Let me see them."

The slender man withdrew a bag the size of a large grapefruit from his jacket pocket and untied the drawstring top. He emptied the contents on the desk. It appeared to be a pile of rocks, most of which were about the size of the end of my thumb.

The scowl disappeared from the big man's face. He produced a jeweler's eyepiece and bent to study the stones.

"How much *geuda* do you have for me?" he asked, without looking up.

"About twenty bags like that, although if you can wait a couple of days, the rain will probably wash much more down from the hills. They can be picked up in yards and streams, and even walkways after a rain like this. And we won't get into the deeper mines for a few days until the water drains out."

"I can wait if you'll guarantee the quantity and if they're like these."

"There's no guarantee, but the track record is good. Heavy rains wash away the soil, the rocks wash down from the mountains, and my people harvest them from the flow areas when the water recedes."

"Ten more bags?"

The slender man smiled. "Yes. I can guarantee ten more bags from a storm like this."

"Good. Put the stones in my car. I'll pay you for these and come back for the others."

"How will you get them out of the country? Since we discovered that the Thais were cheating us, telling us *gueda* was almost worthless, the authorities have clamped down, raised the export fee, and the buyer's bond."

"I've found a way. Are you heating your own now?"

"With what you will pay me from this batch of stones, I'll have the money to buy my first furnace. I've hired a cutter with heating experience." His grin widened in pride. "I'm on my way up in the jewelry business."

"Don't get too cocky," the bigger man scowled. "I'll only buy if you keep your price down, and you keep the quantity and quality coming." Then he smiled for the first time as he rattled a handful of the stones. "Who'd ever guess that a simple heat treatment would turn these ugly little babies into beautiful sapphires worth a fortune?"

"What will these bring you on your market?"

The man with the Spanish accent frowned. "Don't set your sights on taking over my arm of the business. You keep collecting these, and I'll keep paying you."

The two men left the shack. The bodyguard turned off the lantern and quickly followed them to the cars. Twenty bags were transferred from one car to the other, and money changed hands. Just as they were about to get in their respective cars and leave, a circle of lights suddenly lit up the night, surrounding the three men.

"Get your hands in the air—then freeze," a voice shouted out of the rain.

Ed and I hit the ground again—in unison as the bodyguard fired. Two perimeter lights disappeared. A volley of gunfire answered, filling the night with sound and blazes of color. The bodyguard hit the ground and lay still.

"No more heroics. Hands in the air," the voice from the darkness commanded. The man with the Spanish accent and his friend obeyed immediately. "Tie them up," the voice continued. "Get them in the car and let's get out of here."

Just as I thought the worst was over and the two cars were ready to drive away, something jammed against my head.

"Stand up, carefully," a voice immediately behind us commanded.

CHAPTER TWENTY-ONE

"Get to your feet."

My husband swore softly under his breath, then whispered, "Don't say a word."

We got carefully to our feet, hands in the air, and were prodded into the light.

"Who are you?" demanded a voice from the darkness.

"Photojournalists from the States," Ed answered.

"What are you doing here?"

"A story on the sapphire mines."

"Tie them and bring them, too," the voice commanded.

We were dragged to a van, shoved inside, and tied hand and foot. Four men piled in behind us and the van lurched forward. There were no seats in the back of the van, so we were forced to lay on the dirty, wet floor covering. There was a general jostling to get comfortable. One man lit a cigarette, affording a momentary glimpse of the faces that surrounded us. They were not friendly.

I was on my side, facing the front of the van. Ed lay behind me, curled up against my backpack.

"Are you okay?" Ed asked.

"Silence," commanded the man nearest us.

Ed leaned forward. By twisting my head over my shoulder, I could put my lips to his ear and reply.

"Having oodles of fun. You have a lot to explain."

"Hope I get the chance."

I couldn't remember being more uncomfortable, nor more scared. I was soaked to the skin and shivering, with cold, or fright, or both. I snuggled as close to my husband as I could get with the backpack and his tied arms between us, needing his warmth and what little feeling of security that gave me. Even if I'd had a jacket—and I remembered reading that tourists should never go to the cooler hill country without one—it would be soaked, and therefore, useless.

"Raise your head," he whispered, bringing his bound hands up and over my head, so that I lay in the circle of his arms, my head resting on his forearm. Better. Not great, but better.

Our captors, two on each side, leaned against the sides of the van, arms draped over propped-up knees, heads drooping, weapons across their laps. Apparently they were sleeping. The driver chain-smoked one cigarette after another, never speaking to the erect man who rode at his side—the commander, I assumed.

As the miles increased, so did my headache, probably a combination of the smoke, the concussion, and the number of questions rattling around inside my head. I tried to quiet my over-active mind, but sleep seemed impossible, and I had nothing else to do but think about my husband's lies, the name he called me, and try to remember anything from my past. Where had I heard the name Allison recently?

Suddenly the driver slammed on the brakes and shouted at the men to get out. The road was flooded. They'd have to push the van through the high water. The soldiers obeyed immediately, without comment. This same scenario replayed itself a dozen times during the remainder of the drive.

Sometime during the night, the rain quit. We'd been bouncing along for hours before the sky began to pale and night fade. Ed leaned toward my ear.

"Let me do the talking. Answer only if you are questioned directly. Don't lose your temper, and do exactly as I say, when I say it, without questioning me. We may get out of this alive, and we may not. If we don't—know that I love you."

I twisted my head and he brought his ear to my mouth. "Then why have you lied to me? Who is Allison? Do I lose my temper often?" Questions that demanded answers poured forth, but he moved his head and brought his lips back to my ear.

"I hope I have a chance to explain. Remember, no matter how off-the-wall it seems, follow my lead. I wish you'd listened to reason and gone home when I tried to send you."

I twisted my head. "But look at all the fun I'd have missed."

Our captors stirred as the van slowed, stretching arms and legs and yawning widely. I needed to stretch. Actually, I needed a hot shower and a soft bed more than anything right now. My chances of getting that in the foreseeable future didn't seem good, so I'd have been willing to settle for a clean bathroom.

We were nearing civilization. A rooster crowed at the rising sun and the van wove in and out of the first traffic we'd encountered. I wanted to sit up and look out the front window, but when I tried, Ed tightened his arms around me.

"Don't," he whispered. "The less you see—the less you know—the better our chances of getting out of this alive."

I wondered if I had a naturally curious streak or if these circumstances had produced it. I wanted in the worst way to sit up and see where we were, what little town we were driving through, whether we were still in the lush green of the forest or on the plains, or near the water. I'd traversed a goodly portion of an exotic foreign country tonight, and not seen a single mile of it.

Within the hour, I got my wish. We exited the road and bumped over a primitive trail for a couple of miles, then stopped. We were in the forest. But we must also be near the ocean, I reasoned. One of the men, apparently new to the area, was ordered to Matara for food. He'd find his way back by turning at the lighthouse.

Matara. Matara. I'd seen that on the map. But where? Matara. Lighthouse. We were on the very southern tip of the island. The lighthouse at Dondra Head was the southernmost point of land in Sri Lanka. There was nothing between there and Antarctica but the Indian and the Southern Oceans.

The last to exit the van, we were apparently an unplanned inconvenience to be dealt with at their leisure. I hoped we were simply an inconvenience, and not a flaw that would prove fatal—to us. Car doors slammed around us. The commander barked orders in a language I didn't understand, instead of his perfect English of last night. Spanish Accent and his friend, objecting loudly to their abduction, were suddenly silent. Why, I couldn't tell, and I wasn't sure I wanted to know. I was glad he hadn't seen us.

The area teemed with activity outside the van. Soldiers dressed in worn, dirty fatigues scurried back and forth unloading boxes from a vehicle that had arrived after us.

"Okay, I'm ready for some answers," I said quietly to my husband as I struggled to sit up and stretch my aching body. "Talk fast."

But before he had a chance, two men with automatic weapons appeared at the door to the van, removed the restraints from our feet, and ordered us out. Hot tropical sun warmed my bare arms and face. My clothes were still damp from the rain, and I'd never really warmed up during the long, arduous night. Now that we were out of the higher elevation, I knew being warm again wouldn't be a problem.

We were directed through the work area in the front yard to an ancient-looking stone house with a long, low stone porch across the front. I wondered if this had been one of the homes or rest houses of the early Portuguese settlers.

Our escorts were as different as Mutt and Jeff. Both had the dark hair, dark skin, and round face of the Tamils. One was a small, mean-looking man with a scar running from one ear under his jaw to his Adam's apple, as if someone had tried to cut his throat. The other was taller, heavier, and almost friendly-looking. At least, his eyes were. Speaking fairly good English, the friendlier of the two cautioned us severely that we were to be silent—and obedient.

We were taken into the house, which had apparently been abandoned by humans for some time, but used by animals for shelter. It was filthy. The only furniture was a worn, torn, overstuffed sofa that looked like it could walk away by itself if its crawling inhabitants united to move in the same direction.

The commander entered from another room and examined us with cold, piercing eyes, tapping a wooden baton against his hand in irritation. Though a small man, he emanated an aura of extreme power and control. His black eyes reminded me of a wolverine, fierce and savage.

"Lock them in the back room. I'll get to them later," he said, turning his back on us to direct the placement of boxes being carried in, wooden boxes with Arabic symbols. Ed spun me from them quickly. He didn't want me to see what was going on, even if I'd have liked to.

As we left the room, a loud crash indicated a box had been dropped. I glanced over my shoulder to see the commander strike his baton across the head of the clumsy soldier who'd dropped it.

"Idiot! How can we learn to use broken equipment? Drop another and you'll be shot." He continued the verbal abuse on that man and the rest of them in the yard, urging them to hurry, but carefully, or risk a bullet. Their work must be completed before someone arrived at noon. I missed the last part as we were led down a cluttered hall, passing several small rooms on either side, and through a kitchen black from the smoke of countless fires in the huge fireplace. Just as we were about to be forced into a small pantry next to the back door of the house, I turned to the more friendly looking of our guards.

"I don't suppose there's a bathroom in this hotel. I need to relieve myself."

The second, smaller guard curved his lips in what was supposed to be a smile, but was nothing more than a leer.

"I'll take her into the woods. We'll be back in a while."

"I have to go, too." Ed spoke quickly, moving close to me. "How about we all go together?"

The lecherous guard wasn't happy when the friendly guard agreed and led us back into the sunshine. The vegetation was thick and lush, encroaching what yard there may once have been.

Spotting a huge plant with large leaves, I asked if I could be untied to go behind it for some privacy. Lecherous Louie hurried forward, but Friendly Fred stepped in front of me, his gun draped casually across his arm—pointing directly at the chest of the other man. Louie stopped, his angry, dark eyes flashing hate signals. Fred untied my hands and with a caution to watch for snakes and other dangers, turned his back as I stepped into the green darkness of the jungle.

I stood for a minute, eyes becoming accustomed to the deep shade, while I looked and listened for rustlings and movement. Satisfied there was nothing sinister near, I accomplished my task, then turned before leaving to listen to the birds' songs filling the air. The variety of vegetation was astounding. And I spied some of the fruit we'd had for breakfast at the Galle Face Hotel, however long ago that had been.

"Look, there's fruit on these trees," I called to Fred. "I recognize the papayas and mangoes. Is the rest of it edible?"

The large man moved immediately to my side and examined the trees.

"Mangosteen, rambutan, jackfruit, and custard apples. All good to eat. This one, too. Hand-grenade fruit." He smiled at what I was supposed to take as a joke, I think. "It's a durian." He picked a big, green fruit, broke it open and released an aroma that could only be compared to a disgustingly blocked-up sewer. He offered me a bite.

"No, thanks. I couldn't possibly put anything in my mouth that smells that bad. Can I pick some of these others? I'll get enough for you, too. I'm starving."

Ed and Louie joined us, and we soon had enough fruit to supply the entire camp. While I satisfied my immediate hunger on mangoes, papaya, and little pink guava, I picked an orchid, one of several varieties growing wild in the incredible green world. This was, indeed, a Garden of Eden, as Sri Lankans claimed, both beautiful and bountiful.

Complete with serpent. I stumbled backward in horror as the large yellow-and-brown cobra raised his head two feet off the ground. He flattened his neck ribs, giving the appearance of a poufed hood. Weaving sinuously back and forth, he stared at me with hypnotic eyes.

Lecherous Louie dispensed with him instantly in a short burst of gunfire, which brought shouts from the house and soldiers running, guns ready, from the front yard.

Only the fruit we'd picked appeased the commander enough to prevent him from shooting us on the spot, I felt. Our freedom at an end, we were led back to the closet-sized, windowless pantry. The door slammed behind us, and we were left in the dark. Instinctively I reached for the door knob. There was none.

"I didn't have a chance to look for snakes or spiders in here," I shuddered. "Did you?" I leaned into Ed and felt a rush of comfort and security as his arms closed protectively around me. He kissed my temple and my cheek, then pulled me tightly against him and held me, whispering my name over and over, as if to reassure himself that I was there, unharmed and intact.

I withdrew my arms from around him, where they'd gone instinctively when darkness descended on us, and he released me with a reluctant sigh.

"Sorry. I know I promised I wouldn't ask anything of you until you remembered who you are, and wanted me to come to you, but I was so relieved to have you safe and untouched by that scum. Do you have any idea of how close you came to being raped in the woods by that ugly little rat?"

I shuddered again. "Yes, but I was counting on Friendly Fred to step in. Or you with your gun."

"Unfortunately, the soldier took it at the mine. Who's Friendly Fred?"

"A nickname I gave the big one with the friendly eyes. The little one is Lecherous Louie. Apt, don't you think?"

Ed mused, "Amy, you never cease to amaze. We're in danger of being shot any minute because we blundered into something we may not live to tell about, and you calmly announce you have to go to the bathroom, despite the fact you are obviously the only woman that man had seen for eons and he'd been eyeing you all night."

"He couldn't have been eyeing me all night," I argued. "It was too dark to see anything. Like here. I don't dare move for fear of disturbing any current inhabitants who may resent our intrusion."

Ed put his hand in his pocket and fumbled with something. I touched his wallet.

"What are you doing?" I asked.

"Finding my flashlight."

"In your wallet?"

"I keep one of those credit card lights—here it is."

A slender beam of blinding light hit my eyes. Ed scanned the corners, shelves, floor, and ceiling. Even the cobwebs were empty. Or the spiders were hiding. We apparently had the place to ourselves.

I scraped my foot in the dirt on the floor to dislodge anything that might be hidden there, slipped the backpack from my shoulders, and sat on it.

"I thought that had become permanently attached to you," Ed said.

"It's been there so long, I'd almost forgotten what it felt like without it. Okay, husband of mine, we now have plenty of opportunity. Talk. Who is Allison? And who are these guys? Why would there be Arabic words on those boxes?"

"What did they say?"

"I don't remember much. I was so surprised that I knew it was Arabic, and you spun me around so fast, I didn't really have a chance to read them. Some said 'ammo' and others 'explosives,' but that's all I saw. I suppose we've bumbled into something really bad, huh?"

"You could say that." Ed hunkered down on the floor across from me and turned off the light. "I suspect we're right in the middle of a bunch of Tamil Tigers who are being supported by Middle Eastern terrorists. They've apparently just received a shipment of arms. I wish to high heaven you hadn't followed me into this."

"If I'd known where you were going, I wouldn't have. If you'd talked to me, instead of lying to me, I would have been happy to spend the night in a nice warm, dry bed and wake up this morning to a hot shower. Who is Allison?"

"Does the name mean anything to you?" Ed asked softly.

"The question is, what does she mean to you? Is she your mistress?"

"Well, if I can't arouse passion in you, I should be flattered that I can at least incite a little jealousy. No. I do not have a mistress. Until recently, I have not even had a wife."

"But our passport says—"

"There's so much to explain, I don't even know where to start."

"Start with Allison."

"Allison is Bart's wife. They're so much in love you can feel it when you walk into the same room with them."

"More in love than we are?"

"So much more."

The melancholy in his voice made me shiver.

"What's the matter with our marriage?" I asked softly. "You said you loved me. I felt you were telling me the truth. Is the problem with me? Don't I love you?"

I hated asking questions to which I should know the answers. I hated not knowing who I was, who I had been, what I had been. I wanted to stand up and scream and shout and run from this horrible, empty place in my brain that was devoid of all that I should have accumulated over the years.

Ed was silent.

"Please turn on the light for a minute. I can't stand a dark void in my head and one around my body at the same time."

Ed turned the light on. His face was solemn.

"I'm struggling to decide how much or how little I should tell you for your own protection. If these guys don't believe our story, I don't want them torturing things out of you."

"We're not photojournalists, are we?"

"Why do you ask that?"

"Because it doesn't feel familiar. But then, you don't either, so I guess that's not valid."

I hated to ask the next question. It burned in my mind till I could scarcely contain it, but I was afraid to hear my husband's answer.

CHAPTER TWENTY-TWO

I took the coward's way out.

"Who are we? What are we doing in Sri Lanka? What do I know that could be tortured out of me?" I didn't ask what I wanted to know most of all—*Do you love Allison? And do you love her more than me?*

Before he could answer, the noise increased outside—more vehicles arriving, shouts, footsteps pounding past our door to the backyard.

"Listen carefully and digest what I tell you. How you react to it may determine whether we live or not. If these are terrorists from the Middle East arriving, Bart could be with them. He's been infiltrating a group so we could destroy them from the inside. He's disguised as an assassin, esteemed in the terrorist world, hired to teach them how to be more effective in their killing tactics."

"You said we—you, too?" I couldn't believe it. My husband and brother were involved in the world of terrorists and assassins?

"Yes."

"Who are you? CIA?"

"No. I'll tell you when this is all over. The less you know, the better. These people use drugs to find out what they want. If you don't know, you can't tell."

"Is that what all the lies were about? You did know the man in the car that passed us on the road to Ratnapura. The man with the Spanish accent. Who is he?"

"Head of a ring of jewel thieves. We'd heard rumors of sapphires being smuggled into Los Angeles in shipments of clothing manufactured here in Sri Lanka. Apparently he's been buying the stones in their natural form and smuggling them into the States. They're polished and cut, then put through a diffusion treatment, cooked. They're packed in titanium and iron oxide powders and heated for 600 hours near 2,050 degrees centigrade. They come out a brilliant blue, and after another polishing, he has precious sapphires for a fraction of what they'd cost to buy on the open market."

"That important message you were waiting for at the hotel wasn't from our editor."

"No."

"Who was it from?" I pressed.

"Give me a minute to think about this before I tell you any more. I don't want to give you more than you need to know, just to satisfy your curiosity. There's too much truth in the saying, 'Curiosity killed the cat.' Even a little knowledge can be fatal in this business, if you know the wrong thing."

I didn't ask any more questions, just stockpiled the ones that were backing up in my head. Of all the times to knock the memory out of my head, this wasn't one of the best. Had I endangered my husband—and myself—because I couldn't remember anything? That brought up still another question—one of the endless string that already crowded every corner of my head until it began that insidious aching again.

"If this is such a dangerous place, and you're on such an important mission, why am I here with you? Is that why you were so adamant that I leave Sri Lanka?"

Ed was silent for such a long time I thought he'd gone to sleep and hadn't heard me. When he spoke, it was in a low voice tinged with exhaustion, frustration, and, I sensed, even a little fear.

"Our cover as photojournalists gave us an excuse to check on the mines as a source for the sapphires—and the manufacturing shops as a possible means of smuggling the gems into the States. Bringing you into a war zone like this was not my idea. You came because you insisted. I objected. You won. But you're a catalyst for trouble. You have a knack for plunging into the thick of things—right into the messiest, most dangerous part of the problem."

"Am I an agent? Do I belong to your organization, too?"

Ed hesitated, then explained with a sigh of resignation, "You've always accompanied your husband, who couldn't seem to make you stay behind where it was safe."

"Like now?"

"Exactly like now. You manage to get your own way, even when everyone with better sense knows you shouldn't. The best thing that could happen to us right now is that they'll just leave us in here and forget about us. If we had to stay a week, we'd be better off starving than to let those men get their hands on you. Unless this is meant to be a permanent headquarters of some sort, we could wait them out and break out of here when everything gets quiet."

I considered that for a minute.

"No."

"What do you mean, 'no'?"

"I'll take my chances out there. I'm beginning to get claustrophobic already, and the thought of staying in here for a week will have me stark-raving mad inside of an hour. Think of something else, Einstein, because that just won't float."

The only sound he made was a soft groan, then he was quiet. I'd let him think about it, but I was thinking, too. Maybe they'd like the place cleaned up a little. Maybe they'd like their meals cooked. Could I cook? The simplest things for everyone else were gigantic mysteries for me. I mean, how can you not know whether you can cook or not? *Just like you can be married to a man and not recognize him or even rekindle the love you felt for him.*

I stretched my legs out in front of me and felt Ed's stretched beside mine. Comforting. That was the most emotion I could conjure up for this stranger whose wedding ring I wore and whose name I shared. I leaned my head against the stone wall of the pantry, ignoring the possible living organisms that might decide to infest my hair, and closed my eyes.

Relax. Breathe deeply. Close your mind to everything around you. Let whatever images come that will. Let them flow, unbidden. Whatever is hidden in the subconscious, let it flow forth.

Father, please help me remember who I am. Please give me back the memory of the life I've led, the person I am, the people I love. My eyes popped open. Here I was, conversing with deity again. That must be something I do frequently. So be it. I repeated the plea, several times, and then relaxed to see what would happen.

Nothing. The stage of my mind remained as blank as it had been since I woke up with the splitting headache a few days ago. How many days? I tried to remember, but everything seemed such a blur. That had to have been Tuesday. Wednesday we photographed the area, dined with the ambassador, and Thursday we'd driven to the manufacturing plants and Ratnapura. Today was Friday. And still my memory hadn't come back. The thought that it hadn't drove me to my feet.

"What are you doing?" Ed asked.

"I'm leaving. I can't sit here any longer. I've got to be doing something. Anything. What I'd really like is to go for a nice long run and see if it will clear the cobwebs from my head."

Suddenly a memory flashed through my mind—running in the fog to clear my head, the echo of a foghorn through the mist, and a statue of a man with a body draped across his lap. With the image came a knowledge that it had something to do with San Francisco and diamonds.

Ed was on his feet, his hands on my shoulders. "You can't do that. Will you listen to me?"

"Tell me about San Francisco, fog, a body on a statue, and diamonds."

His grip tightened, his fingers digging into my flesh. "You remember?"

"Just that. It was a flash—an instant in the fog—but a memory connected somehow to San Francisco and diamonds."

Ed pulled me to him and rested his cheek against my hair.

"That was when I met you and fell in love with you—and discovered that you were more trouble and could find more trouble than ten other people combined. I know I promised I wouldn't hold you, but if I was certain we weren't going to leave this place alive, I'd renege on that promise in an instant. I'd make love to you right here, right now, so you'd know how precious you are to me."

I hadn't intended to ask it, but the question just slipped out in the breath I exhaled. "More precious than Allison?"

The muscles in Ed's body tensed. As he tried to relax them, his arms loosened enough for me to slip free.

"Your voice betrayed your feeling for her, and your envy at their relationship, as you told me about Bart and Allison's love for each other. I'm sorry we don't have that. You didn't answer my question. Is it my fault? Is it something I've done? What's the matter with our marriage?"

Whatever his answer would have been, I didn't get to hear it. The door was jerked open and Lecherous Louie leered in.

"Come with me," he commanded.

We started from the pantry. He let me pass but stopped my husband with the barrel of his gun poking into Ed's chest.

"You stay."

"Sorry, but where my wife goes, I go. And I think you ought to know that she is a close, personal friend of the new American Ambassador to Sri Lanka. If anything happens to her, the ambassador will move heaven and earth to punish those who were responsible. I'm sure your commander would not wish to draw attention to his little cause from a country as powerful as the United States."

Lecherous Louie spit on the floor.

Out of the corner of my eye, I'd seen a man move silently up the hall toward us. I spoke up quickly and loud enough to be heard at the end of the hallway.

"I'm sure that contempt was for the United States, not for your commander. He's a wise man and wouldn't want you to do anything to jeopardize this little operation. Why don't you ask him if we should be separated?"

Ed picked up on this tack immediately.

"Yes. Ask your commander if this scrawny little piece is worth having the national army called down on your heads. Ambassador Hollingsworth expected us to call in last night. We didn't. He'll already have alerted the police to look for us."

Louie wasn't affected in the least by our revelations. He spat again and grabbed my wrist.

"You stay. The woman comes with me into the woods."

The man in the hall stopped moving toward us and stepped just inside a doorway. I gave one last plea.

"Please talk to your commander before you risk the success of whatever he's planning here. If he doesn't care if the army starts searching—"

Louie had had enough. He shoved Ed back into the pantry with his gun barrel, slammed the door, and pulled me after him toward the trees.

CHAPTER TWENTY-THREE

Oh, please, let that be the commander in the hall, and let him intervene fast, I prayed. The only sound I heard was Ed banging on the door. Where was the commander? I thought I'd seen his baton tapping his palm. Had I only been seeing things? Where was Friendly Fred? He wouldn't let this happen.

Well, neither would I! I had been docilely following Louis as he pulled me eagerly toward the trees. Suddenly I jerked backward with all my might. Louis was thrown off balance and brought around to face me. As he attempted to regain his footing, I kicked him with every ounce of strength I could muster. He might be able to shoot me, but he wouldn't be inclined to rape in the next few hours.

As he doubled over in agony, I raced for the safety of the house before he could recover enough to raise his gun. I ran smack into the commander, standing in the doorway.

I froze. He stared silently at me. Ed was still pounding on the pantry door, yelling at the top of his lungs. I motioned cautiously to the door.

"Can I let him know I'm okay?" I asked. Appearing humble and intimidated before him might be the best way of handling this and it wasn't hard. That fierce gaze would have intimidated the cobra we'd encountered.

He nodded. I hurried to open the door. Ed took one surprised look and threw his arms around me. I could almost have responded this time to the passion in his embrace. But I knew the emotion I felt was only relief.

"How did you get free?" he whispered in a voice husky with tenderness.

I pulled out of his arms and pointed to the man still curled in pain on the ground.

"A well-placed kick. We'll see what the aftermath of that will be soon enough."

The commander watched us without comment, his face void of expression, his dark eyes unreadable.

We stood quietly and waited. The next move was his. He made none. He just stared, in a searing, unblinking gaze, first at Ed, then at me. I met his eyes, and held them.

"Who are you?" he demanded.

"Ed and Amy Teale. American photojournalists," Ed answered quickly, before I could say anything.

"What were you doing at the mine last night?"

"We're writing a story on the sapphire mines. Papio Moreno warned me earlier that day to get out of Sri Lanka. I wanted to know why I shouldn't stick around and do the story. So I went to the mine to see if I could figure out what he didn't want me to find."

"You say 'I' instead of 'we.' You were both there."

Ed started to answer. The commander stopped him and pointed to me. "Your husband has a peculiar way of speaking. Explain."

"Because he thought he was going alone. I followed him."

"In the rain? Why?"

I took a deep breath and decided truth was on our side. Now might be the best time to tell it.

"I was thrown off an elephant the day we arrived in Sri Lanka. I can't remember anything. I've completely lost every memory of my past. I thought my husband was sneaking off to meet another woman. I had to find out, rain or not. So I followed him."

The commander looked at Ed.

"It's true. She remembers nothing, not her own name, not even me. She didn't even recognize the ambassador, with whom she has a very special relationship."

I looked at Ed in astonishment.

"What relationship?"

"You were engaged to be married."

"Why didn't you two say something?" I thought of dinner that night at the embassy. "That's why he was so interested in me. That's what was going on between you two."

"We figured we'd just let nature take its course and you'd eventually remember everything. He didn't want to pressure you with any more memories, since you were having a hard time handling the situation."

At that point, Louie rallied enough to grab his gun and get to his feet. He had murder in his eyes as he staggered toward us. One glance at his commander stopped him in his tracks. He stood, terrified, not moving a muscle until the commander gave a small motion with his baton that sent him scurrying around the corner of the house. His backward glance told me the next opportunity he got, he'd kill me.

The commander turned back to us.

"You will call the ambassador. You will tell him you are the guest of a friend in the hill country, and will call him again when you return to Colombo."

He led the way down the hall and entered the small room next to the front room. It had been set up as a temporary office, with a door taken from one of the other rooms laid across boxes to form a makeshift desk. The commander pointed with his baton to a portable phone on the desk, then to Ed.

"You call. You will say only what I told you. Your wife's life depends on it."

Ed called. He left the message with whoever answered the phone.

"What are you going to do with us?" I ventured, almost afraid to ask.

"Lock you out of my way."

"Please, could I sweep the house, or clean the kitchen, or pick fruit for dinner, or something with a little activity? I'll go crazy sitting in that dark room with nothing to do." I added one final desperate plea. "I'm claustrophobic. Please don't put us back in that tiny, dark room."

Silently, the commander strolled to the window. He remained there, staring out into the tropical sunshine for a long moment. Then he turned and studied us.

"If I leave you out, you will see more than you should. It would then be dangerous to release you. You are a threat to my operation no matter what I do with you. I think I should let Makkim take his pleasure and then kill you."

"Has El Tigre arrived yet?" Ed asked.

A look of surprise flashed across the commander's face, then disappeared just as quickly.

"How do you know of El Tigre?" he demanded.

"He is my wife's brother."

The statement had the impact of an earthquake. The commander leaned across the desk and looked first at Ed, and then at me.

"Elaborate."

"El Tigre is coming to instruct your men. He should have arrived in Sri Lanka yesterday with men from Hamas. He didn't tell us when he would be meeting with you, or where. Just that he'd be with you for a few days, then he'd contact us at the Galle Face Hotel and we'd get together before he went on to train the next group and we left for the States. He doesn't get to see his sister very often, and so we arranged this little Christmas reunion while we were all in this part of the world."

"Why would he tell you this?"

"What you do in your country is no concern of ours. We're here to write a story about the fiftieth anniversary of your freedom and take pictures of your beautiful buildings before you blow them all up. Then we'll go somewhere else and write a story about that. You can make all the trouble in paradise you want. We have no interest in politics. And we've known for a long time what he's done. As I said, we're apolitical."

The commander considered that for a minute.

"You may stay in the rear of the house. Do not come to the front for any reason. Do not speak with my men. Stay out of my way. When El Tigre arrives, we shall check your story. If it is not true, Makkim gets your wife and El Tigre can use you to demonstrate his methods of elimination. Go."

We left.

"I don't think he likes us," I whispered as we hurried down the hall to the kitchen. "Let's make ourselves a little useful."

"And just how do you propose to do that?"

"Let's stir up a little dust in the kitchen in case anyone needs to do some cooking. Then we can go pick some more fruit. Those guys are working up an appetite out front. If we can figure out some way to keep them happy and full, they're less likely to shoot us without just cause."

An armed soldier followed us down the hall and into the kitchen. He didn't speak, he didn't smile, he just stood, gun cradled in his arm, as if waiting for an excuse to use his weapon. Not knowing what else to do, we ignored him and went about our self-assigned task.

Ed improvised brooms out of palm fronds and we swept what appeared to be the accumulated dirt of many years from the floor and cupboard. An old, chipped and dented blue-enameled bowl sufficed for carrying rainwater into the kitchen. Ed tossed the water liberally on every surface including the walls and fireplace, and I swept it back outside.

It wouldn't have passed Martha Stewart's inspection, but it was at least dust free, until the mud in the corners dried. And if there had been food available, the kitchen was now clean enough to cook in.

"I'm not getting enough to eat on this trip," I said as we examined our efforts. "Of course, breakfast was at least three hours ago and consisted only of some fruit. If that's all I'm going to get to eat, we'd better go pick some more. I'm starving."

Ed led the way, and our silent sentinel followed, ignoring the clamor that suddenly reverberated from the front yard. To appease my curiosity, I darted toward the corner to see what was happening. Our guard blocked the way and guided me back to the trees with his gun pointed directly at me.

"Amy, corral that curiosity," Ed commanded, gripping my shoulders. "It'll get us killed yet. Promise me you'll think before you do something stupid like that again." From the expression on his face, only intense self-control kept me from getting a good shaking in the process of my dressing-down. He was right. It was a stupid, impetuous act.

Using our brooms to frighten any cobras or other nasty little beings lurking in the high vegetation under the fruit trees, we headed into the green darkness. It wasn't a nasty little thing we encountered.

A five-foot monitor lizard wasn't happy about his meal being disturbed, and he whirled to face us, his deeply forked tongue flitting in and out of his mouth like a red flag warning danger. When we didn't turn and run, he stood high on his short, powerful legs, stretching his long head and neck, and puffing up his body. His tail lashed back and forth, and his teeth looked like they could easily take my arm off in one bite.

We backed away, relinquishing that portion of the forest to what surely must be the descendant of the fire-breathing dragons of my dreams, and carefully made our way through the undergrowth to other fruit trees, making sure additional members of his family weren't lurking about.

We picked another huge quantity of the same fruits we'd collected earlier, and found king coconuts, pineapple, and bananas, as well.

"Now if we had some good water and some hot bread, we'd be set," I said, spreading our bountiful harvest on the cabinet in the kitchen.

"Both the king coconut and pineapple will quench your thirst, if we had a knife or a machete. Without one, we might as well be stranded in the desert," Ed said. He turned to the soldier who had once again taken his stance in the doorway leading to the hall.

"Do you have a knife? A machete?" No answer. Apparently he neither understood nor spoke English. Ed held up the coconut and made a slashing motion. The guard shook his head. "I'll see if I can snag a thirsty soldier who'll open a couple of these."

"You're not going anywhere without this little shadow. I'm not about to stay behind with Gloomy Gus here." I filled my arms with prickly pineapple, Ed loaded his with coconuts, and we ventured to the corner of the house, with our guard close on our heels just in time to see the commander drive off with a van load of men.

"Wonder where he's going?" I asked, an uneasy feeling overtaking me as I watched the van disappear down the dirt road.

"Probably for lunch."

Our guard decided we had stepped out of our assigned boundaries and prodded us with the barrel of his gun, motioning us back to the kitchen. We obeyed.

Too bad obedience wasn't one of Lecherous Louie's better qualities. He suddenly appeared in the doorway to the kitchen, blocking our entrance to the house. In what must have been Tamil, he chattered something. Our guard argued with him. They went back and forth for a few minutes until Louie lost his temper. He shouted at the man, whipped out his gun and pointed it at the guard's head. Our guard meekly acquiesced, disappearing around the corner.

The uneasy feeling I'd had when the commander left mushroomed into panic. Louie, or Makkim, as the commander called him, broke into the most malevolent laugh I'd ever heard.

"Now who will save you?" he leered, grabbing my wrist and twisting my arm behind me before I could react. With his gun to my head, he ordered Ed to stay put or I'd die. He shoved me into the pantry and slammed the door.

I knew he was going to take my husband into the trees and shoot him as surely as I knew I couldn't possibly get out of the knobless door. I found myself whispering a fervent prayer for Ed's life.

Suddenly a thought came to me. *Get the pen from your backpack.* It was an absurd thought! So I ignored it. Again it came. *Get the pen from your backpack.* What good could a pen do against a murderer and rapist with a gun? The old adage "the pen is mightier than the sword" wouldn't hold true in this situation. I shuddered at the thought of what I knew would happen next. A third time the thought came, with such force I was startled.

Obediently, I fumbled in the dark to find the abandoned backpack, then felt each item within until my fingers closed around the pen. I must be losing my mind. Why would I think of a pen at a moment like this? Granted, it was the only weapon at hand, but still . . .

Clutching the beautiful wood-grain pen, I listened for the shot that would signal the end of my husband's life and the step outside the door that would signal the horror of what would precede my own death.

CHAPTER TWENTY-FOUR

There was no shot. At least I didn't hear any. But suddenly the door flew open and Lecherous Louie grabbed my arm and twisted it high behind my back while I was still blinded by the bright sunlight. He was taking no chances on my getting in another kick.

Where was Ed? Louie didn't seem the benevolent type who would leave witnesses to what he was about to do. Had he used a silencer?

He propelled me across the short expanse of tall grass to the woods and without a pause, we plunged into the green darkness. Louie didn't slow down, thrusting me forward through the lush vegetation until we came to a less dense area under a high canopy of tall, straight trees.

Ed was tied to one of them.

A thin line of blood trickled from above one eye down the side of his face. He didn't appear to be conscious as he sagged against the ropes, head drooped to one side. But he was. He raised his head as we crashed through the undergrowth, shaking it, as if to clear his vision.

"I wanted your husband to see how a real man takes a woman. Then I will decide whether to leave you both here to appease the leopard goddess, or just shoot you. The leopard has been restless. You would make a tasty sacrifice for her." He spun me around, still holding the arm he'd twisted behind my back, and pulled me close to him.

I'd worked the cap of the pen loose with my free hand, and as he brought his face toward mine, I swung the point to stab him, squeezing it with all my might. A sudden puff of gas from the tip of the pen caught him full in the face.

With a howl, he released me, clutching his face in pain. While he was incapacitated, I untied Ed, then raced for the house. When I couldn't hear my husband behind me, I turned back to see Ed securing Louie to the same tree from which I'd just cut him loose. He tore a strip from Louie's worn shirt and gagged him so he couldn't yell.

"Nice time for your memory to come back," Ed said as we hurried from the woods. "Perfect timing, in fact."

"What do you mean?"

"Must have been the trauma of the moment. I understand that sometimes triggers the memory."

"What are you talking about?" I insisted.

Ed stopped at the edge of the trees and turned to me, grasping my shoulders. "Do you remember everything? Did it all come back?"

"I don't remember anything. What's gotten into you?"

He looked at me. "How did you know about the pen if you didn't remember?"

"The pen? Oh. I was as surprised as Louie when that happened. Tell me about that pen and how I came to have it." I stopped, the significance of what just transpired suddenly dawning on me. *How did I know about that pen?*

"You're not going to believe this," I said. "I hardly do myself. But the thought just kept coming to me that I needed to get the pen from my backpack. I tried to ignore it but it was overpowering. I had no idea what I was going to do with it. I just reacted at the last minute. I mean, what else can you do with a pen besides stab an attacker with it? That was all I'd planned to do."

I stared into Ed's eyes. "Why are you looking at me like that?"

"You've done that before. You called it a 'prompting,' I think."

"Well, it came at promptly the right moment. Come on. Let me look at that nasty cut on your eye. Then I think you have *mucho* explaining to do." I stopped. "Do I speak Spanish?"

Ed nodded and took my arm, steering me toward the house. He was quiet as I cleaned his cut with rainwater, wincing only a couple of times when I wasn't gentle enough.

"What did he hit you with?"

"His gun. I whirled on him as we entered the trees, thinking I'd catch him off guard. I'd have killed him with my bare hands to keep him from getting at you, but he was waiting for just such a move. He clobbered me as I turned. The first thing I saw when I woke up was him getting a face full of gas."

"Speaking of which, you have some explaining to do. How did I come to have a pen full of gas?"

Ed's answer was curtailed by another commotion in the front yard that signaled the arrival of several vehicles and many men. As we hurried to the corner of the house to see what was happening, the guard Louie had sent away came around that same corner with another soldier close on his heels. He waved me back toward the kitchen. The other guard pointed his gun at Ed and motioned him toward the front of the house.

I panicked.

"It's okay," Ed said from the corner. "The commander's back. You'll be okay. I'll join you as soon as I can."

My guard hustled me into the kitchen and leaned against the doorpost, blocking the door to the outside so I couldn't leave. I glanced toward the hall. Silhouetted against the bright light in the window in the front room was a tall, lean man with broad, muscular shoulders I hadn't seen before. Probably just arrived. He and the commander were deep in a quiet conversation that I couldn't hear.

He pointed his finger at the commander and spoke, accenting his words with that finger against the smaller man's chest. This had to be a superior officer dressing down the commander. He had an air of authority, an air of intrigue that was compelling. I watched with interest until the tall man spun around and left.

Afraid to be caught watching this scene if the commander looked down the hall, I hurried from the center of the kitchen and busied myself with the fruit we'd brought in. There was no point in starving when the bounty of the land was at my fingertips.

A vehicle roared to life in the front of the house and quickly faded in the distance. I hoped that incident hadn't put the commander in a bad frame of mind. We needed him to be a benevolent dictator in this little camp—although from the noise out front and the foot traffic in and out of the front of the house, this no longer sounded like a small camp.

I remembered Louie in the trees. One more reason we needed the commander in a good mood. I wasn't sure how he'd take having his man tied up in the forest.

Having sated my appetite, I began looking for something to do. We hadn't cleaned the pantry, and on the off chance we might be locked in there again, I decided to expend my energy making it a more acceptable prison.

Through sign language I managed to convey my intent to my guard. He allowed me to gather a few more palm fronds which I put to work sweeping cobwebs, dirt, and an accumulation of ancient debris from the tiny, narrow room. I then doused the whole thing with rainwater and swept it. Looking around, I asked myself, *Would I like to sleep on that floor?*

I swept it again, removing another layer of mud, then wore myself out carting more rainwater until I was content the floor was clean enough to sleep on. If it hadn't still been wet, I would have curled up right there and taken a nap. I was exhausted. Between the heat and humidity, neither of which I was really accustomed to yet, and today's increased activity over my soft life of leisure the last few days, I had no energy left. Added to that was the lack of restful sleep last night. No wonder I was tired.

I didn't add the lingering effects of the concussion to the list. But I did attribute my lingering headache to it.

I sat down on the step and leaned against the doorpost which my guard abandoned rather than share it with me. Now that my body was still, my mind kicked into high gear. Where was Ed? Why had they taken my husband? What was the purpose in separating us?

That was only the beginning of the questions. The pen was James Bond stuff. Why did I have it? Why did I think to grab it when I didn't even know how to use it? Somewhere in the recesses of my mind, I must have retained the knowledge of the gas in the pen. My brain hadn't lost everything. Although . . .

I'd been praying for my husband. Was that an answer to prayer? Oh, Father. This is just too much. Please, let me have my memory back. These questions are too heavy, too many. And if that was an answer to prayer, thank you. I'd welcome any other "promptings" you'd care to send my way.

I lolled in the doorway just out of the hot tropical sun. No place was cool, but this was probably as comfortable as any in the area. Inactivity drove me crazy, but there was nothing more I could do. I retrieved my backpack and examined the contents more closely since the incident with the James Bond pen, looking to see if there were any more hidden goodies I should know about. Other than the funny little telescope gizmo that revealed what was to the side of you rather than in front, I found nothing. However, I thought, that didn't necessarily mean there weren't any.

I wished Ed would come back. He'd know. He knew a lot that I needed to know. I realized now how many things he hadn't told me. In fact, even the questions I'd asked, he'd either danced around or ignored completely. Why? I'd have thought he'd want to help me remember by telling me everything he knew—just to refresh my memory—prime the pump sort of thing. But he seemed almost reluctant to help me remember.

As I pondered this, an uneasy feeling, a foreboding, once again engulfed me. Where was he? Why wasn't he back yet? What if something terrible had happened? The terror of being alone, with all these soldiers, in a foreign country, with no memory of who I was, overwhelmed me.

To calm the increasing panic I felt building within at his prolonged absence, I picked up the scriptures and began reading where they fell open in Isaiah. The verse was underlined in red pencil. "Fear thou not; for I am with thee: be not dismayed; for I am thy God: I will strengthen thee; yea, I will help thee; yea, I will uphold thee with the right hand of my righteousness."

Had I needed that promise at some other crisis in my life? Had I relied on that to get me through another frightening situation? *Oh, Father, please, help me now. And please help me remember all that I've forgotten so that I don't do or say anything stupid in this precarious situation.*

I read until Isaiah had me drowsy, then pulled out the journal and jotted some notes about all the fruits we'd found and some of the things Ananda had told us, keeping it very generic and not mentioning anything about the soldiers or the commander. It wasn't until I found myself squinting to see what I was writing that I realized the sun was setting and it was almost dark.

Glancing into the house, I could see the commander and the man I assumed was his superior officer leaning over some open boxes at the end of the hall in the front room. The lantern highlighted several days' stubble on the tall, lean man's face. It didn't detract from the attractiveness of his rugged profile. He moved with a confidence I liked, an assurance that he knew what he was about. The smooth grace in the ripple of his shoulder and arm muscles as he hoisted one heavy box after another and examined its contents was almost like watching a dancer.

As I observed them, I became aware of a strange fascination this man elicited in me as he moved in the lantern light of the rectangular frame. I couldn't take my eyes off him. When he moved out of sight, I held my breath waiting for him to reappear. *Whoa, lady. You're a married woman, and just a few minutes ago you were terrified out of your mind because of your missing husband. Now you're ogling some good-looking hunk that probably tears up little girls like you and eats them for breakfast.*

I turned my back on him and resumed my praying/worrying attitude for Ed. Where could he be all this time? It had been hours now since they took him away. I could go ask the commander. He'd know. *Or is that just an excuse to see Mr. Universe up close?*

A curious, melancholy mewling began somewhere in the woods, softly at first, then louder and more urgent. I looked at the guard. He bared his teeth and made claws of his hands.

"A leopard?" I asked. "Panther?" He understood neither word. But I was pretty sure that was what he meant. It sounded like a lost kitty—a great big kitty. A cat I didn't want to meet outside of a zoo. Cat. Stirrings of remembrance brought a huge tawny lion to mind—Kat—my friend. The memory astounded me. I'd befriended a lion? When? Where? Maybe I had worked in a zoo in a previous life.

Then I remembered Louie. Lecherous Louie tied up in the jungle with a leopard. I jumped to my feet and hurried to the front of the house. The commander looked up in surprise as my sandals clattered on the stone floor, and he came to meet me before I could enter the front room.

"Sir, I hate to tell you this, but Makkim is tied up in the woods. I think there is a leopard out there. Shouldn't someone go get him?"

"What is he doing tied up in the woods?" he demanded, stepping to the side so the lantern light illuminated my face in the nearly dark hallway.

"He tried to attack me again. I escaped and untied my husband. Ed tied him to the tree in his place. And by the way, I haven't seen my husband in several hours. Where is he?"

"Since I must use one of my men to guard you, I've put your husband to work in his place. They will return soon, and then we will lock you in for the night."

"It's too hot in that little room to spend the night. There are no windows, no air. Please let us sleep in the kitchen, or at least with the pantry door open. I promise we won't try to get away. You know we won't go anywhere without seeing my brother."

The commander frowned at that, and glanced over his shoulder as we heard the voice of his superior officer giving an order on the porch. With a wave of his hand, he dismissed me to go back to the dark kitchen.

"What about Louie, I mean, Makkim?" I persisted.

"We'll see how forgiving the leopard goddess is to an insubordinate soldier," he said as he strode through the front room and hurried out onto the porch. A car engine roared to life before he got to the front yard. I watched him, silhouetted in the red taillights, slapping his baton in his hand. The good-looking hunk was nowhere in sight. As a superior officer, he probably had a nice cool, air-conditioned room in some nearby hotel with a hot shower and a beautiful native woman waiting for him. That was probably him leaving now. The big boss didn't have to sleep in the wild with no running water, electricity, or beds like the rest of us.

Before he moved from the spot, a truck lumbered down the dirt road through the dust stirred up by the departing car, and stopped just in front of the commander. Soldiers spilled from the back, and my husband walked through the beam of the headlights, shoulders sagging, shirt in hand.

My guard retrieved me as soon as he saw the commander was no longer with me. Ed came around the corner of the house and into the kitchen almost immediately.

"Are you okay?" he asked, sweeping me into his arms to make sure that I was.

"I'm fine. Where were you? I've been frantic with worry." I pulled away to look at him, but it was too dark to see him clearly.

"They had us enlarging a cave to stash all these boxes of arms and ammunition where it can't be found. They have enough arms here to level Colombo, I think. And that may be their plan. Did they feed you? Have you had anything to eat?"

"Just the fruit we picked. There's still plenty left. How about you?"

"They made a small campfire and stirred up some rice and beans. Someone brought bread from Matara. Here's a piece I saved for you."

He pulled something from his pocket and put it in my hand. If I hadn't been so hungry for something more solid than a banana or guava, I'd have had second thoughts about eating something I couldn't even see, that had been stuffed in the pocket of a man digging in the dirt.

"What I wouldn't give for a hot shower and a nice soft bed right now. I'm bone weary," Ed said, sinking to the floor by the door. I slid down beside him.

"Unless the commander relents, we're destined to spend the night locked in that oven of a pantry. I asked him if we couldn't please at least have the bit of breeze in the kitchen. This is as soft as your bed is going to get tonight."

"I'm so tired, I won't even notice. It's been a long time since I've done manual labor, and my muscles are screaming in revolt. And—we've got big trouble. I think Papio Moreno saw me this afternoon as they loaded us on the trucks. He'll blow the whistle on us when he knows for sure it's me. And one look at you will clinch it."

"Papio Moreno?"

Ed slapped his forehead with the palm of his hand and groaned.

"Who is Papio Moreno?" I asked again, when he hadn't answered my first question. "Look, I know you've been keeping things from me. I don't know why. I just have to assume that you have a really good reason for not wanting me to remember something. But if we've got more problems, I need to know."

"We interrupted a transaction of stolen jewelry in the Los Angeles airport and called the cops on Moreno and his partner. I don't know how he managed to slip away, but we saw him on the airplane from Singapore to Sri Lanka. He threatened us then to stay out of his way. He's the one we were watching in the shack at the mine. You can bet we'll get the blame for interrupting this second transaction. And he'll sing loud and long about who we are."

"Who are we? You told me you were with an agency, but you just said 'we' interrupted a transaction. And why was I carrying a pen loaded with gas? I think it's time you told me the truth. Don't you think it's too dangerous not to let me know what's really going on?"

Still Ed didn't say anything.

"Are you asleep?"

"No, just trying to sort out what you need to know and what you don't. But I'm so tired, I'm muddled-headed, and I can't decide what I should tell you and what I shouldn't."

"I'll solve that little problem—just tell me everything. Did you ever stop to think that the more you tell me, the more it may help me remember. If I don't have anything to jog those memories, how can they come through? And I need to know what's going on so I don't do something really stupid and get us into more trouble than we're in right now. If that's possible."

"With you, it's possible. Just when I think things can't get worse, you always come up with something that makes current problems pale in comparison. Can I catch a few winks first? Exhaustion isn't the state in which I do my best thinking. Give me a couple of hours. Then I'll tell you what I think you need to know."

It wouldn't have mattered whether I wanted to give him the time or not. He stretched out on the stone floor and in minutes was snoring contentedly. Fortunately he wasn't laying across the doorway, but perpendicular to it. I lay beside him, my feet near the doorstep, hoping to benefit from any breeze that moved between the back door, up the hall, and through the glassless windows in the front of the house.

Had I been in my right mind, which of course, I couldn't find at the moment, I might have remembered Rudyard Kipling's tales of this part of the world. But I didn't. I simply stretched out on the cool, hard, uncomfortable stone floor and with my arm for a pillow, lapsed into dreams of dragons. This time my knight in shining armor did not come to my rescue. And the dragons were creeping up on the kitchen, accompanied by snakes creeping in around my legs.

I screamed and awoke—and found myself staring into the gleaming eyes of a hooded cobra swaying inches above my face.

CHAPTER TWENTY-FIVE

The guard flashed his light on, revealing the menacing creature hovering right above my head. This wasn't a turbaned snake charmer's cobra with poison glands removed. This was the real—lethal—thing. I didn't move. I didn't even breathe. I just stared at him as he dipped and swayed to the music of an unseen flute.

There was no movement in the room except the gentle, deadly swaying of the snake. Even the breeze had stilled. I couldn't hear a single night sound outside. The whole world held its breath.

Suddenly a small furry creature hurled itself at the snake, then scampered away before the cobra could react. Ed grabbed me and rolled me over the top of him and out of striking range of the snake, then held me in his arms to quell my quivering. The guard, on his feet now, kept his light on the snake. Again and again the fierce little mongoose flew in, nipped at the snake, and whirled out of range before the cobra could strike.

My own Rikki-Tikki-Tavi to the rescue. We watched in fascination the battle to the death between the sixteen-inch mongoose and the seven-foot cobra. The mongoose won, hands down. The cobra couldn't tell which direction the mongoose was coming from next, and the swift little creature used that to good advantage, attacking from behind again and again until the fatally wounded reptile lay motionless on the stone floor.

With a chattering farewell that sounded very much like his name, my little hero scurried off into the darkness of the house. Silence descended. I could breathe again. I'd been sitting on my husband's lap, his arms wrapped tightly around me, his breath warm on my neck. It was a comforting position. I snuggled a little closer for a minute, until I realized I must be cutting off the circulation in his legs.

"If you don't mind, I think I'll spend the rest of the night on top of the table with the fruit. I don't think I could handle another encounter with a snake," I said, shivering in delayed fright.

"Go for it. I'd join you, but there isn't room," Ed said with a little shudder of his own. "But I wouldn't mind staying just like this, if it would make you feel better."

"You can't possibly be comfortable sitting on this hard, cold floor, with my full weight on your legs. But thanks. I appreciate the offer."

The guard obligingly shined his light so I could move the remainder of the fruit and curl up where it had been. Then he turned off the light and we all settled down again. The quiet didn't last.

The low growl of a big cat rumbled again in the trees, working its way into a frenzied crescendo of sound. Suddenly a terrified human cry joined the angry roar of the leopard.

I had a feeling I wouldn't be bothered by Lecherous Louie anymore. I shuddered again, not sure whether it was thinking about that man's unfortunate death, or my memories of how close I came to being his victim. And the leopard goddess was no more forgiving about insubordination than the commander had been.

Sleep must have come at some time during the night, because the next time I opened my eyes, the sky was graying with dawn. I lay very still, thinking over every moment since I'd awakened with no memory, remembering Ed's quiet, almost passionate, devotion. And the ambassador. No wonder he was so intensely personal. Had I really been engaged to him? He certainly was handsome. Why had I married Ed instead of Ambassador Hollingsworth?

I remembered the Christmas tree in the Rest House in Ratnapura, and the feeling of melancholy it induced.

Another Christmas tree flashed through my mind. A huge, glittering tree, decorated with elegant gold bows and miniature musical instruments in a lovely room that I instinctively knew belonged in my parents' home—and another, smaller tree in my own little cottage that I shared with . . . with whom?

Someone was there, in the shadows. The image wasn't clear enough to see, but the feeling of love and contentment in that tiny home was so tangible it brought tears to my eyes. Tears of longing to be there again, to take the hand of my husband and pull him out of the shadows, to hold him in the soft, warm glow of the Christmas tree lights.

My heart ached with longing to be in his arms again. I glanced at my husband stretched out on the kitchen floor below me. Why did I feel so differently about him now? What had happened to the love I'd felt in that cottage? Had I changed? Had he?

I started counting days. My world began on Tuesday when I woke up without a memory. My journal said that had been December 20. Today was Saturday, December 24. Tonight was Christmas Eve. I couldn't remember how I usually spent Christmas Eve, but I'd bet this was as different as it could possibly get.

I sat up and stretched. Every muscle and bone in my body complained as I moved, reminding me just how much abuse it had received in the past few days. I glanced at the guard. He was sleeping as soundly as my husband. Why couldn't we just leave? We had to be fairly close to a town. I didn't want to spend Christmas Eve—or Christmas Day—in these dirty, primitive surroundings, in my same filthy clothes, prisoners of a tyrant with a baton he used like a scepter.

I slipped off the table and knelt beside my husband, covering his mouth with my hand.

The minute I touched him, he was wide awake and ready to fight. I motioned for him to quietly follow me outside. Creeping toward the door, I quietly scooped up my backpack as I went by the guard. Ed was right on my heels.

We got as far as the step.

"Going somewhere?"

I stared into the dark, stern eyes of the commander, his displeasure apparent even in the pale light of dawn.

"Yes," I said defiantly. "To take a hot shower, shampoo my hair, brush my teeth, and generally improve my appearance and sense of well-being. If I can't find that, then I'll just have to settle for a short trip into the weeds to take care of my morning bodily functions."

"You were sneaking away from the guard," the commander accused, pointing the ever-present baton at me.

"I don't really like strangers watching me take care of personal hygiene. Besides," I added, "he was sleeping so soundly, and we had such a wakeful night, I didn't want to disturb him."

"You gave me your word you wouldn't try to get away."

"Yes, I did. And we didn't even try to escape last night, though we probably could have. So I kept my word. And now, if you don't mind, I really need to step into the bushes. And I'd prefer to do it in private."

I turned and walked toward the high vegetation at the edge of the high grass and weeds, praying nothing else was awake at this hour. Ed grabbed a fallen palm frond and, stepping in front of me, rustled it before him as he made his way into the brush. Satisfied that the monitor lizard and his family had vacated the area, the leopard was sleeping off her midnight snack, and nothing else was of major danger at the moment, he motioned me to join him.

I sent Ed back to keep our guard at a distance, then when I'd taken care of my needs, I picked a couple of fresh mangosteen. I'd developed a taste for the tangerine-size fruit with the dark purple skin. Inside, the pure white segments, shaped like an orange, had a sweet-sour flavor, sort of like eating grapes and strawberries together.

We sat on the back step to eat them, sharing with our guard. He squatted on the little path we'd made between the house and the woods.

"So much for our escape," I said softly, sure that he couldn't understand what I was saying, but feeling a need for caution nevertheless.

"Actually, I'm not anxious to leave until we've seen Bart. He may need us to help him, or our being here may totally screw things up for him. Wish I knew. Unfortunately, I'm afraid I've been drafted for manual labor again today. If they come for me, you keep a very low profile. Stay out of sight, but keep your eyes and ears open for Bart. Since he didn't show up yesterday, he'll probably arrive today or tomorrow. If I'm not here, you'll have to find out what he wants us to do."

"How will I know him?"

The commander's leather-soled shoes padded across the kitchen, and he appeared in the door above us.

"Come with me. It's time to return to the work at the cave."

I grabbed Ed's arm and whispered, "How will I recognize him? I don't remember what he looks like."

The commander smacked his baton in his hand. "Now."

Ed leaned to kiss my cheek. "Trust your instincts," he whispered. And he was gone.

Trust my instincts. The only thing my instincts told me was that I needed to get out of here and back to the Galle Face Hotel. As quickly as possibly.

I spent the morning, for want of anything else to do, perusing the books on Sri Lanka that were in my backpack, memorizing a few phrases of Sinhalese and Tamil, and reading the scriptures. In the Book of Mormon, in Alma, I came across an interesting verse that I had previously underlined in red. As with all the other marked scriptures I found, I wondered why I'd marked this particular one and what special meaning it may have had when I did it:

> *Counsel with the Lord in all thy doings, and he will direct thee for good; yea, when thou liest down at night lie down unto the Lord, that he may watch over you in your sleep; and when thou risest in the morning let thy heart be full of thanks unto God; and if ye do these things, ye shall be lifted up at the last day.*

I pondered that for a while. Counsel with the Lord. Did that mean tell him what I needed, or did it mean to ask him for help? Since I had nothing else to do, I looked up every footnote at the bottom of the page: Joshua, Lamentations, and Psalms in the Old Testament; Hebrews in the New Testament; Jacob in the Book of Mormon, and section three in the Doctrine and Covenants. I found my answer.

I wasn't to counsel the Lord but to take counsel from him. And wait on him. And to have a grateful heart. Then the reward: ye shall be lifted up at the last day.

The last day wasn't my chief concern at the moment. I needed help today. Now. Because if I didn't get it, *this* might be the last day. But I wouldn't counsel him. I'd simply explain how things were in case he didn't know, and ask for his suggestions on how to get me and my husband out of here and back to the safety of civilization.

I did have a grateful heart for what I could see as blessings in this situation—I hadn't starved to death; in fact, there was more fruit than

I could possibly eat in the next millennium. I'd been protected yesterday from Lecherous Louie, and last night from the cobra. My memory was returning in tiny bits and pieces, a flash here and there. I had a husband who truly cared for me, and even if I hadn't had a resurgence of that same love for him, I guessed it would eventually come back.

About midmorning, a car rattled up the dirt road, the only man-made sound I'd heard for hours. The jungle was full of sounds, dozens of different kinds of birds calling, croakings, rustlings, an occasional growl or roar, but since nearly all the soldiers were gone to the cave, it had been very quiet.

I'd settled in my favorite spot in the kitchen doorway that led outside, as much to catch any breeze that might happen by and relieve the oppressive heat, as to watch what was happening in the front of the house, directly up the hallway.

Digging the telescope gizmo from my backpack, I pretended to observe the colorful birds flitting from tree to tree in the jungle. By sitting in the doorway with my back to the doorframe and looking straight ahead, I could see everything that was going on directly to my right or to my left.

I focused on the hallway to the front of the house. Occasionally the commander strode from his makeshift office to the front room, removed something from a box, then returned, but he was very quiet about it.

I watched to see who had arrived. My heart quickened. Maybe it was Bart. Would I recognize him? Would I be able to tell it was my own brother? He would, of course, recognize me. But if I wasn't supposed to be here, maybe he would pretend not to know me. Then what would the commander do? He was waiting for Bart's arrival to determine our fate, but if Bart thought it best not to acknowledge me . . .

The commander went to the front porch to greet whoever had just arrived. They didn't come back into that front room where I could have seen them, or even move in front of the open window where their silhouettes would have been easier to identify. I sat quietly, forcing myself to be still. I recited all the reasons I shouldn't go up front and just look to see who it was.

First, if I saw someone I shouldn't, the commander might simply shoot me right there. Second, if it was Bart, and our being here would endanger him, I didn't want to force things immediately. Third, if it wasn't Bart, but was the superior officer that was here yesterday, I didn't want to call attention to myself. He might order the commander to shoot me on the spot and get rid of a witness before Bart could come.

In a few minutes, the commander entered the front room and bent over a box that was opposite the door to the hall—directly in the line of vision through my little spyglass. The superior officer appeared, his profile rugged and clear-cut, his bearing confident, almost arrogant, oozing power and authority with every gesture.

This time the man was shirtless, revealing an admirable physique and a four-inch bandage wrapped around his midsection. He carried a box that must have been extremely heavy. When he put it down, he stayed bent over with his hands on his knees to catch his breath, then felt his side under the bandage as if to check for bleeding. As he straightened, his back squarely to me, I gasped in astonishment.

Angry red scars crisscrossed from his neck to his waist. He'd been savagely scourged. The scars had healed, but nothing short of plastic surgery would ever wipe out the reminder of what he had suffered.

Sympathy surged through me. My heart reached out to the ruggedly handsome man who'd been so severely whipped. I yearned to stroke the scars and rub away their pain. Suddenly I caught myself and realized what I was thinking.

Jumping up, I gave myself a good talking to as I paced back and forth in the back of the house out of sight of the two men in the front room. He probably deserved it. He'd probably been caught stealing, or blowing up something, or some other horrible thing these terrorists did. Maybe he'd even killed someone. He'd probably earned every one of those lash marks.

But all my analyzing didn't do much good. In the middle of citing a reason why he'd been so brutally beaten, I'd find myself thinking of the restless energy in his movements, the rugged, vital strength that attracted me, and the desire to be held by that powerful-looking man, despite the despicable things he may have done.

Whoa. What had come over me, thinking such forbidden thoughts? I was being disloyal to my husband—and way out of line harboring such taboo feelings. It must be the heat, the exotic climate, the danger we were in. I could think of a dozen reasons, but none of them were more than rationalization.

Suddenly I sank to the ground. Was that what was wrong with my marriage? Was I an unfaithful wife? The thought made me sick. But it made sense. My marriage was on the rocks, apparently because I was drawn to attractive other men. Not even nice men, evidently. How could I possibly be attracted to a terrorist? What was wrong with me?

Ed deserved a better wife than this. From all appearances, he was a devoted husband, and if I'd been a more loving wife, he wouldn't have to be envious of Bart and Allison's relationship. I resolved then and there to be all he needed—to reciprocate the love and passion he declared with his eyes each time he looked at me. From this moment on, I would be the most loving, faithful wife a man ever had. Ed would never dream of Allison again.

I had no time for more self-recrimination or resolution. The commander appeared in the doorway with his superior officer directly behind him. One glance into those azure blue eyes staring at me over the dark hair of the commander, and I was mesmerized. All the guilt I'd just felt for being attracted to this man flooded back. My resolve to be a loving, faithful wife wavered uncertainly in the electric gaze of those compelling eyes.

CHAPTER TWENTY-SIX

The piercing blue eyes narrowed in disbelief. The tan, handsome forehead wrinkled in a frown. I sat motionless on my heels and held my breath. In one swift movement, he pushed the commander out of his way, and in two long strides reached the spot where I knelt. Powerful hands plucked me from the ground. He crushed me against him, holding me so close I couldn't breathe, all the while murmuring something softly in my ear, kissing my hair, my forehead, my cheek.

My body responded to him, to the trim, hard form pressed against mine. I leaned into him, answering the urgency I felt in his embrace. It felt so—right. So very good. Like I belonged here. My arms went around him and my fingers found the scars on his back. A flash of memory. Tibet. A beating in a Red Chinese prison.

"Oh, Princess. My own Princess. It's been so long."

Horror shot through me. My body went rigid. Bart. This man was my brother.

I pulled away quickly, thoroughly ashamed at the very unsisterly feelings I'd experienced. How could I react like that to my own brother!

"Bart? Is that you?" I whispered, forcing the words out when nothing wanted to come.

He held me at arm's length and stared. "You don't recognize me?"

The commander, not to be left out of this little reunion, spoke up.

"So she is your sister? Her husband said she was, but I tended to believe it was simply a ploy to keep from being shot."

"Husband?" Bart looked at me, waiting for an explanation.

"Ed is working at the cave." I dropped my gaze. I couldn't bear to look into those beautiful blue eyes, with my heart still pounding from his touch. How could I not remember him? How could I be so attracted to my own brother?

"Well, this is about the biggest surprise I've ever had. What are you doing here?" he said, looking from me to the commander.

I hesitated. The commander prompted me. "Go ahead. Tell him."

"As you know, we came to do a story on the fiftieth anniversary of the independence of Sri Lanka and planned to meet you when you finished training these men. But we were picked up by the commander at the sapphire mine the other night and we've been his 'guests' ever since."

Bart turned to the commander. "And her husband is digging at the cave while she's here alone?"

"I provided a guard for her. Since I had to use one of my men, I simply put your brother-in-law to work in his place. They'll be back tonight."

Bart put his hands on my shoulders and ran them down my arms to my hands, which he held very firmly in his. He wouldn't let go, even when I tried to gently pull away. He just watched me, those eyes the color of Ceylon sapphires boring all the way through me.

"Something about you is different. What is it? There's something in your expression . . ." Without letting go of my hands, he whirled to face the commander. "What's happened to her?"

The commander, apparently fearful of the fury of this giant of a man who towered a good head and shoulders over him, explained quickly that I had amnesia.

Bart turned to me. "Is that true? What happened?"

I nodded. "I was thrown from an elephant—and landed on my head. When I woke up, I didn't recognize myself in the mirror, didn't recognize my husband, couldn't remember my name, or anything about me. The only reason I had any knowledge of you was that I found your inscription in the scriptures you gave me. Ed said you'd given them to me when we joined the Church."

He looked stunned.

"What did the doctor say? Is it temporary? You don't remember anything?"

"Dr. Armstrong said my memory would probably come back in bits and pieces, and hopefully at any time. But, of course, he couldn't guarantee anything. I did have a severe concussion. I've only had little snatches return here and there. Mostly I have this huge void where my memory bank used to be."

Bart's eyes darkened with sudden pain. He gathered me into his arms again and stroked my hair, murmuring how much he loved me. I pulled quickly away, hating my body for responding as it did to his touch even now.

"Ed kept telling me what a wonderful, loving brother you were," I said shakily, trying to recover my equilibrium.

"He's right. You're my favorite woman in all the world," he said, keeping my hands tightly in his, as though he thought I might run away.

I looked at him in surprise, then realized he had to be teasing.

"Ed also told me that you and Allison are so very much in love, it's tangible. So I know you're pulling my leg. But that's okay. To someone who can't remember anything about herself, you can't imagine how comforting it is to know that there's someone around who really loves you. Besides my husband, of course."

"And how are you two getting along?" Bart asked, his eyes probing the depths of mine.

"What do you mean?"

"Is he good to you? Is he being a loving husband?" There was a strange timbre in his voice, an undercurrent to the question I felt, but didn't understand.

"Yes. He sat for hours by my bed, holding my hand while I tried to climb out of that dark, painful void I'd plunged into. And he has been, ever since, in every respect, the most loving, devoted husband I could ever imagine. I see his love in his eyes every time he looks at me. I'm going to make him as happy as Allison makes you."

The brilliant blue eyes clouded, and the slightest hint of a scowl appeared on the handsome face. I wasn't sure what had displeased him, but something had. He ran his finger softly down the side of my face, tracing my chin.

"Where is my Allison right now?" he said so softly he couldn't have been speaking to me. "Will I ever get her back again?"

"What?" I asked, not sure I'd heard what he said.

His eyes misting, he looked at me without speaking for a long minute. Then he squeezed my hands and straightened up.

"Look at you. You're a mess. How long has it been since you've had a bath?" Bart said, wrinkling his nose.

"Too long. There's nothing I'd like better right now than a hot shower, and then a lovely, soft bed with clean sheets in an air-conditioned room," I answered wistfully.

"I think I can grant your wish, Princess," Bart said with a pleased smile. He turned to the commander.

"I'm going to take my sister to my hotel. She can shower and clean up, and spend the afternoon in bed. I'll be back in about an hour."

The commander squared his shoulders.

"I don't think so, sir."

"What do you mean, you don't think so? I said I'd be back in an hour." Bart's voice dropped to a cold, clipped, don't-mess-with-me tone.

"I know that's what you said. But until you have fulfilled your part of the agreement, I'd feel much better if I can keep your sister where I can see her. It's not that I don't trust you," he added hurriedly, "but I think you'll finish here much more quickly and efficiently if you continue to be concerned about her welfare. There will not be as much postponing if you're anxious for your sister to be comfortable."

Bart's voice was cold. "Any postponement was because you hadn't done your homework. It was not because of me. We should have finished today, but you weren't ready. I don't want my sister here with this rabble you call an army."

"El Tigre, humor me," the commander spoke patiently. "Please see it as I do. Tomorrow you train my men. Then you can take her to a hot shower and clean bed."

Bart considered the commander's words, noting the guard with the gun resting across his arm just behind the commander, and the other two soldiers who appeared at the side of the house. He put his arm around my shoulder and pulled me close to him.

"Okay. We'll get your men trained tomorrow. But my sister won't be out of my sight for even a minute until I'm through here."

"Agreed. She is free to do as she wishes as long as she is within sight of the two of us. Let us continue in the house."

Bart kept his arm possessively around my shoulder as we left the bright sun and entered the shaded interior of the house. Ed had said I idolized Bart. That's what these feeling were—the adoration of a younger sister for her handsome big brother. Nothing more. Any little sister would recognize what an attractive, charismatic man her brother was. I'd simply reacted to that masculine charm. That thought soothed my unsettled conscience somewhat.

When we walked into the front room, one look at me amid the boxes loaded with arms and ammunition, and Bart dispatched a new plan.

"Send one of your men to bring back all your soldiers. The cave can wait. Let me start their training now, today. You can finish your hiding place after I leave."

The commander thought about that for a minute, then called to one of the men guarding the road to the house. As he spoke to the man in the doorway, giving instructions, Bart turned to me.

"What name are you using?" he whispered.

"Ed and Amy Teale. That's what our passports say. Isn't that who we are?" Of course not, dummy, I thought. Where's your brain? If your husband is in some kind of agency, he wouldn't go around the world using his own name. I wanted to ask what our names really were, but the commander turned back to Bart and they busied themselves with the equipment in the boxes.

Why hadn't I realized Ed would be using an alias, and as his wife, I would be, too? That was the reason for the brown contact lenses. And for the secrecy. Ed hadn't wanted to tell me anything that I might give away inadvertently. It was no wonder, since I was apparently extremely slow-witted.

I settled myself on the ledge in the glassless window and watched my brother explain the various pieces of equipment to the commander. He was knowledgeable and articulate, as well as a skilled teacher. The commander was a quick learner, with intelligent, probing questions. Bart had all the answers.

In a few minutes, the soldier returned in Bart's car, followed by the truck rumbling down the road, stirring up the dust. Ed jumped out and ran to the house when he saw me sitting in the window. Bart strode forward and grasped his hand.

"Ed, I'm surprised to find you out here instead of in Colombo. I'd hoped you'd take better care of my sister than that, although she has tried to assure me that you're being a most loving husband."

The agitation in Bart's voice surprised me. Granted, I wasn't in the best of shape, but it certainly wasn't Ed's fault.

"El Tigre, you, of all people, know how hard-headed Amy is. I tried to send her home after her accident, but she stubbornly refused to go. If I'd forced her on the airplane, she'd have faked a heart attack or labor pains and had the pilot turn back. So I figured the next best thing was just to keep her close and keep an eye on her."

Bart dropped his voice so I could barely hear him. "And how close was that?"

I didn't hear the next thing he said, but Ed wasn't smiling anymore. I jumped down from the window and looped my arm through Ed's. The least I could do was give him a little moral support.

Bart glanced down at me and quickly looked away, but I'd already seen the pain in those blue eyes. I didn't understand what was going on here—neither the words nor the undercurrent of tension flowing between my two men. Was my mind still so muddled from the concussion?

We sat on the waist-high stone partition that enclosed the front porch while the commander gathered his men in the clearing below us.

"Instructions?" Ed asked Bart quietly.

"Get her out of here. Our guys show tomorrow. I put off the training, hoping they'd arrive today, but your being here forces my hand. I'll have to begin their training now, make it look good, and hope our guys don't let any of them slip through their fingers when they come in." Bart dropped his voice even lower. "And, buddy, remember whose wife Allison is, will you?"

I shook my head. Did Bart say what I thought he said? Was Ed really having an affair with Allison, even though he'd denied it? And just when I'd resolved to be a more loving, caring wife. This was one nightmare after another.

The commander's appearance put a stop to their conversation. Bart motioned Ed to take me and leave. We returned to our relegated abode in the kitchen.

"Now what?" I asked.

"Anything happen when you saw Bart?" Ed asked.

A flush of guilt shot through me. "Like what?" I asked.

"No memories? No flashes of anything?"

How do you tell your husband that you've just found your own brother more attractive than you find him?

"One instant when I touched the scars on his back. Tibet came. What happened?"

"He was on assignment in Tibet when the Red Chinese captured him. They kept him for six months, torturing him, before he escaped to Nepal with the help of some lamas. That's where he was converted to the Mormon church—by a Frenchman who was a prisoner there."

"Ed, if he hadn't called me Princess, I wouldn't have had any idea who he was. He was here yesterday. For a long time. From observing them together, I thought he was the commander's superior officer. Had I known who he was, I could have told you. Not that it would probably have made much difference . . ."

Ed interrupted. "No harm done. As you said, it probably wouldn't have made any difference. But he's right. I do have to get you out of here. There'll be a lot of fireworks, and you don't need to be anywhere around when that happens. I need a plan quick and hope we get a chance to run it by Bart. It's apparent the commander doesn't trust any of us, and he's not going to give us any opportunity to put our heads together if he can help it."

I left him to think while I pondered the strange behavior of my husband and brother, but my head commenced throbbing as the emotional upheaval escalated. Thrusting aside the thought that my husband was having an affair with my brother's wife, I blanked every thought from my mind and busied myself with the fruit I'd picked this morning.

I shared some with the guard whom I now considered another appendage, he was always so close at hand. He was nervous. He kept looking out into the woods, and when there was any noise out there, which there had been frequently during the day, his hands quivered and his dark eyes darted from corner to corner as if to find a place to hide.

The next time I saw the commander enter his makeshift office, I hurried up the hall.

"Makkim said something about appeasing the leopard goddess with a sacrifice. Is there a group that worships the leopard?"

As if to brush away an annoying insect, the commander flicked his baton at me.

"Some believe the leopard goddess can change to a human form and walk upright, moving among humans as a woman. A foolish, primitive belief. They stake animals to be eaten by the goddess so she'll leave their animals alone and bless them because of their generosity. Foolish superstition."

He bent his head over papers on his desk, dismissing me by the act.

I walked slowly back to the kitchen, wondering how we could use this little bit of information to our advantage. I felt sure our guard was totally spooked by the sounds in the jungle, and I felt just as sure that they were made by leopards. If there was some way we could play this up . . .

I was about to suggest a brainstorming session to Ed when another vehicle approached. The second truck full of soldiers had arrived from the cave. Suddenly there was a loud commotion out front as the man with the Spanish accent demanded to see the commander. I watched from the doorway to the kitchen as the commander stalked out of his office and into the front room.

"Ed, I think we've got big trouble," I warned. "Your Spanish friend is probably ratting on you at this very moment."

"On us," Ed amended. "I think this might be a good time to take another walk to the woods. Put a little distance between us and the commander and see what happens."

As we headed for the kitchen door, our guard blocked the way, his eyes wide with fear. He shook his head. There was no way he was going out where he thought the leopard waited, and so we couldn't go either. Which probably wasn't a bad idea, as I thought about it. I didn't believe in his leopard goddess, or I might have appealed to her for help, but I did believe there was at least one of those incredibly dangerous animals out there in those trees, and joining it wasn't the brightest of ideas.

Since we couldn't leave by the back door, we headed for the front entrance to see what was happening. Staying just out of sight of the enraged Moreno, still loudly demanding to speak to the commander, we could hear Bart shouting orders as the group of men disembarked from the truck.

"Get these men lined up ready to march. You two. Fall in, right behind me." Bart pointed at Papio Moreno, and the man from the mine who was selling Papio the raw sapphires, the *guedo.*

The new arrivals joined ranks with the group already assembled in the front yard, and Bart marched the entire troop, on a run, into the green darkness of the jungle. Moreno hadn't had a chance to connect with the commander.

But how much of Moreno's message had the commander heard? I tried to remember what Moreno had actually said and what the commander could have concluded from that.

"What do you think?" I whispered as we hurried back down the hall to the kitchen.

"Bart caught on fast to Moreno. I don't think the commander heard enough of his rantings to guess at what Moreno wanted to tell him. All we can do is hope that the illustrious leader thought Moreno wanted to complain about being forced into manual labor."

I hated waiting. I hated having nothing to do. I hated most of all being in the same clothes day after day. I hated not being able to shower. Thank heaven I'd grabbed my backpack with my toiletries in it. At least I could brush my teeth with the rain water and wash my face. The climate was so humid, I could have foregone moisturizer, but it was one of the only luxuries I had here, so I indulged.

And with nothing else to do, I decided to indulge some more.

"Would you mind bringing in some more rainwater?" I asked my husband, who was pacing the floor in frustration and boredom.

"I'd be glad to do anything you ask," he smiled. "Especially get you out of here. But I haven't figured out just how yet."

I handed him the old battered blue enamel bowl and began communicating to our guard what Ed was going to do. In sign language and a couple of phrases I'd picked up from the guide books on Sri Lanka, I informed him that Ed was going for water but I was staying, so he didn't have to worry about going out near the woods.

It made him very uneasy that one of his charges would venture near the trees, but as long as he didn't have to go, he apparently would allow it.

When Ed returned with the bowl full of clean water, I stepped into the pantry, and posting Ed at the partially closed door so I could have both a little light and privacy, I proceeded to take a bath in the bowl. I wasn't going to face Christmas Eve, whatever it would bring, looking like something the dog dragged in. I washed my face, then wiped the rest of me and lathered my hair with shampoo.

Scooting the bowl of dirty water out the door, I asked for a fresh one, and when Ed had dutifully pushed the bowl full of clean water into the pantry, I knelt on the floor, stuck my head in the bowl and rinsed the suds off.

"Another one, please, if you don't mind," I said, pushing the bowl out a second time.

If only I had some clean clothes. I'd splashed through the rain, rolled in the mud, and worn these for two days straight in the heat and humidity of the tropics. They were only fit to be burned at this point.

But when my hair was squeaky clean, my teeth brushed and gleaming, my face soft with refreshing moisturizer, I dabbed a bit of perfume on my wrists and temples and felt almost human again.

Until the shouts came from the jungle.

"El Tigre is dead!"

CHAPTER TWENTY-SEVEN

Unable to speak, I grabbed Ed's arm, staring into his gray eyes with the question caught in my throat.

His arms went around me, but I pushed him away.

"He couldn't be. He couldn't be," I whispered over and over, shaking my head in disbelief.

"Let's go see." Ed grabbed my hand and pulled me down the hall. Just ahead of us, the commander hurried from his office. We joined him on the front porch, waiting for the terrified soldier to catch his breath and report.

"El Tigre and the men in front of the march were attacked by the leopard. They are dead," he panted.

"Did you see the leopard? Did you see it attack? Did you see El Tigre?" I blurted before the commander had a chance to question his informant.

"No. We just heard them. El Tigre screamed at the leopard, then told us to flee. There was a terrible noise in the jungle, men screaming, shots, the leopard roaring as it attacked."

"You stay here," Ed ordered, pointing a finger at me. "I'm going to see for myself."

The commander nodded in agreement and motioned for his soldier to show Ed where they had been attacked. The reluctant man, prodded only by his greater fear of his commander, jogged back into the jungle with Ed at his heels, passing the rest of the returning soldiers.

Not one to waste time and manpower, the commander, with a glance at his watch, ordered a truckful of soldiers to the cave to finish preparations for hiding arms and ammunition there. I was relegated back to the kitchen.

My guard was thoroughly spooked by this time, having been informed by one of the returning soldiers what had happened. Had there been a back door on the kitchen, I know he would have locked it against the dreaded leopard.

Dread. I understood that emotion. I dreaded Ed's report. Bart couldn't be dead. I'd only had him for a short couple of hours. I needed more than that. He was a link to a past I couldn't remember, a link I had hoped to use to trigger my lost memory. And his presence had been incredibly comforting.

I paced the rock floor in the kitchen. I paced the long hallway to the front of the house and back. I pushed past the guard and paced the backyard, and then started over. What was taking Ed so long? Why wasn't he back yet?

Was it better for him to be gone long, or to return quickly? Which would signal the best news.

As I paused in the doorway to the hall, the commander, returning to his office, glanced up at me. For a brief second, our eyes locked. He looked quickly away and proceeded into his office, but that fleeting glimpse revealed more than he intended. If Ed returned with confirmation of El Tigre's death, we would not be allowed to live through the night.

We'd probably join Lecherous Louis tied to a tree in the jungle, a sacrifice to the leopard goddess. Then our bodies, or what was left of them, would be turned over to the American Ambassador by local natives who "just happened" to find two unfortunate Americans who must have become lost in the jungle.

He didn't need witnesses to what he was doing here. Only the possibility that I was El Tigre's sister had protected us thus far. And when Papio Moreno reported his tidbit of information, the death sentence might be worse than being left in the jungle for the leopard.

A plan. I needed a plan to get away before that could happen. If I went to meet Ed and intercepted him on the way back, we could overpower the soldier with him and escape into the jungle. I'd take my chances with monitor lizards, cobras, leopards, and whatever else the jungle held, any day, over the cold heart of a greedy, power-hungry human.

But, the logical side of my brain argued, you're assuming that your brother is dead. Is he? Or has your husband been gone so long because he's caring for the wounded, and Bart is still very much alive?

True. I had assumed that Bart was dead. So now I was back to pacing and waiting. The wait was interminable, the suspense excruciating. When I'd finally had all I could take of both, I stormed into the commander's office to beg to be allowed to go and find out what had happened to my men.

As I did so, the babble of voices in the front yard heralded the return of the search party. I rushed to the front yard with the commander close on my heels.

Ed and the soldier emerged from the jungle, one on each side of the tall man who had sold the sapphires to Papio Moreno. He was bleeding and badly injured, able only to walk with their help. There were just the three of them. No one else followed.

I stared at my husband, at the message his eyes flashed. Those bleak, gray eyes said it all. My knees buckled under me and I slid to the steps, unable to stand. A numbing sadness enveloped me, as gray as the twilight descending on the jungle. It felt as though someone had torn my heart from me, had plucked all passion from my soul.

The tears flowed freely. I made no attempt to hide them or wipe them away. I wept for what had been—for what I couldn't remember and for what might have been—and all that I'd never know. And for Allison, the wife who loved Bart so dearly.

I listened to, but barely heard, Ed's report to the commander. Bart had jogged in front of the double column of men through the dense underbrush in the near darkness. Papio Moreno and the mine manager were several feet behind, with the soldiers on their heels. When the leopard roared, the soldiers started shooting. From the sounds in the brush, it had been wounded by their shots. El Tigre yelled at them to retreat and suddenly disappeared into the undergrowth, dragged off by the injured leopard.

When the smoke cleared, so to speak, Moreno was dead and the manager of the mine had been wounded by the wild gunfire of the soldiers. The leopard got El Tigre.

"Are you certain El Tigre is dead?" the commander asked the wounded man.

The mine manager was certain he could not have survived the rage of the wounded leopard. The noise was terrible, the thrashing in the brush, the screaming of the beast, the cries of the man. No one would have survived.

"Did you see the leopard with your own eyes?" the commander demanded.

"No, but to hear it was enough to scare a man to death," the manager replied. "I will never forget that sound the rest of my life."

I found myself praying that if Bart hadn't escaped, that he at least had not been eaten alive by the leopard. That would be a gruesome death. The thought produced another fountain of tears.

As I prayed, I had a completely irrational thought. *Get your backpack.* I stopped crying and sat dumbfounded on the step. *Backpack.* It came again. I stood without a word, entered the house, and walked down the long, narrow hallway to the kitchen. Ed followed immediately, with our omnipresent guard close behind.

I picked up the backpack, opened it, and stared inside. What was I looking for? Why had I thought of the backpack? I looked blankly at Ed, expecting him to want some kind of explanation for my strange behavior. He smiled instead.

"Get your journal and write down your feelings. I've heard that's a good cathartic exercise for deep sorrow. Come on. We'll sit here on the step. There's barely a few minutes of light left before the sun sets."

He pulled me to the doorway and we settled on the familiar stone where I'd already spent so many hours. Our guard wanted nothing to do with the out-of-doors and was more than happy to watch us from inside the kitchen.

When we were seated with our backs to the guard, Ed took the journal and pried opened the padded cover. A gun nestled in the padding. I stared into Ed's triumphant eyes.

"How did you know that was there?" I whispered.

"I watched you put it there. I'd planned to keep it as an emergency backup. This is the emergency. We're getting out of here now. Our chances are better in the jungle than here with *El Commandante.*"

"What's your plan?"

"Exit stage left, as they used to say in the cartoon." Ed stood and pulled me to my feet. "I'll take care of the guard."

"Not till I get my backpack. There may be some other goodies in there you don't know about and I don't remember." Smiling at the guard, I picked up my backpack, and put the now empty padded journal back inside, then looped it over my shoulder and grabbed a handful of bananas. I waved the guard over and offered him his choice of the fruit on the table.

Ed joined us, and as the guard reached for a mangosteen, Ed clobbered him on the head with the gun, catching him before he hit the floor. We dragged him to the pantry, put him on the floor, relieved him of his gun, and shut the door behind him.

"You're a crack shot with this," Ed said, pressing my gun into my hand. "Use it if you have to."

We raced through the high weeds of the little yard and plunged into the jungle.

"Where are we going?" I asked as we skirted the clearing and headed in the direction of the dirt road.

"The road curves. If we cut through the trees, we'll come to the road in a few minutes. Hope we've got that long before the commander decides to check on us."

We didn't. As Ed spoke the words, I could hear the commander shouting at his men to find us and bring us back. Soldiers yelled, lights flashed behind us, and the jungle was alive with the sounds of men crashing through the underbrush.

We had no light. The sun was below the horizon, and what sunlight remained didn't penetrate the thick vegetation. I couldn't see where I was going until I was right on top of whatever obstacles were in my way. My ankles and sandaled feet took a real beating from thorns and stickers. My heart pounded as I ran, with fear as much as with exertion.

The jungle seemed suddenly to have a heartbeat that pulsed with life. Life that was bent on keeping us here, on slowing us down so we'd be captured. Branches reached out to clutch my clothing and scratch my arms and face. Roots and vines tangled around my feet, tripping me constantly. Only Ed's tight grip saved me from falling.

Suddenly I smacked my head on a low branch. The force tore my hand from Ed's and knocked me flat. Ed stopped, put me on my feet, and with one arm around my waist propelled me on through the trees. The blinding headache returned with a vengeance. I knew what they meant by seeing stars before your eyes, only I saw flashes of brightly colored lights.

I was so dizzy I could hardly stay on my feet. I wanted to lay down, to stop this stupid, exhausting race through the dark and just go to sleep.

"Don't give up on me now, baby. Keep moving. You can do it."

He murmured a steady stream of encouragement in my ear. I wasn't sure how long I could stay on my feet and keep moving. My head didn't just ache. It throbbed. It pounded. With every step I took, with every jostle and jolt, it threatened to explode. My knees kept buckling, but Ed would propel me along until my feet caught up again.

I could feel the dark closing in, not just the dark of the jungle, but the sweet darkness of unconsciousness and oblivion. I was ready to succumb, more than ready to escape from the pain in my head, from the beating my body was taking.

"Don't give up. It's not far. Hang on. We're almost there."

He didn't quit. He just kept making promises—promises that I could do it, that we could make it together. Promises of wonderful things waiting just ahead. Promise me a bed and a hot shower, and I'll do anything, I thought, fighting to keep from succumbing to the welcome oblivion. Promise me I'll spend Christmas, clean and safe, with Bart. That's all in the world I want.

The thought jolted me as much as the jogging. Christmas with Bart. Our first Christmas together. That didn't make sense. Growing up together, we'd have spent many a Christmas together. Flashes of memory, tiny vignettes of color and people and events, flickered through my mind, none of which made sense. I needed to stop, to sit quietly, to let it come back, and to fit together the pieces of the puzzle that flew by as quickly as the palm fronds we raced past.

Through the throbbing in my head, I was suddenly aware of someone crashing through the brush just behind us. I tried to increase my pace, to do my share and take the load off of Ed. If he wasn't burdened with me, he could get away. I'd slowed him down. Now we were caught.

As we plunged on, with the sounds of our pursuer coming closer and closer, I kept expecting to hear the command to halt, or simply to hear or feel the shots in the dark. Couldn't he see us well enough to shoot, or did the commander want us alive?

Suddenly he was right behind us. I could hear his heavy breathing, even over my own gasping breath.

Then he was there, with us, matching stride for stumbling stride through the sharp-leaved ferns and undergrowth in the dark.

"I've got her," came a voice almost next to my ear, and I was wrenched free from Ed's aiding arm.

CHAPTER TWENTY-EIGHT

He didn't stop or even slow his pace. He kept racing through the jungle as he swung me into his arms. Ed didn't object or miss a step, but raced beside us as we continued the wild plunge through the dense undergrowth. I thought about using the gun I still clutched in my hand, but was afraid if I shot him or hit him over the head, he'd land on top of me and break something. At least we were going in the right direction.

"Hang on to my neck, Princess, and wrap your legs around my waist."

Bart! My heart leaped at his voice. I obeyed immediately, snuggling my head against his neck and locking my ankles behind his back. I clung tightly to him so his arms were free for better balance and to push aside branches.

"Here, take these," he said, thrusting something at Ed. "Night vision goggles."

No. Not at Ed. At Oz. That wasn't Ed Teale running beside us. It was Oswald Barlow. And he *wasn't* my husband.

The pieces of the puzzle were beginning to fall into place, jolted there by the jostling, no doubt, and by the whack on the head I'd taken.

"Almost there," Bart said between breaths. "Veer left up here. There's a waterfall. Bikes are behind it."

We stopped at a waterfall not much taller than Bart's six foot four inches. He plopped me on a rock while he wheeled one motor scooter from behind the liquid curtain and headed back for another. Oz stopped him.

"No. Leave that one here for me. I'll stay and cover you. You get your wife out of here. Take her home and give her lots of babies to keep her busy."

Your wife. Me. I was Bart's wife. What about Allison?

I was Allison. Yes!

Bart started to object, but Oz interrupted. "I mean it. Get her out. I'll blow up the stuff at the cave and come out with the team. You told me where they'll be. I'll join up with them and see you back at Santa Barbara before New Year's. Chill a bottle of sparkly and we'll celebrate."

"You lied to me. You told me you were my husband. You told me Bart was dead. The next time I see you . . ." I couldn't think through the headache what I would do, but something drastic. I tossed him my gun before I impulsively shot him with it.

Oz laughed and kissed my cheek.

As the sounds of men searching the jungle echoed through the trees, Bart grasped Oz's hand and thanked him for watching over me. Oz stopped him.

"I have to tell you, man, keeping my distance from your wife was the hardest thing I've ever done in my life. One sign from her when she lost her memory, one flicker of invitation, and I don't think I could have resisted. Even when your wife thinks she's supposed to be married to somebody else, she only loves you."

"You're a good man. Now get lost before I start this up and lead them here," Bart said to Oz. "And take care."

Bart put me on the back of the scooter and wheeled it at a trot along a narrow footpath that ran beside the little stream.

Oz disappeared into the jungle in the opposite direction. Bart gave him a minute, then cranked up the noisy scooter and we roared into the night. I hung on for dear life with my arms around my husband's middle and my thumbs hooked in his belt loops on the front of his pants. The scooter bounced clear off the ground at times. I leaned my head against Bart's back, feeling his scars through the thin cotton shirt, remembering now the many times I'd stroked and soothed them.

I laughed out loud—partly from the pure joy of finally knowing who I was—but mostly, I think, from the knowledge that I wasn't a wicked woman who was turned on by her own brother. The relief of knowing that Bart was really my husband, and the sensual emotions I'd experienced were completely legitimate, was even more overpowering than the relief at escaping the soldiers.

"What's so funny?" Bart asked over his shoulder.

"It will take me a month to tell you everything," I shouted, "husband of mine."

The dirt road, when we finally hit it, wound back and forth through the jungle. We didn't seem to be making much progress forward. I kept looking over my shoulder expecting to see the lights of our pursuers any minute. Just before we hit the main road, they appeared through the trees behind us.

How could we outrun them on this little putt-putt of a bike? Once they reached the road, they'd catch us in no time. But we didn't stay on the main road. We'd only been on it for a minute when we turned off onto a secondary road.

We drove through a housing area, nestled in tall palm trees and almost hidden by the same lush, green vegetation we'd experienced the last two days in the jungle. Suddenly a gate barred our way. We were on a Navy compound.

Bart skidded into a turn and followed the fence until we came to a pedestrian opening. Whipping the scooter through the narrow opening, we sped down a rock-lined dirt path toward a tall, snowy white lighthouse whose bright beacon split the blue velvet sky.

"I'm going inside to signal our rescue boat. Let me know if anyone comes." He slid the scooter around the lighthouse to a tiny entryway and jumped off the bike, pulling something from his pocket as he ran toward the door. In a few seconds, he'd unlocked the door and disappeared inside.

I leaned against the lighthouse, legs quivering, head splitting, and listened for our pursuers. Waves crashing against rocks and the breeze rustling in the palm trees were the only sounds in the warm night air. A pale moon played peekaboo with a long slender cloud on the eastern horizon. On the surface, a perfectly lovely night.

Or had been. The perfect stillness of the night was shattered by the sounds of a truck gearing down. It stopped. Peeking around the octagonal corner of the lighthouse, I could see the soldiers at the gate. Sure that it wouldn't hold them back for long, I slipped into the lighthouse to alert Bart. The place was barren, save for innumerable stairs winding to the top. I called, then ran back to watch the soldiers.

Bart clattered down the stairs as the truck roared through the locked gate and sent it flying.

"Do we run for it, swim for it, or make a stand?" I asked as he burst through the door.

"Maybe all three. Hop on."

We jumped back on the scooter and Bart turned it toward the beach, staying on the hard-packed sand as long as he could. When we hit the soft, deep sand, the scooter bogged down and we abandoned it, heading straight for the line of white water crashing on the rocks ahead.

"Get behind those rocks. Our boat should be here to pick us up in a few minutes. If we're lucky, the truck was making too much noise to hear the scooter and didn't see us come down here."

"Dreamer," I said, as I waded into the surf and then down the beach a hundred yards to a cluster of big rocks. The beach in front of the lighthouse was one rocky outcropping after another. The sandy swimming areas spread down the beach on either side of this wide expanse of rocks and boulders.

Bart scrunched down beside me on one knee behind the rock. "You'll never know how good it is to see you, Princess." His hand caressed my back and shoulders, his fingers ruffled through my hair, as we watched and waited for the soldiers to appear. "You said Oz lied to you. Did you remember something?"

"That I'm Allison—and that you're not my brother. Thank heaven. And that I've missed you so much these last few months . . ." My words were muffled as Bart pulled me down on his knee and covered my mouth with his in a hungry kiss. I answered his hunger with every fiber of my being. I loved this man so much it frightened me. And I wanted him so much I almost forgot the soldiers tracking us.

"Whoops. Heads up, Princess," Bart said breathlessly. "We've got company." He pushed me back on my feet and turned his face to the soldiers who had fanned out when they found the abandoned scooter.

"How did you do that?" I whispered, watching the two who were following our tracks in the sand to the water's edge.

"Do what?" he asked, never taking his eyes from the enemy.

"Seem totally involved in the passion of the moment, and yet stay so detached you know everything going on around you."

"It's almost impossible when you're around," he said, pulling me down for another quick kiss, "but I have big plans for this Christmas Eve, and nothing is going to interfere, not even the Tamil Tigers."

The soldiers had split up at the water's edge, one going right and the other heading straight toward us. A soft, low whistle, like a song bird, floated across the water. Bart whirled me to face the waves.

"That's the signal. Get in the water and stay low, behind that string of rocks. Someone will take you out to the boat. When you get to the point, they'll signal and I'll come. Move it."

There was no arguing, though I hated to leave Bart behind. As I slipped into the water, all the terrible things that could happen to him flashed through my mind. And all that I'd been through without him. I started to turn around and go back, but as I turned, strong arms wheeled me around and pointed me toward the boat.

"This way, *noona*. He'll be right behind you." Without giving me a chance to swim on my own, the man propelled me toward the point, nearly drowning me in the process. At times the water was so shallow, I skinned my knees on the rocks, but he never let more than his head out of the water. When it was so deep I couldn't touch bottom, he never let go of my waist, never ceased thrusting me forward.

As we reached the end of the rocks, a tiny fishing boat bobbed gently in the rolling surf. Another pair of strong hands reached out and pulled me aboard as the soft bird-like whistle went out again across the water.

"Lay down in the bottom of the boat. You won't bother the fish. They're dead."

I flattened into the narrow bottom of the smelly boat on top of the night's catch, and came eye to eye with a silver, scaly specimen that still had some life in him. He flipped his tail in my face, then lay still. The smell was so overpowering, I knew I'd never, in this lifetime, be able to eat another fish.

Paralyzed with fear, I listened for the gunshots that would signal the soldiers had found Bart. They never came. But neither did Bart. Suddenly the boat started moving through the water.

"What are you doing? Where's my husband?" I demanded.

"In the other boat. These boats won't hold more than two people, especially with the bottom full of fish," he explained, leaning toward me so his voice wouldn't carry over the water.

"Where are we going?" I asked, wondering how far I'd have to go with my aromatic traveling companions in my face.

"Just around the corner. There's a ship waiting off shore to get you away from here."

I turned my head around enough to get a look at my benefactor. As I'd suspected from his accent, he appeared to be a native Sri Lankan, dark-chocolate skin, with deep lines etched in his forehead. Silver moonlight shimmered on the short, bristly, white beard and moustache covering the bottom half of his face and the thick white hair that covered his chest. His head was wrapped in a turban and a short sarong covered him from waist to mid-thigh.

My examination was cut short by his command.

"Tigers. Cover yourself with fish, quick."

CHAPTER TWENTY-NINE

Of course. The commander would call for naval reinforcements rather than let us slip through his fingers. We could pinpoint his arms cache. He didn't have time to move it before we could have the Sinhalese army there to destroy it.

Slipping the backpack off that I still wore, I buried it in fish above my head, then burrowed under the disgusting, slippery, smelly creatures myself. But the water in the bottom of the boat was too deep to lay face down. I rolled over. Just my face peeked out of the reeking water. Covering my nose and mouth with my arm to keep the fish at least that distant, I piled them around and on me, and with the help of the old man, soon became one with the catch of the day.

As a boat bore down on us, the throb of an engine vibrated through the water. The powerful beam of the searchlight penetrated the layers of fish. Could they see me as easily as I could see that light?

In a language I didn't understand, probably Tamil, someone directly above us shouted in a demanding voice what appeared to be a question. I felt the load diminish on my legs. The old man must have held up a couple of fish, but he said nothing.

Again the voice rattled the phrase, slowly, more distinctly. It was Tamil. I recognized it from the phrase book in my backpack. "What are you doing?" The old man answered in Sinhalese. "I fish." For a long moment the light played over the boat, glittering through the translucent fish scales above me. I lay frozen, not daring to breathe. Then the engine roared to life and the boat sped away, leaving us bobbing wildly on its wake.

It stopped again, and the scene apparently repeated itself at the fishing skiff just behind us. I held my breath, praying Bart wouldn't be discovered. In a very long minute, the engine roared once again and soon was lost in the sound of gentle waves sloshing against the side of the skiff.

The old man removed the fish from my face, but cautioned me to leave the rest in place just in case the Tamils came back. So I remained in the fetid water in the bottom of the boat, covered with reeking fish, and thought of Christmas Eve with my husband.

How romantic could it possibly be with both of us smelling to high heaven from our ordeal? I thought of the strong odor that clung to the skin after just a few minutes of handling fish. How would we ever rid ourselves of the odoriferous scent after soaking in the stuff?

I thought of Oz. Good old dependable Oz. I would kill him when I saw him again. Making me believe he was my husband! What if he hadn't been the good guy that he was? Or what if I'd given him just a little bit of encouragement? What if? What if?

Remembering what we'd just come through, I decided I ought to be very grateful that Oz was an honorable man. I should thank him, instead of skinning him alive.

I watched the stars twinkling in the midnight blue heavens above me, watched a satellite streak across the sky, and the beam of the lighthouse flash its life-giving light as regularly as a heartbeat—minute, after minute, after minute. It had even aided us on this clear, moonlit night, bringing our rescuers to us.

I thought of another Christmas, of other stars, and one bright one in particular, and of the Savior it heralded. I remembered now, I'd wanted this Christmas to be so special, since it was my first as a member of the Church. I'd planned to wrap a package for Christ and put in it a list of things I would do for him next year—my gift to him in return for all the gifts and blessings he'd constantly given me.

Suddenly a ship loomed above me, blocking out the stars.

"We are here. You may shed your fish skin," the old man said, pulling his smelly treasures from my legs.

I sat up and looked around as the other skiff pulled alongside.

"What a sight you are, Princess," Bart laughed, "but a sight for sore eyes."

"I can't possibly look as bad as I smell," I lamented, rolling over the side of the skiff into the warm tropical water. As I rubbed and scrubbed my skin and doused my hair, Bart surfaced beside me.

"I don't care how you look, and my sense of smell is ruined for the moment." He wrapped me in his arms and I twined myself around him as we sunk beneath the waves in a liquescent kiss. If I died at this moment, I would die a happy woman, I thought. When we surfaced for air, a rope ladder dangled at our heads.

"Up you go." Bart held the bottom rung of the ladder while I looped my foot in it and pulled myself onto it. I turned before I started the ascent, and thanked the old man for helping us. He handed me the backpack I'd forgotten. I was sure everything in it was soaked and ruined, but I looped the old friend through my arm and hauled it to the top of the ladder anyway.

Bart conferred with the two old fishermen, then scurried up the ladder and joined me at the top to wave them off.

When I looked around, I was standing on a work of art—a two-masted, junk-rigged, work of art that looked like it had floated out of a legend. Polished mahogany and teak wood gleamed in the flickering tiki lights.

Exquisite statues tucked in corners and elaborate teak furnishings on the deck could have come from a museum, or a palace. Candles flickering in cut-crystal sconces cast a thousand points of light mirrored in the gleaming wood. A visual feast.

Bart smiled down at me. "Like it?"

"It's incredible. Where did you find it? What is it? And look what I'm doing to these teak floors. I'm dripping all over them."

A sarong-draped, barefoot native appeared from below with huge, plush, Turkish towels, then disappeared. I draped myself in one and slipped out of my dripping, sloshing sandals.

"So much for those. And for these clothes. They're only fit for burning." Then I stared at Bart. "I have nothing to wear."

"Oh, well," he smirked. "What a shame." He stripped out of his wet clothes and wrapped a huge towel around him. After a moment's hesitation, I did the same.

"We don't want those clothes smelling up the honeymoon suite, do we?" he asked softly as his lips caressed my cheek, brushed my eyelids, and found my mouth.

"I don't know what I would have done if you had really believed you were married to Oz," he whispered.

"You'll never know how glad I am that you're not my brother," I said softly, snuggling closer. "And that the leopard didn't get you. Was there really a leopard?"

"Remind me to roar for you someday," he murmured. "Have I told you lately how much I love you?"

"No, but I'm a captive audience, so go ahead." I pulled away and looked up into those deep blue eyes reflecting the moon shining over my shoulder. "Before you do, though, I have one question. Well, I have a lot, like where did this boat come from, and how was it so conveniently waiting for us? But the most immediate one . . ."

"Yes?" His forehead wrinkled in a slight frown.

"Does this beautiful boat have a hot shower?"

Bart stared at me, then leaned back his head and laughed. Swooping me into his arms, towel and all, he headed below deck.

"It does, and while you're enjoying it, I'll see if the cook has some concoction that will neutralize the fish smell, short of scouring off the first layer of skin. If you take your time, I'll join you. It's been far too long since you've had one of my famous back scrubs."

The sudden remembrance of his back scrubs was delightful. "I promise to take my time."

With his towel still wrapped around his waist like a sarong, he left me standing in the middle of a luxuriously appointed bedroom that was cleverly designed to give an impression of spaciousness.

Large windows framed the twinkling lights of the night fishermen bobbing in the bay and the Dondra Head lighthouse flashing its friendly beacon. A king-sized bed draped in native tapestry was the centerpiece of a collection of beautiful Thai antiques, including lovely porcelain plates and statues and magnificent wood and ivory carvings.

I suddenly realized this was one of the converted Thai rice barges I'd read about in a brochure at the Oriental Hotel. Several had been restored after the fashion of the famous royal barges of Bangkok, the favorite transportation of Thai kings. And it was fit for a king. But what was it doing in Sri Lanka?

A knock at the door interrupted my thoughts. The native who

had furnished the towels bowed slightly, and with a knowing smile, handed me a rice bowl full of an interesting smelling concoction.

"To get rid of the fish smell?" I asked.

He smiled again and bobbed his head enthusiastically up and down as he backed away from the door. The smell must be even worse than I thought.

Cradling the bowl carefully in one hand, I opened a couple of louvered mahogany doors before I found the bathroom. What a bathroom it was! Burnished brass faucets gleamed above pink marble sink and huge jacuzzi tub. The shower was a work of art with lotus blossoms etched into the glass door and deep pink and white lotus blossoms hand painted on royal blue tile.

The shower beckoned and I answered the call, delighting in the hot water streaming over me, washing away the dirt and grime and salt and sweat of the past few days. I covered myself liberally with the mixture from the rice bowl, and rubbed it vigorously into my hair as well. When I finally felt clean again, I realized I had been in the shower a long time, far longer than I should have been there alone. Where was Bart?

As I towel dried my hair, puzzling over my missing husband, a memory of our honeymoon returned. I knew why I'd finished my shower alone. My husband must have slipped into his Interpol mode and forgotten all about me. It had happened before.

From the closet I'd discovered as I searched for the bathroom, I took a sari, made from yards and yards of soft, white cotton bordered with gold and sapphire blue threads. I wrapped it around me, imitating the folds and drapes used by natives, and stood back to view my handiwork. Not bad for a novice.

I fluffed my short dark hair with a brush, and removed the brown contacts. Barefoot, I made my way along the teak and mahogany paneled hall to the stairs to search for Bart on deck. As I reached the top of the stairs, a tremendous explosion thundered across the water. The jungle blazed with flames leaping high into the night sky not far from the Dondra Head lighthouse.

Had Oz just blown up the ammo? I turned to the pilot's house, expecting to find Bart there. He wasn't. Captain Leung Ek bowed and introduced himself.

"Where is my husband?" I asked, almost afraid to hear the answer.

"He had to go ashore, but said to tell you he will be back before Christmas is over so you can celebrate together."

"Where did he go?"

The captain hesitated. "He said he had to get something important and he would return shortly."

"Captain Ek, I think you know where he went and what he's doing. Please tell me."

Again, he hesitated, and turned to look out the window at the flames that were still visible from the explosion.

"He didn't go back there, did he? Back to the Tamil Tigers' camp?"

Without looking at me, the captain nodded.

"Why?"

"A message came just after you arrived. The men he expected to take care of the Tigers and bring out your friend were delayed. He had no way of contacting your friend, so he went after him. He notified the Sinhalese Navy at Dondra, and the Sinhalese Army is also on its way to round up the Tamils."

"What about the Tamil Navy? They had boats on the bay when we left Dondra. Are they still patrolling these waters?"

"Yes."

"And he went right by them? How did he get to shore?"

"He took the small motor launch."

"But if they're still around, they could have seen him or heard the boat."

Captain Ek's somber eyes met mine. "Yes."

"Why didn't you stop him?" I turned to watch the flames eating away at the jungle. My heart pounded in my chest. This couldn't be happening. Just when I thought it was finished, it had to start all over again. I looked up into the narrowed eyes of the captain.

"I'm sorry," I apologized. "You might as well try to stop a typhoon."

Suddenly a smaller explosion, at the foot of the lighthouse, echoed across the water. A tiny fire blazed momentarily, then went out.

I stared at the captain in terror.

"Bart's launch?" I asked. The words came out in a whisper.

Captain Leung Ek nodded gravely. "I fear it was."

CHAPTER THIRTY

I could hardly force the next question through my closed throat. "Would he have been in it?"

Captain Ek shook his head. "No. He signaled when he landed. He has been on shore nearly twenty minutes."

Could I have possibly been in the shower so long?

"How long did he think he'd be?"

"He said if he had not signaled in an hour, I was to return with you to Bangkok immediately. From there you could fly to America."

Over my dead body, I thought.

"How is he going to get back to the ship if they've blown up his transportation? Are the old fishermen still around?"

"No, their job was finished." He fell silent, his eyes focused on the lighthouse.

"Then how will he get back?" I persisted.

There was no answer.

"You think he's not coming back," I said slowly. Dondra Head was crawling with Tamil Tigers. A truckload had been on the beach searching for us less than an hour ago. They'd been joined by how many from the sea, I didn't know. The commander would leave no stone unturned to find us. And Bart had rushed headlong back into the melee.

"Do you have any other small boats on this ship? Something to get me to the lighthouse?"

Captain Ek turned from the window, disbelief gleaming from dark, narrowed eyes.

I repeated the question when he stared without answering.

"I need to be there when he and Oz make it to the lighthouse, and bring them back to the ship. Do you have another small boat?" I wanted to shake the silent man before me.

"Just an inflatable lifeboat," he finally said.

"Does it have a motor?"

"A small one."

"Please get it ready, right now. I've got to hurry."

Captain Ek rang for the native who appeared immediately, then scurried off, returning in minutes with the small four-man life raft, already inflated. The captain started to instruct me, but it was similar to one I'd handled—when? Recently. Somewhere. I couldn't wait for the memory to return. It was enough to remember that I knew how to use it.

"Do you have a gun?"

The captain produced a small handgun and an Uzi with an ammo belt.

"I'll take them both. Thanks. And don't leave without us. We'll be back."

They lowered the inflated life raft into the water and held it under the ladder while I hiked the sari above my knees and climbed down to board the awkward little craft.

"Let me send Manawa with you," Captain Ek asked for the second time.

I shook my head. "No. Even as small as he is, that would be too much weight in the boat. We may need to hightail it out of there in a hurry."

Leaving the *Manohra Song* behind me, I headed the boat toward the lighthouse, praying mightily all the way.

"If there's anything I need to know now, Father, I'm listening. Please guide me safely through to Bart, and bring him and Oz safely out to where I'll be."

It wasn't until I said that that I realized what a difficult task I had just undertaken. Discounting the danger from both land and sea, how on earth would I know where Bart had left his boat? How would I know where, in that long stretch of beach and among all those rocks, he'd return, expecting to find his transport back to the ship?

And how could I navigate the rocky bay in the dark, with no knowledge of where a deeper channel might be, where to avoid running over a jagged rock or coral formation that would rip the bottom right out of the inflated boat?

The enormity of it almost overwhelmed me. I had no idea what I was doing. Once again, I'd plunged impetuously into the fray without thinking. It was a familiar feeling. A memory of people discussing this aspect of my personality surfaced. My parents. Anastasia. That was the group Bart and Oz were with. I was one of them. And the question had been, was I too impetuous to be a professional agent?

Spray blew into my face, soaking my clean, dry sari as I bounced across the waves. I thought of what Oz had said as we parted. "Take her home and give her lots of babies to keep her busy." He may have been onto something there.

I'd even forgotten to ask the captain what Bart's signal would be. I could blunder right into the Tamil Tigers as they flashed some kind of signal to their boats out here. I imagined my guardian angels shaking their heads in disbelief at this stupid woman they constantly had to extract from trouble. That, too, was a familiar memory.

Don't let them give up on me just yet, Father. I really need them right now. And maybe a few more than usual, if you have any that aren't too busy.

As I neared the coast, I let up on the throttle, slowing the little craft to a lazy crawl. The moon was halfway up the sky now, illuminating land and sea. There were no boats visible anywhere near on the water, at least, none that I could see. I watched the beam from the lighthouse sweep the sky several times, lighting the empty waves. Even the night fishermen bobbed far down the coastline toward Matara.

I scanned the moon-drenched beach. It was empty. Nothing moved except the tall palms that swayed in the tropical breeze. There wasn't a glimmer of light anywhere. I moved the little boat closer to the shore, mindful of the rocks, watching for the white foam to signal where the waves met them.

When I was straight out from the lighthouse, I saw a point of rocks ahead and swerved the boat back to deeper water to round the point. There, floating behind the rocks, smoldering pieces of wood flared into flames, then flickered out, doused by the waves. Then another small flame flickered as it found a bit of oil, and when it had exhausted its fuel source, died.

Bart's boat! Thank you, Father. Now, please bring them safely here.

With the motor idling, I waited, not daring to turn it off in case it wouldn't start again. Not sure how mechanical I was, I certainly didn't need to be trying to figure out how to restart a dead engine when they appeared.

I glanced back in the direction of the ship I'd just left, not expecting to see it because of the curve in the bay, but there it was in all its glory. Captain Ek had moved in closer. Or was he leaving? Before I had time to worry about it, gunshots echoed across the beach.

My heart rate accelerated. My mouth went dry. My eyes burned from searching the darkness behind the beach. Suddenly two figures burst from the trees, running fast on the hard-packed sand. Bart's long legs carried him faster than Oz's short ones, but they were making good time until the shots behind them kicked up sand all around their feet and ricocheted off the rocks next to them.

Oz went down. Bart rolled in the sand and crawled back for him, scooping him over his broad shoulder. He stayed crouched, next to a rock, watching the beach. I moved the boat in closer to shore, then whistled, trying to imitate the songbird sound we'd responded to. Bart whirled around. I waved and turned the boat so it pointed out to sea, ready to escape.

A light flashed at the edge of the beach, and another. Dark figures moved toward the lighthouse. Bart jumped to his feet and raced to the boat, dumping Oz into the bottom. Catching the Uzi I tossed at him, he whirled and fired. I hit the throttle of the little craft. And prayed.

The boat responded, leaping forward through the waves. I tossed Oz the handgun as Bart continued to pepper the beach with gunshots, keeping their pursuers behind cover until we were out of range.

"What do you think you're doing?" Oz asked from the bottom of the boat. "I thought you were supposed to be safely out of harm's way."

"Someone had to rescue you two. Since I was all that was available, you'll have to settle for me."

Bart leaned across the motor. "What are you doing here?"

"They blew up your boat. You didn't have transportation."

"So you flew to our rescue."

"You lied to me. You said you'd come and scrub my back. You

never showed up. If you think you're going to get out of it that easy, Charlie, think again."

He leaned across and kissed me.

"While you two lovebirds are billing and cooing, I'm bleeding to death," Oz complained good-naturedly. "How about some help?"

"Why couldn't you just leave him in the jungle? He's going to spoil my whole Christmas Eve," I said.

"We could always just toss him overboard," Bart countered.

"We could, but you'd probably feel sorry for him and go in after him, and then I'd have to rescue the two of you again. Normally I could handle you both, but I'm not quite up to par tonight. Think of something else."

"Somebody will have to patch him. You or me?"

"He may have to bleed to death. Look behind you."

Skimming across the waves in hot pursuit, a boat ten times the size of ours, with probably ten times the power, bore down on us from behind a jetty. It was even bigger than the first Tamil boat that had stopped us. We were too far from the *Manohra Song* to make it before they caught us, and they were sure to have enough firepower to blast us out of the water.

"Okay, Sherlock. What do we do now?" I asked, testing the throttle to see if it had any more power hidden somewhere. It didn't.

"Just keep moving. I'll try to think of something."

Our options disappeared with every tick of the clock. Just as Bart was ready to fire on them, which would probably have triggered some high-powered response, a bright searchlight caught us in its beam.

Across the waves, a loudspeaker blared something in a foreign tongue.

"I suppose that means stop or we'll shoot," I said.

Bart nodded. "Probably."

The message was repeated.

"Do I stop or do they shoot us out of the water?"

"Stop," he said. "I don't think they're Tamils. I think it's the Sinhalese Navy."

"Why do you think that?"

"Because they haven't blasted us out of the water yet," he smiled.

It was the Sinhalese. Bart identified us as Interpol. We bobbed silently in the life raft caught in the spotlight with guns aimed at us while they checked Bart's ID code name with their headquarters. An officer returned shortly. Our identity had been verified. We breathed a collective sigh of relief. Their headquarters also sent word that the majority of the Tamil Tigers at the camp had been rounded up. The sweep would continue through the night and until the Sinhalese felt certain the rebel Tamils were contained.

The officer reported they had also received a request from the Ambassador of the United States to keep their eyes open for two Americans. Would we be the ones? Yes, Bart replied. He asked them to notify the American Embassy we were safe. We'd contact them later.

The Sinhalese Navy escorted our little life raft to the *Manohra Song* with Bart at the helm. I knelt in the bottom of the boat to check Oz's wound. He'd been hit in the thigh, and it was bleeding profusely.

"You did this on purpose, just so I'd feel sorry for you and not kill you the next time I saw you."

Oz grinned up at me. "Are you really that mad?"

"You let me think I was married to you. You lied to me up one side and down the other. You are a despicable creature who doesn't deserve the least bit of sympathy." I relented. "But thank you for being a gentleman. I guess I owe you big time for that."

"You'll never be able to repay the debt," he said, enjoying my chagrin.

"Well, it doesn't include ruining a perfectly good outfit to bandage you," I said, pulling his shirt off of him and ripping it in two. "So we'll use your clothes instead of my sari." Folding one piece of his shirt, I made a pressure bandage, and with the other I tied it securely in place.

"There. If you bleed to death, it will only be because you deserved it."

I was overjoyed to see the two-masted junk loom above us once again. We waved off our Sinhalese escort, and I hurried up the ladder. Bart, with Oz slung over his shoulder, climbed the rope ladder to the deck where Captain Ek met us with Manawa at his side. They carried Oz below to a stateroom on the other end of the hall from ours.

"Manawa will care for his leg. He is experienced with bullet wounds," Captain Ek assured us.

Oz lay back on the pillow and offered a weak smile. "Take the bullet out, sew me up, and I'll be as good as new. I'll even join you under the Christmas tree later, if you have one."

"We'll see about that," I said.

As I left the room, I whispered to Manawa, "Clean him up, sew him up, and shut him up for a couple of days. Complete bed rest. He's not to be seen or heard until we get to Bangkok."

Manawa nodded his head knowingly and, with a conspiratorial smile, bowed deeply.

Bart shut the door behind them. "I'm ready for that shower now. Want to join me?"

"Promise you won't leave me there alone again?"

"I promise," he said, leading me down the hall toward our room. Then he stopped and opened a door on a large stateroom as we passed. A beautifully decorated Christmas tree filled one corner of the room with gaily decorated presents spread underneath. A table was set for two with golden flatware, gold-rimmed china, and gleaming crystal.

"When we're cleaned up, we can eat here if you wish, or we can sit on deck under the moon and stars, sip sparkly, and catch each other up. You have a lot to tell me about your 'marriage' to Oz."

"And you have a lot to tell me about a certain beautiful girl in Bangkok named Mai Li who just appeared in my memory when I saw an injured man in bed. And how you came to have this boat, complete with Christmas tree, and presents, and chilled sparkling cider. And a table set for two. Do you travel like this often? And who were you expecting to travel with you?"

Bart backed me up against the sleek mahogany paneling, his arms on either side of my shoulders with his face close to mine, his body just tantalizing inches away. He kissed my temple.

"You wouldn't be jealous, would you?" he whispered, his breath warm in my ear.

"Me? Of course not," I said, knowing he didn't believe me for a minute.

"Or worried that there would ever be another woman in my life for even an instant?" His blue eyes probed the depths of mine.

I hesitated, searching his face, searching my heart. "No," I answered softly. "No. I trust you implicitly." I cupped his face in my hands. "I may not trust other women, but I do trust you." I kissed him gently. "But you'll explain about the boat anyway?"

Bart slid his finger down my cheek, a sly smile playing at his lips, his eyes full of amusement.

"I slipped away from Hamas Monday when we reached Sri Lanka long enough to call the control center in Santa Barbara. Mom said you and Oz went to Bangkok to find me and, failing that, would wait at the Galle Face Hotel for my message."

His lips moved down the side of my face and kissed my ear.

"Anticipating us together in paradise, I decided to finish this caper by Christmas. Our first Christmas had to be the best, so I had a friend in Thailand send Captain Ek with the *Manohra Song* to Colombo, complete with Christmas tree, presents, and Christmas dinner for two."

His lips found mine and brushed gently over my lower lip, nipping it between his teeth. "Guess we'll have to share dinner with our unexpected guest," he lamented softly.

"Unfortunately, Oz will miss Christmas this year," I replied, running my fingers slowly down his bare chest. "And I'll have you all to myself."

"How do you plan to accomplish that?" he asked.

"Trust me," I smiled. "It's already been arranged."

His mouth moved softly across my cheek, hovering just over my mouth. His sensuous teasing was more than I could handle. I wrapped my arms around his neck and pressed against him, closing the distance he'd kept between us. He stepped back.

"Before that happens, I have one more thing to do. Do you mind?"

"Let me guess," I sighed. "You've just teased me into a state of rapture and now you're going to go play Interpol agent again."

"One phone call, Princess," he promised, flashing the beguiling smile that always melted me. "That's all. And just to make sure, you can come along while I make it."

"Actually, I guess I need to make a phone call, too. Ambassador Hollingsworth needs to know we're all right."

"Your former fiancé?"

"That's what they tell me."

Bart looked at me. "Just how much do you remember?"

I sighed. "Enough to know that I'm not the kind of person to leave Oz drugged over Christmas, as much as I want to be alone with you. How about if we ship him off to the embassy, let Dr. Armstrong take care of him tonight, then we can go ashore tomorrow and bring him back. You need to meet Milton. Or he needs to meet you. There needs to be a little closure there, I think."

Bart made his phone call to Interpol to identify the link with the sapphire smugglers and the manufacturing shops Oz had discovered. Interpol would notify the proper authorities in each country, and by the new year the smugglers would all be out of business. At least, for a while.

Then we remembered another call that needed to be made—to the control center in Santa Barbara to Bart's folks, who would relay the message to the rest of Anastasia. That triggered a wonderful idea.

"Instead of bringing Oz back here, let's put him on the first flight to Los Angeles. Mai Li can nurse him back to health. They both need special attention right now. I think they'll be good for each other."

"Meddling in people's lives again?" Bart asked with a knowing smile as he leaned against the teak paneling of the pilot house.

"No. Just collecting a couple of strays and getting them together in a warm, snug environment conducive to healing hearts, bodies, and minds."

"Any more little loose ends you need to tie up or are we through now? Can we go get that shower?" Bart asked, clearly ready to remove the effects of his night's work.

While I was thinking about his question, he pulled me down the stairs and into the stateroom containing the Christmas tree, excitement evident in his boyish expression. He retrieved a tiny package hidden among the branches.

"Here. Open this. I can't wait to see your face when you do."

He folded my fingers around the tiny package and kissed my cheek, then watched as I untied the golden satin ribbon, peeled off the gold foil paper, and found a black voile ring case. When I opened the lid, an exquisite sapphire ring sparkled from its black velvet cushion.

Two large Ceylon sapphires, the color of Bart's eyes, were intertwined in a golden lover's knot that included twenty-two small deep blue sapphires. A note tucked inside said, "A memento from your first assignment in Interpol. The light blue sapphires come from the mines in Ratnapura, the darker stones from the Kanchanaburi mines in Thailand, your first areas of endeavor. Love, forever. Bart."

My eyes misted. "How could you do all this and still be entangled up to your eyeballs with terrorists? I can't believe you were thinking of me and planning this while you were in danger for your very life."

Then I stopped. I looked up at him with dismay. "I don't have a Christmas present for you."

A smile played at the corners of his mouth. He picked up the gold satin ribbon I'd discarded and, looping it around my neck, slowly, deliberately, pulled me close to him with it, never taking his eyes from mine. He gently tied the ribbon at the base of my throat, fashioning it into a bow.

"I have the best present of all, Princess, and I'm going to savor it every hour..."

I slid my arms around his neck and interrupted him with a gentle kiss. "Merry Christmas," I murmured. Then I pulled away and tipped my head back to look up into the warm depth of Ceylon blue eyes. "What did you say your name was?"

With a laugh, he picked me up and carried me toward our stateroom. "Maybe a shower will jog your memory."

It would be a wondrous Christmas.

Yes, this was the season of miracles. And I'd just had mine.

ABOUT THE AUTHOR

Lynn Gardner is an avid storyteller who does careful research to back up the high-adventure romantic thrillers that have made her a popular writer in the LDS market. For her first novel, *Emeralds and Espionage,* she relied on her husband's expertise as a career officer in the Air Force, interviewed a friend in the FBI, and gathered extensive information on the countries in which her adventure took place. Additional research in Hawaii, San Francisco, and New Mexico allowed her to create exciting stories with realistic settings for her other novels.

Lynn and her husband, Glenn, make their home in Quartz Hill, California, where Lynn is director of the stake family history center. They are the parents of four children.

Among her many interests, Lynn enjoys reading, golfing with her husband, traveling, beachcombing, writing, family history, and spoiling her four granddaughters and two grandsons.